I was thrown from my feet and slammed into one of the mechanical horses. Her rage was terrible to see and she reduced my cloak to ribbons as she sought to claw my flesh. I responded in the same fashion, and we rolled back and forth across the linoleum floor, which was soon streaked with our tainted blood. My left ear was a bloody ruin and a deep gouge ran from my right shoulder down across my ribs. Eventually my greater physical strength worked to my advantage, and I shattered her forearm when she unwisely lunged toward my throat. It would knit within a few hours, of course, but in that instant she reeled back, clearly disconcerted, and rushed from the gymnasium before I could interfere.

MANAGANSETT PRESS

Paula Sheffield is the author of:

Dark Mistress
Dark Muse

DARK MUSE

Paula Sheffield

Managansett Press First Edition 2015

DARK
MUSE

WHAT HAS GONE BEFORE

A cache of documents has been discovered that suggests that Bram Stoker was very selective about which information he included in his account of the battle against Dracula. Reconstructing the actual course of events from these fragments has revealed that the Count had long since repented of his evil ways and had set about destroying the few remaining undead before ending his own existence. His greatest enemy is the immortal daughter of a Sumerian king, Enheduanna, who was the first vampire and who has actually never died, although she has faked her death many times over the course of centuries.

Enheduanna had been posing as Mina Murray, later Mina Harker, using the hypnotic power of the glamour to ease her way into the lives of others. Although she initially enjoys the prospect of a battle with Dracula as a way to deal with the boredom of existence, she eventually realizes that he poses a genuine threat to her survival. She then manipulates her companions into chasing him back to Transylvania, where they apprehend his wagon and destroy him. In the process Quincey Morris is mortally wounded and Mina/Enheduanna attempts to transform him before he dies and is buried. Although she is convinced that Dracula is dead, there is reason to believe that a substitute may have been made and that it might only have been one of his servants who was dispatched. As a precaution, she kills Van Helsing and Jonathan Harker and fakes her own death. Arthur Holmwood has been driven insane by his experiences and Dr. Seward has disappeared.

Letter from Edward Palmer to James Chatsworth, dated June 26, 1920.

    So much has happened since last I wrote that I don't know where to start and my hand wants to jump ahead and write things that will make no sense to you until I have explained what went before. Let me first relate as promised how I learned of the existence of those enigmatic documents I have already sent you.

    As you know, I make a fair living cleaning up manuscripts or creating them from whole cloth for members of the upper class who fancy seeing their name listed as the author of a book on one subject or another. I supplement my income as well by occasional pieces of my own, some of which have attracted considerable favorable comment, if I do say so myself.

    In any case, I was laboring in my office several weeks ago, trying to turn Sir Robert Cosgrove's scribblings into actual prose, when a large man with Slavic features but the attire of a gentleman entered my office. He had a cultured voice with just the slightest trace of an accent.

    "Excuse me, but do I have the honor of addressing Mr. Edward Palmer?"

    I confessed to being so named and he introduced himself as Josef Straban.

    "I am somewhat familiar with your work, Mr. Palmer, both that which appears under your name and much that has not."

    That made me immediately wary as the nature of my business requires me to be discrete about my clients' authorial accomplishments. "I have some skill in literary matters, Mr. Straban. Are you seeking assistance in some project? A travel book perhaps? Or a family history?"

    His smile came and went so quickly that I almost missed it. "Although my family history has its moments of drama, it is not any work of my own which I wish to discuss with you. Rather, I am in a position to point you toward an existing, unpublished work which might, if suitably edited, prove to be quite remunerative."

    I have dealt in the past with more than my share of crackpots, and I might have relegated my visitor to that same class if it had not been for the calm self confidence with which he spoke. There are some men who exude an aura of absolute power which is palpable enough to touch the consciousness of the rest of us, and so it was with Josef Straban.

"That may be so," I admitted cautiously, "but I'm afraid that I have an ample workload at the moment." That wasn't precisely true; the project for Sir Robert was in its final stages and I had no other certain work in sight.

"I am sorry to hear that." He removed a small card from his pocket and handed it to me. On it was written an address in Piccadilly. "This house is occupied by an elderly woman named Bates. She does not own the property but is employed as its caretaker by another person whose identity is unknown to her, receiving her stipend from a solicitor's office here in London. She is the third individual to occupy this position. Part of her charge is to safeguard a box of diaries and manuscripts which have been stored in the house since 1875."

"I'm sure that's all very interesting, but what has any of this to do with me?"

Straban ignored my question. "As was the case with her predecessors, Mrs. Bates has instructions to release these documents only in the event that certain conditions are met. These conditions are twofold. In order to receive them from her custody, you must display this." His hand hovered over my desk and an ornate, tarnished ring fell from between his fingers, too small for a man. "You must also repeat the phrase 'The Lady requires her past' before she will relinquish them."

This all seemed a bit too mysterious for me and I said so. Straban nodded. "I can only assure you that you will be more than rewarded for any awkwardness you might feel." He started to rise.

I glanced down at the ring. "I'm sorry, sir, but I cannot in good conscience accept this engagement on your behalf."

He smiled but did not resume his seat. "It is not on my behalf that you will act, but on your own. I merely wish for the truth to be made known. How that is accomplished and who profits by it is of no interest to me."

"Nevertheless, I feel you should look elsewhere." I stood up and pushed the ring across the desk so that it was within his reach.

We stood motionless, both of us, for some time. My visitor finally relaxed his shoulders and reached inside his jacket, removed a considerable amount of currency and placed it on the desk without bothering to count it. "I see that I have misjudged the situation, Mr. Palmer. Perhaps you will allow me to repair the damage by making this a matter of business rather than a mystery. I would like to retain you to secure these documents for me as I have described. You are to safeguard them in whatever manner you feel adequate until such time as I return or send further instructions. During the interim, I give you a free hand to examine them and make whatever use of their content you find appropriate, including publication in whole or in part."

I glanced down at my desk. The funds lying there were probably equivalent to at least six month's income, even in a good year. "Under those circumstances, I believe I could find the time to act as your agent. If you will give me a moment, I will write you a receipt."

He raised an admonishing hand. "There is no need. I trust you implicitly." And then he was gone, almost as though he'd never been there in the first place.

My visitor had piqued my curiosity as well as my avarice, but I refrained from acting until the following morning, even though I was so distracted that the work I did for the balance of that afternoon probably worsened rather than bettered Sir Robert's prose, if such a thing is possible.

The following morning I took a carriage to the address on the card, but exited a block distant. I examined the house from that vantage point, purchased a few items from a pushcart to avoid appearing conspicuous. It looked to be in good repair, though so heavily shuttered and curtained that I could not glimpse the interior. There was no sign of life from within, and after perhaps half an hour I approached, feeling somewhat uncomfortable.

Eventually I became impatient with myself and strode forthrightly to the door, used the small brass knocker to announce my presence. There was a long pause and I was raising my hand to knock a second time when the door was suddenly ajar.

"Yes? What is it?" I could see one eye and the hint of a nose, but nothing else.

Feeling rather foolish, I spoke as directed. "The Lady requires her past."

There was no initial reaction and I began to feel more the fool than ever. Then the door edged shut and, red faced, I started to turn away, stopped when I heard the distinct sound of a chain falling loose.

"Come inside, if you please sir."

My hostess came barely to my shoulder, and I am not a tall man. She was thin, with sharply chiseled features and her skin was almost as gray as the clothing in which she was dressed. I entered a small vestibule, to the left of which was arranged a small sitting room, amply if not regally furnished, clean and orderly, though poorly lighted.

"Would you be Mrs. Bates?" I asked.

"I suppose that I am." She indicated that I should take a seat, but made no move to do so herself, so I remained standing.

"My name is Palmer, Edward Palmer. I've been employed to fetch some materials which you have held in safekeeping. I trust that you know what I am referring to."

"The diaries and papers. Yes, they are all quite safe. I have always watched out for them, just as I agreed to. You are supposed to have something to show me."

"Oh, yes. I had forgotten." I produced the ring and handed it to her. She bent closely over it, eying it critically, then crossed the room to a small wooden cabinet. I waited patiently while she slid open a small drawer and extracted what, from a distance at least, looked like the exact mate of the ring I'd carried. She held the two up to her eyes for almost a full minute before sighing and putting them both into the drawer.

"Looks like the right one."

"I assure you it is not counterfeit. And the documents?"

But she didn't seem to hear me. "What's to become of me then?"

"I beg your pardon?"

She turned and looked at me, and I realized she was quite advanced in years. "Will they be putting me out of this house then, now that you've come? Is it to be the streets for me?"

I had no idea what the arrangements were for the maintenance of the property and told her so. "But I have no instructions to say anything to the solicitors who pay you or anyone else, so I see no reason why you should not continue to live here." I hoped that what I was telling her was the truth, but I had no idea what chain of events would follow once I had completed my task.

She seemed resigned if not reassured, and led me down a short, narrow corridor to the rear of the house. The room we sought was kept locked with perhaps the heaviest device I had ever seen outside a bank, and the door itself was lined on both sides with sheets of lead. Mrs. Bates produced a key and led me inside, lighting a small lamp. The room was bare except for a plain table that sat in its direct center, and on top of which was a wooden box.

"They're all there, every one of them."

The top was unfastened and I lifted it to one side. It was about half filled with small bound volumes and a bundle of loose papers and newspaper clippings. "Have you read any of this?" I asked.

Mrs. Bates shook her head vigorously. "Never had no call to. None of my business, was it? I did what I was employed to do and nothing more." She was sounding a bit more belligerent now so I decided to hasten my departure.

The box was heavier than I expected, but quite manageable. I thanked her for her non-existent hospitality and bade her a good day, then waited outside with my foot resting on the box until I was able to hail a carriage and return to my office.

I had planned only a quick glance at the documents that day, but it wasn't long before I realized the nature of them, their relationship to Stoker's novel, and detected enough of the anomalies to realize I had stumbled into, or been pushed into, a situation quite extraordinary.

It took two full days to arrange everything chronologically and mark the significant passages. When the task was done, I was torn between believing myself the object of a very elaborate practical joke and sensing that I was on the brink of revealing a secret that would reshape how we think of our world. It overwhelmed me and for the next few weeks, the box and its contents remained hidden in the closet of my office while I struggled to complete Sir Robert's book.

Then we had our conversation at the Sullivans' party the other evening and the renewal of our old friendship reminded me of how easily you were able to plumb the depths of every problem that presented itself when we shared quarters at Oxford, and I knew that I had found someone who could look at the evidence coldly and logically and suggest an explanation for what appears to be an elaborate fantasy.

One more thing before I close.

I made inquiries concerning Josef Straban. I could find no one who knew him either socially or professionally, although I obviously lack the resources to conduct an exhaustive investigation. The address on the card he left with me was a hotel in Piccadilly which proved to be rather less elegant than I might have expected.

The desk clerk informed me that no one of that name was presently registered at the hotel, but he reached under the desk and brought forward a sealed envelope and handed it to me.

"The gentleman said that I should give this to anyone who inquired about him."

I thanked him heartily and took a seat in the lobby, tore open the envelope, and read the brief note contained therein. It will be enclosed with this letter. I am off to Scotland for a few days, for reasons which should be obvious.

Handwritten note addressed to Edward Palmer but neither signed nor dated.

If you are reading this, then it is probable that you have in your possession a collection of documents whose authenticity you will most certainly doubt. I have reason to believe that a second cache is being watched over in similar fashion in the vicinity of Cruden Bay, Scotland, where Bram Stoker spent the declining years of his life. Unless I have misjudged your character, you will find it difficult to avoid pursuing the tale to its end. I wish you the best of luck, and hope that we will meet to discuss the matter at least once more.

JS

Letter from James Chatsworth to Edward Palmer, dated June 30, 1920.

I was tempted from the outset to believe that you had made up this entire elaborate story simply to bedevil me the way you once did while we shared quarters, but knowing your animosity toward anything that hinted of the irrational or supernatural, I found it in that respect totally out of character. I also took the liberty of asking some of my learned colleagues to examine samples of the documents you forwarded to me, and they agree that the condition of those materials is entirely consistent with their stated age. What few verifiable details I could identify also agreed with external sources.

So if this is a hoax, it is one that was conceived before either of us was born. I am more inclined to believe that it was some elaborate form of written playacting engaged in by one - or more likely several - individuals for some purpose we may never learn. Whether Stoker participated in its creation, or made use of selected portions later, is a question that remains unanswered. It certainly explains why his other literary efforts were so markedly inferior. Whatever the truth might be, it is almost certain that they represent a valuable literary find, and perhaps have commercial value as well.

That all being said, I am somewhat concerned about this mysterious Mr. Straban. Although he has offered you no harm, I suspect his motives. It would not surprise me to discover that it is he who is behind the mysterious funding of Mrs. Bates. I fear this letter will not reach you before you depart, and that even if it did, it would not deter you from going, but I pray that you will use the utmost caution as well as discretion in pursuing your inquires. I feel an almost premonitory sense of danger.

Your friend always,

Charles

Edward Palmer's Travel Diary

June 28, 1920

I have never previously kept any sort of journal or log other than some informal notes about my work, but I have decided to do so on at least a temporary basis. It would be amusing to claim that I have been inspired by the examples of Jack Seward, Mina Murray, and Vlad Tepes, but the truth is rather more prosaic. It is too soon to guess what truth lies behind the elaborate façade I am exploring, but whether it is a hoax, self delusion, or actual history is irrelevant. I propose to document my investigations and discoveries, perhaps produce a book of my own. If Sir Robert Cosgrove's name can grace the frontispiece of a treatise on England's moral decline, then certainly I can pen the true story behind one of the most notorious literary works of the last century.

Departed today by train for Cruden Bay. I have made arrangements to stay at a local hotel. Sir Robert's manuscript is as ready as it will ever be, and I have sent it off by messenger so that he may peruse it at his leisure and discover how brilliant an author he really is. With no other projects pending, I have decided to spend a portion of Josef Straban's funds by treating myself to what may well be a waste of time, but will at least serve as a long overdue holiday.

June 29

Too exhausted yesterday to write a full account so I will need to catch up this evening. I am reasonably comfortably ensconced in a small suite of rooms at the Cruden Bay Hotel, a quite modern establishment situated within easy walking distance of the town and the shore, surrounded by tennis courts, a bowling green, and croquet fields, and conveniently close to the new golf course. I arrived by rail from Boddam in the midst of a miserable drizzling rain which persisted for the balance of the day, and then by tram from the station to my lodgings. Unable to rest while en route, I lay fully clothed on my bed and dozed for several hours, then turned in quite early that same evening.

The sun was up this morning and so were my spirits. It is quite a beautiful place, named for some glorious victory of the Scots over the Danes hundreds of years ago. The local harbor was constructed in the late 1870s, just after the death of Vlad Tepes if we accept these things as true, but it attracts more tourists than commercial vessels.

There is a fishing village directly south of here, called Whinnyfold, facing the Skares of Cruden, a series of upthrust rocks of forbidding aspect which linger off the shore like carrion birds seeking prey. The desk clerk assures me they are haunted and that if

I wait around long enough, I might see the ghosts of those who perished in shipwrecks as they walk above their watery graves.

The village proper is called Hatton and seems unprepossessing, though after London's hustle and bustle I must say the more relaxed demeanor of the local inhabitants is positively refreshing. I am told that I must not leave without visiting Slains Castle, which was restored some years ago and until recently had been regular host to the nobility. The Earl is bankrupt now, apparently, and the property has passed into new hands. Much has changed following the War even in these remote regions.

North of us the scenery is reputed to be quite spectacular along the coast, which is lined by eroding cliffs and features a dangerous chasm known as the Bullers. Cruden Bay itself is crescent shaped with an attractive and extensive beach, although the water is rather cold. It seems a quite ordinary and modern place in some ways, but overlaying it all is a cloak of superstition that seems entirely complementary to my mission.

During the course of my trip, I concocted a cover story to explain my activities. It is not entirely satisfactory and will not hold up to close investigation, but I am relying on my charming manner and glib tongue to see me through. Tomorrow will be my first test.

June 29, 1920

I met today with the clerk who maintains the records for the Episcopal Church of St. James, which sits so prominently on its hill that it commands the eye for miles in every direction. He is an elderly but likable chap named Henry Potter, and has held his position for many years. My appointment was for mid-morning but he was not immediately about when I arrived, having forgotten it entirely. A village lad fetched him for me when I tossed him a copper, and he was suitably apologetic.

His office was small but neat, compulsively orderly I would be tempted to say. "Now, Mr. Palmer," he said after sending the boy for some tea. "How is it that I may help you?"

I had rehearsed my story several times and felt confident that it would hold up. "I have come down from London to do a bit of amateur sleuthing. My uncle is a solicitor and he has recently been handling the estate of a rather wealthy but eccentric gentleman of substantial means. The client, whom I am not at liberty to name, had been more than a bit dotty the last few years, and dispersed a number of his assets in such manner that the heirs are having great difficulty securing them."

Potter nodded. "The aristocratic blood runs thin at times," he said judgmentally.

"Yes, so I would imagine. In any case, some of these assets consist of properties scattered about the countryside. Their maintenance is provided for by funds held in trust by individuals whose names were never properly recorded. In most instances, a caretaker is hired to live in the property and to see to its upkeep in exchange for a stipend and, of course, the free lodgings. As far as I know, these caretakers remain completely ignorant of their employer."

Potter nodded, but his eyes were straying, so I moved directly to the point. "Among the effects of the deceased were papers which hinted that one of these properties was located in or in close proximity to Cruden Bay, and that this particular property might hold a number of valuable documents which are known to be part of the estate. I wondered if you might be aware of any of your parishioners who lived in such circumstances."

"Oh, dear me, I can't say that I am, Mr. Palmer. Our membership consists entirely of families, most of them well to do and hardly in need of such employment. You might try the Old Church near Hatton. Mrs. Tinsdale would be the person to whom you should speak. She has a sharp eye."

The tea had come and I accepted a cup, although I was impatient to go. Potter launched into a history of the church while I sipped, informing me that it was originally built to commemorate the defeat of the Danish invaders. I turned down the offer of a biscuit, pleading a late breakfast, and managed to depart without wasting too large a portion of the morning.

I had hired a bicycle from the hotel and made my way without haste to Old Church. There I managed to locate Mrs. Tinsdale without great difficulty, a formidable woman who pinned me to my seat with her eyes. I repeated my light fantasy about the missing legacy and was met with a prolonged and awkward silence that led me to suspect that Mrs. Tinsdale didn't believe a word of it.

"There's naught I can tell you, Mr. Palmer," she said at last, somehow managing to make my name sound like an insult. "It is no business of mine the circumstances of others, nor do I have any obligation to pass on such gossip to a newcomer on their say so."

"I assure you, Mrs. Tinsdale, that my intentions are entirely honorable. It is simply as a favor to my uncle that I agreed to pursue the matter. If I were to discover the identity of those who currently benefit from the arrangement, they will not lose as a consequence." Actually, I didn't know if that was true or not.

"And what would be the consequences for the poor soul you discovered, pray tell? The property reverts to the estate, I should think, and any prior arrangements for its stewardship would come to an end."

""Well, yes, probably." I could see where she was steering the conversation, but could not think fast enough to alter its destination.

"Then if I was to tell you and you was to determine that someone who had entrusted their situation to me was no longer entitled to their living, it would be me who would be responsible for their losing their home, would that not be the case?"

"I am sure that some sort of arrangement could be made." It sounded weak even as I spoke the words, and I began searching for an escape route. My little prevarication was not going to work this time. "In any case, it is only right that the truth be brought to light."

"That's as may be. I cannot help you, Mr. Palmer, and while I do not wish you good luck, I do wish you a good day."

I felt like a Dane rushing from the field of battle.

June 30, 1920

After being disappointed by Potter and repelled by Mrs. Tinsdale, I ended yesterday feeling disappointed, frustrated, and totally inadequate. A night's rest and a hearty breakfast has improved my spirits somewhat, and when I outlined my imaginary quest to the desk clerk, he even offered a concrete suggestion. Two of them, in fact.

The first was that I visit the local constabulary and request their assistance. I am loathe to do so because once any official interest is aroused, it may be pursued far enough to unmask my little fiction and cause me significant discomfort. The second was to engage a local solicitor, a Mr. Ormsby, who specializes in real estate transactions. It might well be that this Ormsby is in fact the administrator of the place I seek and, if so, he would certainly be in a position to enlighten me quickly. I have made an appointment with him this afternoon. I am determined to see this through. My father used to charge me that I was easily deflected when an obstacle was placed in my path, but this time I shall rise above my own limitations.

Later

I did not care for Mr. Ormsby, and I have the distinct impression that he reciprocated. To put it succinctly, the man is a snob, obviously considered my intentions suspect, asked entirely too many questions I did not want to answer, and was almost insultingly unwilling to provide any assistance whatsoever. His clerk, whom he called Miss Dobbit repeatedly, as in "Can you believe such a wild tale, Miss Dobbit?" and "I could not get involved in such a morbid effort, could I now, Miss Dobbit?", apparently shares my opinion. She sat out of his line of sight throughout our interview and made small disapproving faces behind his back, sometimes so exaggeratedly that I nearly burst out laughing. The man's insufferable arrogance and overbearing attitude angered me sufficiently that I found my own temper rising before the interview ended.

Ultimately I was dismissed. "Please see the gentleman out, Miss Dobbit." His tone made it clear that the term 'gentleman' was a compliment I scarcely deserved.

I was shaking my head in exasperation as I made ready to leave, but Miss Dobbit placed a restraining hand on my arm when we reached the outer office. "Wait here a moment, sir, if you will." She hurried into a small room to one side, then returned bearing a calling card which she thrust into my hand.

"I don't know if he can help you, but we have employed Mr. Moore as our agent in the past, and he has almost always provided satisfaction."

I thanked her profusely but she cut me off. "Be gone with you now before he comes out. The old bear is actually as softhearted as they come, but he has an exaggerated sense of his own dignity. In confidence, I assure you that none of our clients is a likely prospect, but Mr. Moore casts his net considerably wider than do we."

It was too late to seek another appointment, so I have returned to my rooms. There still remains some hope, but I am beginning to understand the thin substance of my quest, and wonder if I'm making a fool of myself.

July 1, 1920

I have met the most charming young woman.

After finishing yesterday's entry, I retired to the hotel dining room, only to find it extremely crowded. The staff were uniformly apologetic but insisted that I might have to wait as much as the better part of an hour before I could be seated. The nearest inn was within a few minutes ride, but I was tired and a bit depressed and had no intention of setting forth again before the morrow.

I was about to turn away and return to my room to pass the intervening time when a waiter hurried over and informed me that one of those seated within had offered to share a table with me. Naturally I was of two minds about accepting. The prospect of finding myself impaled upon a lance of incessant chatter by a variant of Mr. Potter, or skewered for my lack of breeding by a supercilious pseudo-Ormsby dimmed my appetite, but at that crucial juncture my stomach rolled and protested audibly and I accepted defeat.

Imagine my delight at finding myself joining a quite attractive young woman of approximately my age. She introduced herself as Miss Shirley Appleton of Toronto, Canada. She is of slightly above average height for a woman, with an attractive if somewhat slender figure, but her most remarkable feature is a sweep of rich, auburn hair which she unstylishly allows to fall loose about her shoulders.

I introduced myself briefly and thanked her for her charity toward a starving man. "I hope you will return the favor by rescuing me from a dull evening," she replied easily. "I was supposed to meet my cousins here, but they have sent word that they have been delayed on route and will not arrive until tomorrow. I am terribly ill suited to entertain myself, I am afraid."

"Are they also Canadian?"

"No, my father emigrated when he was eighteen. I have been back to visit twice before, but this is the first time I have dared make the trip on my own. I assume you are here for the golfing?"

I shook my head. "Never had time for that sort of thing. Too busy making a living."

"You are in commerce then?"

"Not exactly." I had always felt a certain amount of embarrassment explaining my profession to others, even though it was by no means dishonorable and certainly paid my bills. Most of the time, at least. "I provide a research service to various authors," I began my usual explanation, then halted, inexplicably unwilling to mislead my new acquaintance. "But for the most part, I turn barely literate manuscripts into prose so that spoiled dilettantes can delude themselves into believing themselves capable of writing a decent sentence."

"Have you no ambitions of your own then?" Her eyes were quite remarkable and they never wavered. I felt as though she could read a lie before it left my lips.

"I dabble occasionally in the creative arts. With lamentably little success to date."

"So is this a vacation or are you here on business?"

I wasn't sure how to answer that. "A bit of both. I find myself ahead of the bills at the moment, and there is a bit of a mystery that I'm trying to clear up. It may, perhaps, result in an interesting subject for an article."

She leaned forward over clasped hands and her eyes sparkled. "Do tell me about it. I love a good puzzle."

I provided a reasonably accurate but heavily edited version indicating that I was searching for a cache of documents rumored to be in the vicinity of Cruden Bay, and alluded to those already in my possession, although without mentioning the specifics of their content or their relationship to the Stoker manuscript. She questioned me quite closely and I reluctantly described the probable arrangements made for their safekeeping. Fearing that I had revealed too much, I attempted to bring the conversation to a close. "The details are, I am afraid, somewhat confidential."

"Then I shall not press you for them. But it does sound like wonderful fun. Is there any way that I could be of assistance?" There was a childlike quality in her voice and I reassessed my judgment of her age. Early on she had carried herself with the authority of a woman in her mid-twenties, but I mentally shaved five years off that estimate.

"I'm afraid it is all going to be very tedious. I hope to engage a local man tomorrow to pursue the matter, but short of knocking up every house in this part of Scotland, there seems to be little else I could do."

"You might post a notice in the local papers."

That had never occurred to me and upon reflection I doubted it would have any result, but the small effort required was certainly worth the investment. I thanked her for the suggestion and asked about her cousins. She was silent for a moment, then seemed to accept my redirection of the conversation and we finished our meal in companionable discussion of inconsequentials.

When she had finished, I offered to escort her to her door but she declined. "It is my habit to take a solitary walk after the evening meal and reflect upon my day." She smiled pleasantly. "And you have given me quite a bit to reflect upon. I wish you the best of luck, Mr. Palmer, and I hope that you will further enlighten me before you leave."

"If that is at all possible, Miss Appleton, it will be my great pleasure to do so."

This morning I rose early, finding my sleep plagued by dreams in which I was lost in a series of nondescript, poorly lighted, and extremely dusty rooms, searching for some unknown treasure and pursued by an indistinct but vaguely frightening presence who whispered just below the threshold of audibility. It was quite unsettling and I woke twice in a cold sweat, finally rising unrefreshed and fretful.

A hearty breakfast helped dispel the fog in my head, and I set off on my bicycle in considerably improved spirits. I found Mr. Moore's establishment with minimal difficulty, a small, blocklike building with closely shuttered windows, a gabled roof, and an understated sign that read simply "Quentin Moore, Inquiries".

The gentleman who opened the door for me was a head shorter than I and appeared pale and undernourished. The lenses of his spectacles were so thick that his eyes were distorted. He introduced himself as Alfred Lembic, Mr. Moore's secretary, and ushered me into a small office whose walls were lined with books from floor to ceiling. A second door leading to the rest of the building was closed. There was a heavily cluttered desk in one corner and three chairs arranged so that each faced the other two.

"I wish to discuss a matter of business with Mr. Moore if he i available."

Lembic gestured that I should take a seat. "I am afraid Mr. Moore is not in at the moment. He is occupied with certain," he paused dramatically, "inquiries of a delicate nature."

I had started to sit, but now stood up. "I see. Could you suggest a better time then? Might I make an appointment?"

"That won't be necessary. I have full authority to take down the particulars of your request and relay them to my employer, who rarely has the leisure to interview prospective clients. If Mr. Moore feels that he can be of any service, he will contact you."

Let me say outright that I cared very little for the man. His manner was one of sly obsequiousness. I also sensed that something lay hidden behind the eyes, something judgmental and unkind. Nevertheless, I repeated my cover story, again refusing to put a name to my fictional parties. "I am afraid I have been enjoined against revealing that information."

"Quite right, I'm sure." Lembic glanced away briefly and I thought that, just for a second, his expression betrayed amusement, and I wondered if he had seen through my little fable. "I expect to hear from Mr. Moore later today. Where can we reach you?"

I gave him my room number. "I shall be in and out today and this evening, but a message left at the desk will certainly find its way to me." I stood up, impatient to leave, and Lembic followed me to the door.

"Have you seen the Bullers yet, Mr. Palmer?"

"No. I've been told about them, of course."

"You really mustn't leave without visiting them, if I may say so. They are quite extraordinary."

Finding myself at loose ends, I wandered about Hatton rather aimlessly for the balance of the morning, ate a light meal at a picturesque tea shop where the chatty hostess regaled me with tales of the local tourist attractions. I listened intently, hoping for some clue that would assist me on my mission, and heard more local gossip than I cared to. Unfortunately, none of it cast any light upon the specific darkness facing me.

After escaping Mrs. Geoghan's, I decided to take Lembic's advice, rented a bicycle, and received instructions for the four mile journey to the coast. Even had there been no sign, I could not have missed the Bullers of Buchan, for the roar of water crashing down into the chasm was audible long before I had any visual cue. As Lembic had suggested, it was really quite spectacular. The ocean rushes in through an open arch and falls approximately seventy meters. I must have spent an hour watching the descending water. It was quite exhilarating and much to my surprise, I found myself grown hungry again. Fortunately there was a pub in the small village nearby, cramped and poorly lit, although the fare was quite respectable.

After that I walked along the cliffs for a bit, enjoying the scenery, accompanied by a great number of seabirds who followed me as attentively as street beggars might have done back in London. The sun seemed to decline rapidly after that, and I hastily reclaimed my bicycle and pedaled back to the hotel, arriving at dusk.

Three young women were sitting at an outside table when I arrived, and I recognized Miss Appleton when she waved me over. I was a bit tired and dusty and not really in a sociable mood, but her enthusiasm was contagious and I finally agreed to join them at their table for a few moments.

Rachel and Lucinda Campbell were quite evidently sisters, although I had to struggle to find any features they shared with Miss Appleton. Where she was fairly tall, they both tended to be unusually short. Rachel was clearly older than her sister, and temperamentally she seemed far more mature. Both had dark hair and pleasing features, though Rachel seemed a bit too finely chiseled and Lucinda, Lucy that is, somewhat gaunt. I wondered if she had been recently ill. I have never been good about guessing ages, but if as I now suspected Miss Appleton was barely twenty, then in all probability she was closely bracketed by her cousins.

The sisters were planning to spend a fortnight in Cruden Bay before Thomas Campbell, their father, arrived following a trip to Scandinavia. "Your father is in business then?" I inquired politely.

"Actually he works for the Crown," Rachel informed me with a hint of pride.

"He's a spy is what he is," effused Lucy, leaning over to clutch my arm. "He still refuses to talk about his duties during the War."

Rachel's glare should have scorched her sister's skin, but Lucy seemed oblivious. "Our father works in naval intelligence," she told me levelly. "In a purely advisory capacity and sometimes as liaison with certain foreign governments."

"Will you be going back to Glasgow when he arrives?"

"Shortly thereafter. But then we are to visit London and a hop across to Paris." Rachel's solemn posturing cracked a bit at that point and I asked if this would be their first trip to the continent.

"We went once before, but I don't remember much of it. Our mother was still alive then, and Lucy was just a baby."

"And will you be accompanying them, Miss Appleton?"

"I certainly shall. And how are your investigations going, Mr. Palmer?"

This necessitated yet another rendition of my story, this time for the benefit of the Campbell sisters, who surprised me by being very attentive and asking a number of probing questions, particularly Lucy. I made a quick mental reassessment; for all her frivolity, Lucy was an astute, intelligent young woman as was her sister and cousin. Fearing that one or another of them would find some fatal flaw in my masquerade, I changed the subject, but Lucy returned to it a short time later.

"You must let us assist you, Mr. Palmer. It sounds like great fun."

"It's all rather tedious actually. I would not want you to waste your holiday in such trivial and probably pointless pursuits. In any case, I have made arrangements with a local man and hope to resolve everything shortly."

I made my reluctant excuses a short time later, because I began to feel that I was intruding. It would be dishonest of me to pretend that I was not attracted to Miss Appleton. She had a way of appraising one with her eyes that might have seemed rather forward if it had not been immediately obvious that she was a good hearted and transparently honest person. It would not be unfair to say that I was no longer in a great hurry to find the answers to my questions, at least not for the next fortnight.

Midnight

I had not thought to write more here until tomorrow, but I am strangely restless and wish to summarize recent events while they are still fresh in my mind.

After leaving Miss Appleton and her cousins, I dined alone, then shared brandy with two gentlemen from Cornwall who had come for the golf. We discussed nothing of consequence, and I forgot both of their names even before we parted, although they seemed likable enough. It was a clear, cool night, and I went outside for a smoke before returning to my room. When I did so, I found that I had a visitor.

He must have been waiting in the shadows of the corridor, because he was at my side the moment my key touched the lock, although I had had no hint of his presence.

"Mr. Palmer?"

"Yes." I watched him rather warily. He was a tall man, large through the shoulders, wearing a well tailored suit that seemed somewhat incongruous because of his rough features, a shock of ink black hair that fell well below his collar, and a rather extraordinary moustache that extended beyond the sides of his head.

"My name is Quentin Moore. I believe you spoke to my secretary earlier today." His voice was deep and betrayed a faint but discernible American accent.

"Ah, yes, I did indeed. I had hoped to meet with you, but not quite so informally."

"I apologize, but I have just returned to Cruden Bay this evening. Lembic described the inquiry you suggested, but lacked some particulars. He was unable to indicate the degree of urgency, so I came over straightaway. If another time would be better for you, I would strive to be at your service."

"No, no." I unlocked the door and pushed it open. "Come in, please. I appreciate your prompt response."

We seated ourselves inside and I told my story once again. Moore listened intently, almost without moving. When I was done, he let the silence hold for an uncomfortably long time before speaking.

"You give me little to work with, Mr. Palmer. If in fact such a cache of documents exists in this area, their presence is likely a closely held secret. I don't know how many solitary tenants might be found in the vicinity of Cruden Bay, but there are certainly a good many of them, and for that matter, what assurance do we have that this particular lot, granting its reality, is not guarded by a married couple, or perhaps an entire family?"

"None at all," I admitted. "Is the situation completely hopeless then?" I felt suddenly deflated.

He sat forward with his hands on his knees. "Not necessarily. There are certain lines of inquiry that might prove fruitful. The peculiar circumstances of the financing, for example. Very few of the local residents live without visible means of support. And there are other possibilities." He let his voice trail off.

"What possibilities might those be?"

Moore shook his head. "If I revealed all of my resources, I would never secure any trade. You must trust me to pursue the matter in my own way. Might I inquire why you have not simply placed an advertisement?"

Lucy Campbell had suggested this very thing, and I had a flimsy story ready. "The family wishes to avoid any public mention that might reveal the sad mental state of the deceased. We are specifically prohibited from doing so, or we would naturally have pursued such a course long since."

"Yes, of course." He laughed softly. "I am an American, as you must have realized by now, and I confess that the English sense of propriety continues to amuse me even though I have been exposed to it now for many years."

I wondered if I should feel insulted, but Moore gave me no opportunity to do so.

"It is an intriguing problem that you have presented me, Mr. Palmer, and I confess that that I am not currently overburdened with work. I suggest that you employ my firm to conduct some initial inquiries, with further efforts conditional upon our mutual agreement that there is some ground for hope. If that is agreeable to you, we could meet again, say, two days from now."

I could think of no objection and said so. "How much is this likely to cost me, Mr. Moore?"

He quoted a quite reasonable rate for the preliminary work, more reasonable than I might have hoped for, and I realized that expenses here were undoubtedly a lighter burden than in London. Or perhaps he was desperate for work. I paid him half the agreed sum in advance, and he wrote me a receipt on a page torn from this very notebook. I offered to buy him a drink in the hotel bar, but he declined.

"I have traveled a considerable distance this day, Mr. Palmer, and I am frankly rather weary. It's home for me, a quick meal, and some much needed rest so that I can arise alert tomorrow on your behalf." And a moment later he departed.

Letter from James Chatsworth to Edward Palmer, dated June 30, 1920

Dear James,

Upon sober reflection, I am more convinced than ever that you are involved in some immensely clever hoax. I cannot imagine why you would be the target of such an effort, but it is entirely possible that ultimately you are not, that misleading you is merely a preliminary step in a larger plot whose object we cannot yet determine. Consider the arguments against proceeding.

Primus, the question of authenticity. We would have to admit the existence of the animated undead among us. Although it is understandable that the uneducated residents of remote and undeveloped continental regions should fall prey to such superstitious nonsense, it would be inexcusable for rational men such as ourselves to allow ignorance to conquer reason. Segundus. One might argue that the authors of these documents were to varying degrees deluded but believed themselves to be telling the truth. Mr. Stoker then constructed his story from selected portions of the text. His motivation for doing so is at best obscure, but I can think of no circumstance in which this would prove advantageous for you. At best, one might excite some interest among scholars interested in the novel's literary antecedents, but frankly, my recollection is that the book was of dubious moral probity and doubtful literary value. Tertius. Even if the unthinkable were true, what purpose would be served by revealing the existence of these documents to you, who have no connection with the named parties? What has this Straban to gain? I can only suggest that this is part of an elaborate hoax whose ultimate purpose is to separate someone from their fortune.

There is one course of action which you might well consider, although I wonder if this entire charade was designed to urge you in that direction. Mr. Stoker's widow remains alive and active in society. Perhaps she could cast some light on the issue?

Your Concerned Friend,

James

Edward Palmer's Travel Diary

July 2, 1920

I found myself at loose ends today, so I decided to devote myself to tourism. I have refrained from taking a proper holiday for several years now – the expenditures would be difficult to justify - and since there seemed to be nothing productive I could do, I talked at length to the desk clerk. Once I had convinced him that I positively had no interest whatsoever in the game of golf, he admitted that there were other things to see and do. Slains Castle seemed the best bet for a bit of hiking.

"There is no admittance to the castle proper at the moment, but the courtyard is open, and the gardens, though they are rather overgrown, I'm afraid. There are usually peddlers about so you can get yourself a bite to eat if you're not too fussy, and if you would rather, you could pedal down to Port Eroll, what has some good taverns." He suggested two in particular and gave me directions and advised me to leave my bicycle at the base of the cliff. "There's usually a boy or two about who will watch over it for a few pennies. Pick one who has a number in his charge already if you can. More likely to be reliable."

It was an extraordinarily pleasant day and being in no hurry, I dawdled through the morning and took twice as long as I might have otherwise before reaching my destination. There was indeed a young lad offering to take my bicycle in charge. "But I'm off at dusk, so if you're not back afore then, it's on yer own head."

The climb was lengthy but not arduous, and the castle was worth the effort, though clearly it had been neglected in recent years. The lawns were unkempt and overgrown and the gardens had pretty much gone wild. The castle itself is a sprawling, blocky structure whose highest point is perhaps four stories, the tower house. The doors and windows were all heavily barred, and the interior so dark that I could see very little even peering through the open spaces. The roof was intact insofar as I could determine but showed signs of wear. I knew the castle had changed hands recently but there was no evidence that the new owner was planning a significant restoration.

On the other hand, the view to seaward was magnificent. The castle is so close to the cliff edge that it seems almost an extension of the surrounding rocks. The waves striking far below make the air and ground shiver in response. I had a bad moment when I turned my ankle on a loose stone near the edge, and I left a respectful gap between myself and the precipice thereafter. A young couple had also made the climb, but they seemed more interested in each other than in the castle. The promised peddlers were not in evidence, although an older couple on a hiking trip were brewing tea and offered me a cup, which I found quite refreshing.

I might have stayed longer but my stomach protested such mistreatment, so I reluctantly descended the path, found my young bicycle guardian soundly asleep, rewarded him with an extra penny anyway, and pressed on toward the harbor.

The King Canute Tavern was the first I encountered. It was not one of those the desk clerk had recommended, but I was famished and in no mood to be epicurean. I parked my bicycle and entered, and was greeted almost immediately by a young man who was devastated to tell me that there were no tables open but that I could take a seat at the bar and order a meal there. No sooner had I done so, however, than history repeated itself. Someone tugged on the sleeve of my jacket and I turned to discover Miss Appleton standing behind me.

"It seems to be my destiny to rescue you from dining alone, Mr. Palmer. There is a vacancy at our table if you would deign to join us."

I glanced in the direction she had indicated and spotted the Campbell sisters sitting in the far corner of the room. Lucy grinned and waved while Rachel simply nodded and touched her lips with a napkin. "It would be my great pleasure, Miss Appleton."

"Must we be so formal? This is the third time we've spoken and I much prefer to be called Shirley."

"Very well," I hesitated, "Shirley it is then. And I am Edward."

She raised one eyebrow. "Not Ed, or perhaps Ted?"

"No, I'm a bit too stuffy for that. I was Neddy for a while, but then I learned to walk and it was Edward henceforth."

I told the barman that I was joining a party already seated and followed Miss Appleton, Shirley, back to the table. Lucy greeted me with her usual effulgence and Rachel condescended to smile briefly. They had, I realized, almost finished their meal, and in fact by the time my ale and a bowl of lamb stew arrived, the table had been otherwise cleared. The press of people around us was ebbing as well, and we were able to talk normally almost from the outset.

After the usual pleasantries, the details of which I could not have recalled even moments later, Shirley asked if my investigations had advanced at all. "In no particular," I confessed. "I am at the mercy of an expatriate American and his staff. He offered me scant hope, I'm afraid."

"Are you no longer pursuing the matter personally?"

"Not at the moment. I've just visited a ruined castle and nearly fallen off a cliff, otherwise my life has been uneventful these past few hours. Until encountering the three of you, of course."

"Well, we have been pursuing the matter for you!" said Lucy brightly. Rachel glared at her and Shirley looked amused and guilty simultaneously.

It was Rachel who explained. "I hope you won't feel that we've been interfering in your affairs, Mr. Palmer. I assure you that we have been quite discrete. Lucy was flirting with a young man in Hatton." This time it was the younger sister who glared, but she held her peace. "He mentioned in passing that he lived adjacent to a reclusive woman who almost never left her home and who lived without visible means of support. Lucy endeavored to discover the address, but he misinterpreted her interest and became rather too familiar, so I was forced to intercede and he left in rather a huff."

"But he did say that his house faced down onto the harbor here!" Lucy was quite animated and her voice was raised enough to attract the attention of our fellow diners. Rachel shushed her and she continued in what was now an exaggeratedly conspiratorial and no less noticeable voice. "We hired a car and came out to take a look. And lucky us, he also mentioned a cobblers' shop across the street.

There are only two such in the village, and only one facing a private residence. The mysterious neighbor must live on one side or the other."

I struggled to find an appropriate response. "And were you planning to knock on their doors and ask them to reveal their secrets?"

"More or less," replied Shirley. "Don't worry, Edward. We haven't been revealing any of your business. You would be surprised how much three transparently silly young ladies can learn if they set their minds to it."

It was an awkward meal that followed. On the one hand, I greatly enjoyed their company, even warming somewhat to the rather grim Rachel. On the other, I had no wish to involve them in what might be a fruitless enterprise, or even a dangerous one, and I was concerned that they might inadvertently let slip something which would jeopardize my cause. And so I accompanied them on their investigation, and spent more than an hour sitting on a stone wall watching the ocean while they drank tea with an elderly woman whom they misled with some elaborate fantasy about searching for a lost branch of their family.

"I'm afraid we have wasted your time, Mr. Palmer," Rachel said quietly when they rejoined me. "Mrs. Hobson is living on her late husband's pension. She is extremely nearsighted and has trouble walking over uneven surfaces, so she rarely leaves her home."

"But she was delighted to entertain us," added Shirley. "Her neighbors apparently believe she practices witchcraft and will have nothing to do with her."

I took my leave a short time later, declining their offer of a ride even though it would have been quite possible to carry my bicycle in the boot. Instead I rode into Hatton to make a few purchases and send off a couple of wires. I only record that visit here because of a most peculiar encounter.

I had just purchased a new journal at the local stationer's shop and was trying to decide if there were any other errands I needed to complete before starting back when I glanced across the narrow street and saw Miss Dobbit, the solicitor's clerk, emerging from a small shop. She recognized me as well, but rather than nod a greeting or acknowledge me in any normal manner, she recoiled in what was quite obviously dismay and confusion. I might have called out to her, but she hurried off without speaking, leaving me sorely puzzled.

Perhaps she regrets having assisted me despite her employer's intransigence. I hope that she did not jeopardize her position by so doing.

From a Letter by Edward Palmer to James Chatsworth, dated July 3, 1920

Your suggestion regarding Mrs. Stoker is a good one, and I shall almost certainly act upon it when I am done here. I considered writing to her, but there are so many questions I have to ask that it is better if I endeavor to seek her out in person.

As you have surmised, I am in no hurry to leave Scotland. It is my first real holiday in too long a time and I am enjoying every bit of it, as well as the refreshing exercise and beautiful scenery in the area. I might even take up golf. And I confess as well that I am much taken with Miss Appleton and regardless of my success or failure, I shall probably remain in Cruden Bay until her uncle comes to fetch her away. She is remarkably intelligent and mature for her age, and her buoyant spirit makes it impossible to remain solemn in her presence. I know that I vowed to remain a bachelor after that disastrous situation with Kitty Hargreaves, but perhaps I was overly hasty.

Edward Palmer's Travel Diary

July 3, 1920

Nothing much to report today. My appointment with Moore was not until after lunch, so I spent the morning exploring the shoreline facing the Skares. Nary a ghost was to be seen, although the constant spray, the clinging morning fog, the persistent and erratic winds, and the odd shadows cast by the standing stones onto the rolling waters all combined to give the area a suitably supernormal appearance. It is easy enough to see where the superstitious might impose form upon chaos. If ever there was a place suitable for the dead to rise, I have seen it today.

I ate alone at a small pub whose name I have already forgotten, then proceeded to Hatton and the offices of Mr. Quentin Moore. Once again I was greeted by the unpleasant Mr. Lembic, who expressed his employer's regrets.

"Mr. Moore was called away unexpectedly, but will return later today. I have been instructed to advise you of our progress to date. Please come in; I have just brewed a fresh pot of tea."

Mr. Lembic was extremely solicitous and I made a conscious effort to overcome my aversion to the man. He assured me that every effort was being made. "I have combed through the lists of local property owners, successfully eliminating the vast majority from consideration. Mr. Moore is personally investigating those who seem to best fit your requirements. You must realize, of course, that in addition to Hatton, we are dealing with a significant number of small farming communities, and a handful of fishing villages."

"Yes, I visited one yesterday. I can probably strike one candidate from your list, in fact." Lembic listened intently to a recital of my adventure of the previous day.

"These three young ladies are friends of yours?" He inquired politely.

"Recent acquaintances only," I assured him.

"It was our understanding that this was to be a confidential inquiry." This time he sounded faintly displeased.

"And so it is. Trust me, the ladies have been quite discrete. This is all a game for them, and they will move on to another amusement as soon as a better one offers itself."

We parted shortly thereafter. Lembic assured me that Moore would be in touch within a day or two, and declined to accept a further partial fee. "There will be time for that when you and Mr. Moore come to a final reckoning, Mr. Palmer. If we did not believe you to be a gentleman, we would not have accepted the commission at the outset."

July 4

I returned to the hotel after yesterday's appointment hoping to find Shirley on the verandah, but there was no sign of her or the cousins. The desk clerk told me they had gone off in a hired car again only an hour before, after receiving a phone call from an unknown party. He made no effort to avoid smirking at my dismal effort to sound casual, and I am afraid I grew rather red faced. So I smoked a leisurely cigar and had a drink in the bar before going up to my room for a short nap, though sleep escaped me. My room was at the front of the hotel, and I found myself rushing to the window whenever a motor sounded from below.

They had not returned by dinner time so I finally ate alone, barely tasting what was probably a quite excellent piece of mutton. Feeling unaccountably sorry for myself, I drank rather more than is good for me, but avoided further embarrassment by leaving quietly before it became obvious to my companions. I managed to only partially undress myself before falling asleep lying diagonally across my bed.

It was too late for breakfast when I rose this morning, and I doubt in any case that I could have faced eggs without losing my composure. Although not ordinarily fond of coffee, I let a perceptive and sympathetic waiter talk me into having a cup, and I confess that it was quite bracing, though rather bitter.

I was at loose ends. It seemed impolite to bother Moore or Lembic again so quickly, and I was too shaky to consider bicycling into Hatton or walking the cliffs. My preference would be to spend the day talking with Shirley Appleton, although I was simultaneously reluctant to have her see me in my present condition. Her quick mind and keen eye would no doubt have identified the cause of my malaise in an instant.

I sat outside for a while, dozing in the warm sunlight, and woke shortly before noon with my head almost cleared and much of my normal energy restored. Having forgone breakfast, I was suddenly quite hungry, and entered the hotel intent upon ordering an early lunch. Instead, I found several members of the hotel staff and not a few of the guests hovering in the lobby, talking in small intense groups.

I had made a point of cultivating all three desk clerks and the present one, a nice young man named Waverly, nodded as I approached. "What's going on? Have I missed something?"

He nodded, looking distinctly unhappy. "It's a terrible situation, Mr. Palmer. That sort of thing just doesn't happen to us. Our clientele is very proper, I'm sure."

"Has there been an accident?"

"Not an accident. Murder!" He made it sound obscene, as perhaps it was.

A sudden presentiment left me speechless, and I had the strangest sense of déjà vu as Waverly continued to speak. "One of our guests, sir. A young lady."

I reached across the counter and grasped his arm, perhaps a bit roughly as he recoiled and his distress became alarm. "Which young lady?" My voice was like that of a stranger.

"One of the Misses Campbell, sir," he answered in a shaky voice, slowly withdrawing his arm.

"And what of the others? Miss Appleton and the sister?"

"I'm sure I don't know, sir." Having freed himself, Waverly chose to be offended by my manner, but frankly I didn't give a damn.

It took a few minutes to learn the particulars, or at least enough of them to give me some direction. A motorist had spotted their automobile in a ditch halfway between the hotel and the coast and had stopped to offer help. The vehicle was completely deserted and he was about to leave when his attention was drawn to a spot of color in the underbrush. He looked more closely and discovered the body of a young girl.

"Perhaps she was thrown from the car," I suggested to my informant, "during the course of their accident."

"He is quite certain that is not the case. The authorities have been called."

There was no word concerning the fate of the others. I approached Waverly again, who informed me with a trace of malice that there were no vehicles available for me to rent today, so I resorted to my bicycle, pedaling furiously. The constable's van passed me just as I was leaving the hotel property, and by the time I reached the scene, at least a score of figures were moving about.

I identified myself to a uniformed officer as a friend of the Campbells. He asked me to wait a moment while he conferred with his superior, then waved me over. Inspector Morton had a coarse, jowly face and his voice was gravelly. "You are acquainted with the deceased?" He stared at me as though this in itself were grounds for suspicion.

"I have spent some time with the Campbells and their cousin, yes."

"Would you be willing to confirm the identity of the remains?"

I nodded, not trusting myself to speak. He led me off the road and through the brush to a small declivity. An indistinct form lay in its center, covered with a blanket. Another uniformed officer stood just beyond, shifting his weight uneasily from one foot to the other. Morton lifted one end of the blanket, just enough to reveal the head and shoulders of Lucy Campbell. Her eyes were wide open, and there were streaks of blood on her face. I saw the ruin of her throat, so badly mauled that her spinal cord was exposed, and turned away with a shudder.

"Can you identify the victim, sir?" Morton's voice had softened, though just slightly.

"That is Lucy Campbell, the younger of the two sister." I forced myself to breathe deeply for several seconds. "Have you found the others yet?"

"We're organizing a search party now. Your assistance would be welcome."

I nodded, then followed Morton back to the roadway where he asked me to wait for further instructions. More than a dozen vehicles had arrived by now, disgorging both those professionally involved and those merely curious. I recognized a pair of golfers from the hotel, a shopkeeper I had done business with in Hatton, and then – most improbably of all – I spotted Miss Dobbit.

I am habitually suspicious of coincidences. This was the third time I had crossed the woman's path since arriving in Cruden Bay, and I was employing a man whom she had recommended. For a moment I considered greeting her, but then I noticed something furtive about her actions. She spoke to no one, kept her distance from the clusters of people ranged about her, and slowly made her way along the verge of the road to the point where the marks of the tires indicated that the Campbells' car had turned onto the grass. There was no indication of a particularly violent passage, and in fact although the vehicle was canted at a sharp angle it did not appear to be badly damaged at all. Shirley had mentioned that Rachel was an excellent driver and there seemed to be no reason why their vehicle would have gone out of control. The road was straight and in good condition and the weather had been fine for days.

No effort had been made to keep people from approaching the ditch. I took advantage of a low hedge to follow Miss Dobbit unobserved, and saw her bend at one point, then secret something inside her blouse. It looked very much like a man's handkerchief. Her mission apparently accomplished, she turned abruptly back, and I fell to the ground to avoid detection. When I dared look again, she had passed me and I hurriedly followed, then hid my face. Miss Dobbit was astride her bicycle and headed toward Hatton.

The rest of the day and early evening I spent searching the brush and woods in the company of perhaps three score other men. Constable Morton dispatched us in long lines and we methodically combed the countryside, but by nightfall we had found nothing, no trace of Rachel or Shirley, nor of their attacker. I had had nothing to eat but dry biscuits and cold tea before I finally returned to the hotel, but I left half my meal half uneaten and fell asleep immediately upon retiring.

It is early in the morning of July 5 now, and the kitchen staff is just beginning to stir, so I have completed yesterday's entry while sitting at my window, watching a strange fog slowly creep across the grounds. Despite the evidence, I have all along believed the Dracula documents to be fantasies. That has changed now. The death of a stranger, even under bizarre circumstances, can be dismissed as a hoax, a strange accident, or the result of twisted human malice. The death of an acquaintance, however casual, makes the act far more personal. Lucy Campbell was a child, flirtatious, flighty, and eminently likable. That final expression on her pretty face was stamped indelibly in my mind. So also was the fact that despite the extreme violence done to her throat, the only signs of blood were a few spatters on her cheek and forehead. The grass around her body was unstained.

Where had the rest gone? I think that I know, and the only thing that prevents me from packing my bags and returning to London by the first available train is the possibility that Shirley Appleton and Rachel Campbell may still be alive. And if they are, they are in peril of their very souls.

July 5

No fresh news this morning. The search will not be renewed today. If the authorities have any open lines of inquiry, they are not making them public. I stopped by Moore's office this morning, but the lights were out and no one answered my knock. After walking aimlessly about Hatton for two hours, I found myself in the vicinity of Mr. Ormsby's office. Responding to I know not what stimulus, I drank tepid tea at a shop that provided a relatively unobstructed view of his door and sat in silent vigil. Twice I saw expensively dressed gentlemen disappear inside, and twice I watched them depart. Then, quite early in the afternoon, the door opened and Miss Dobbit appeared.

It was surprisingly difficult to follow her without being observed. There were people about, but the streets could hardly be called crowded, particularly by London standards, and it was with some difficulty that I did not betray my presence. Miss Dobbit seemed quite nervous; her head turned from side to side constantly as she walked, and she stopped on more than one occasion to gaze back along the path she had followed, as if sensing my pursuit. I tried to remain on the opposite side of the street at all times, sheltering in doorways and hesitating before turning corners. Twice I almost lost track of her, but upon each occasion I was able to remedy the situation. And finally she reached her destination, a small but quite well maintained cottage set back so that it lay in the shadow of a rather rundown hostelry.

Someone opened the door for her as she approached and she disappeared inside without a word. There was no convenient public place for me to wait without looking suspicious, so I rather brashly concealed myself in a private garden, continuing my surveillance through a gap in an ivy covered trellis. I was beginning to feel rather foolish when she emerged less than an hour later, but doggedly followed her all the way back to Ormsby's offices.

Although I did not actually suspect her of being involved in the attack on Shirley and the Campbells, I was grasping at straws. The prospect of drinking more inferior tea and watching Ormsby's door all afternoon held no appeal, so I strolled off, initially planning to return to the hotel. My feet had a mind of their own, however, and I found myself retracing my earlier route to the nondescript cottage. Arriving, I hesitated only a moment, then walked directly to the front door and rang the bell.

The door opened only a hand's width and an elderly woman peered out at me. "Yes? What is it?"

I removed my hat and made a little bow. "Pardon me for disturbing you, madame, but I'm looking for the Dobbit residence."

"I'm Mrs. Dobbit. What do you want?"

"Actually it is your daughter who I have come to see. I am an old friend." I was suddenly painfully aware that I had no idea what might be Miss Dobbit's first name. She seemed like one of those people who only required the patronomic.

"An old friend is it?" She sounded marginally less unfriendly.

"Yes. I arrived in town unexpectedly and I thought I might pay my respects. Is she at home?"

"No. She's out, won't be back until late. Wait there a second." The door closed and I heard the bolt being undone. Then the door opened, giving me a look at a dark but orderly and well furnished sitting room. I was immediately reminded of Miss Bates' house, and experienced a rare epiphany. "Would you care for a cup of tea, Mr. . .?"

"Hemming. Donald Hemming. That would be most gracious of you, Mrs. Dobbit."

The tea was really quite excellent, though the small biscuits she served with it were rather stale. Mrs. Dobbit moved slowly and deliberately, and at first I thought her frail. It was only as we talked that I realized her vision was so bad that she had to consciously focus on things she wished to see. I managed to fend off her questions about my acquaintance with her daughter by inquiring about Miss Dobbit's livelihood. "I believe she was employed as a clerk when last I spoke to her. I confess it has been more than a few years."

The old woman nodded vigorously. "She work for a barrister or some such, though he doesn't pay her much and works her far too many hours to my way of thinking. Odd hours too, the middle of the night sometimes. If it wasn't for my special arrangement, we'd have trouble keeping food on the table."

My instincts had been right. "I have a confession to make, Mrs. Dobbit. I'm not really here to see your daughter. I'm here about the special arrangement."

I saw her knuckles whiten where she held onto the arms of her chair. "I don't understand you, Mr. Hemming."

"The Lady requires her past."

For a few seconds, I thought Mrs. Dobbit was going to have a stroke right in front of me. She shook so badly that the chair creaked. Then she visibly regained control and nodded. "I've been expecting you or someone like you, of course. Not this soon, but eventually. She hasn't come to me now for almost ten years, though I had a letter a few years ago."

My heart was racing, but I kept my voice level. "Do you have something for me?"

"Of course I do, young man. I swore to watch over them and I always keep my word. They're perfectly safe." She rose to her feet and made her way methodically across the room to a mantle clock. I waited while she fumbled with it, opening a small door on the back, and removed an object I could not see. "I must see the ring, you know." She walked toward me, extending one hand, on the palm of which rested a small object.

I remembered the ring that I had surrendered to Miss Bates in order to secure the first lot of documents. She had never returned it to me. "I am afraid I have forgotten it, Mrs. Dobbit."

Her fingers curled closed and she stopped in the middle of the room. "I cannot give them up without I see the ring, Mr. Hemming. She was most specific on that point. Most specific."

"I understand completely." My mind raced furiously. "Might I examine the ring for a moment. I've been retrieving her property from several sources and all of the rings are different. I could return tomorrow with the correct one if that is convenient."

She hesitated, but then opened her palm. I examined it quite closely. It did not appear to be particularly valuable, nor was the pattern unusually intricate. I committed the color and rough form to memory, then thanked her and rose to depart.

"One other thing, Mrs. Dobbit. It would be best if you refrained from telling your daughter about my visit. The one for whom I act would prefer that we keep this just between the two of us."

The woman nodded, and I felt slightly guilty about taking advantage of her. But only slightly. "I've always done as the Lady asked. I'm not about to stop now." She paused, then touched my arm. "The special arrangement. That doesn't end now, does it?"

"So long as you don't tell anyone about our business, it will continue," I reassured her, hoping I was telling the truth. "That's another reason not to tell your daughter. She might let it slip at the wrong moment."

"She doesn't need to know any more than she does already," Mrs. Dobbit responded firmly. "She has her own secrets what she doesn't want to tell me, so I don't see why I can't keep my business quiet as well."

"Exactly. I shall call on you tomorrow about eleven, if that is all right."

"I'll have the tea ready, Mr. Hemming."

And I made my escape.

Later

Received a brief missive from the mysterious Mr. Straban, from a new address in Aberdeen. I cannot imagine how he has found me but I have made no secret of my movements and I suppose it required little effort to track me down. I have written in reply, describing today's discovery as well as the death of Lucy Campbell. Although I am still uncertain of Straban's motives, it is possible that he can throw some further light on matters, and if there is any chance of helping dear Shirley, I must take whatever risks are necessary.

Letter from Josef Straban to Edward Palmer, received at the Cruden Bay Hotel on July 5.

Dear Mr. Palmer,

I trust that your inquiries are progressing. I am at present involved in complicated affairs which demand all of my time, but I would appreciate a summary of your progress sent to my address here appended. I have every faith in your resourcefulness, but let me encourage you to be cautious. There is reason to believe that you may be actively as well as passively resisted. There is, as you no doubt are aware, an elaborate and wide reaching conspiracy to prevent the documents in question of being more widely disseminated. I trust to your judgment concerning their publication or exposure. I ask only that I be provided with a copy, or access to the originals, before they are presented to any other audience.

If the funds which I have advanced to your have proven insufficient, please let me know. I ask no accounting from you at this time as I continued to have every confidence in your integrity. I expect to remain at this location at least through the end of the month.

Yours,

Josef Straban

Edward Palmer's Travel Diary

July 6

Still no news about Shirley and Rachel. According to the local papers, they are believed to have been abducted by person or persons unknown, and the police are pursuing "certain lines of inquiry" which probably means they have nary a clue to work with. Hoskins, the hotel's evening bartender, has a brother who is employed as a constable and he told me in mock confidentiality that the police believe Lucy was killed elsewhere, which might explain the lack of blood at the scene.

I hired a motorcar and was in Hatton early this morning, and as luck would have it I found a ring in a small jewelry shop that might just pass as the duplicate of the one Mrs. Dobbit showed me. I must trust that her poor vision will work to my advantage. That task completed, I stopped by the offices of Mr. Quentin Moore.

Lembic was in, and was his usual repulsively enthusiastic self. At least until I told him the purpose of my visit. "I wish to make final disposition of our business, Mr. Lembic. I've decided this is a fool's errand and will waste no more of my uncle's money on it."

"But we are pursuing some very tangible leads, Mr. Palmer."

"Nevertheless, I must call a halt." He grudgingly examined his ledger and quoted a number, rather less than I had anticipated, and I paid him gladly.

"Will you be leaving Cruden Bay then, Mr. Palmer?"

"Not immediately. I am on holiday after all."

"Then I wish you the best." And he saw me out.

Mrs. Dobbit was waiting for me and opened the door before I had a chance to knock. I pretended to slip as I entered, falling headlong and banging my hand against the stone fireplace, scratching the ring I now wore on my right hand. Mrs. Dobbit was quite agitated, but I insisted that I was perfectly fine and was soon drinking her very spicy tea and another stale biscuit while she crouched over the two rings, holding them very close to her eyes.

"They don't look exactly the same," she said querulously.

"I may have damaged mine somewhat in the fall, but I assure you that this is the ring I was given by the Lady." Not entirely untrue, since it had been sold to me by a young lady.

When Mrs. Dobbit continued to resist, I became desperate and pursued a course I had hoped to avoid. "Well, if you cannot be persuaded, I shall just have to return to the Lady and tell her so. She will have to come herself to collect her property in that case, and I only hope that she will not feel so inconvenienced that she changes the special arrangement."

The threat was quite effective. Minutes later Mrs. Dobbit was opening a concealed panel in one wall. There were two large parcels inside, both stuffed with documents, and I carried them way as quickly as possible, suddenly terrified lest Miss Dobbit come home early and find me looting the family treasure. I made a hasty departure, assured Mrs. Dobbit once again that her special arrangement was safe, secured the parcels in my panniers, and rode back to the hotel.

I have arranged the documents chronologically, spreading them all over my bed and throughout the room. A significant number of them are badly damaged, charred beyond recognition in some cases, others water stained. They were obviously damaged in a fire at some point. Although I have not yet read the material in any detail, the names I have seen already send thrills through my body. If they are authentic, as I now believe they are, this trove contains letters and accounts of the activities of any number of famous and powerful people, some still alive. I have asked that dinner be sent to my room, as I fully expect to spend the entire night trying to weave them into a coherent account.

I shall make notes as I do so, highlight the significant passages, and pack these materials so that they may be sent back to London. I will entrust them to James for safekeeping. I cannot leave myself because of the uncertainty about Shirley Appleton, whom I now suspect I have come to love.

Enheduanna's Journal
December 1, 1875

I have been remiss in recording my history these past many weeks, but there has been much to arrange, obstacles to overcome, plans to be laid, and a new identity to be constructed. Mina Harker is no more, and I shall not greatly miss her. She was too limited in potential to be a satisfying performance for any great length of time. After arranging the deaths of the happy couple, I sojourned briefly in London, taking my prey from among the streetwalkers and drunken dockworkers, most of whom will never be missed. With Godalming an invalid with an ailing mind, and all the others but Seward dead, I felt reasonably safe from discovery. Then while walking along Maiden Lane near the Strand, I happened upon Singleton, the consulting detective who accompanied Inspector Cotford to Hillingham following the death of Mrs. Westenra. Although I assured him he had mistaken me for another, his eyes were troubled and I felt them lingering on my back until I was out of his sight.

One does not live a life as long as mine without learning caution, and I left London the following day. I have cached all of the journals and other papers relating to the Mina Murray phase of my life, as I have done periodically in the past. Most of my earlier histories reside in moldering tombs, or in the empty coffins of those who briefly served as my children, now all perished except perhaps for Quincey, if he has managed to survive the transformation. Mina's cache has a living guardian, however, and a firm of solicitors has been engaged to ensure that she is succeeded in due course by another equally trustworthy. In this fashion they remain more accessible. When I next feel the need to refresh my memories of the past, I shall retrieve those earlier accounts from Persia, the Ethiope, and elsewhere and bring them all to England, perhaps consolidating them at last. From time to time, episodes fade in my overcrowded memory, but they can be restored from the journals, just as an artisan breathes fresh life into an old landscape by cleaning and freshening the paint on the canvas.

Fortuitously, I had already made the acquaintance of Philippa Balcombe, who was briefly in London. Her husband had just completed an assignment in India and the family was taking an extended holiday before moving to their new home in Dublin. They have four daughters who are universally dull and incurious. If they pooled their efforts, they still could not muster the spirit of even a Lucy Westenra. James, their father, is as distant, unimaginative, and uninvolved as was Henry Westenra, and Philippa is a woman terrified of life. She already had retreated into a slavish dedication to her husband and daughters when I met them and habitually dosed herserlf with laudanum, which weakens the will. It required only the faintest touch of the glamour to induce her to invite me to dine with them, and over that meal I touched the minds of all the others. They were uniformly malleable and I was already half convinced to make use of them before Singleton's appearance forced the issue.

My true reflection has been forbidden me for so long that I no longer remember my own features, although mortals apparently still see me as I was when I stopped aging. Although I cannot clearly see myself in a mirror, the general shape has remained consistent throughout the centuries and I have learned to alter my hair, clothing, and composure to mimic a reasonable range of ages. When Philippa commented upon my likeness to her youngest daughter, I realized that I resembled the Balcombe girls sufficiently that no one would think to question my identity if I numbered myself among them. At first I considered posing as the oldest, but that would inevitably lead to pressure to marry, so instead I decided that my age would be sixteen, with two older and two younger sisters. I shall be Florence, named for one of my favorite cities, or at least such it was when my name was Medici. I have not returned there for over a century and it might be a far different place by now. No matter.

It was not difficult to cultivate the Balcombe family. Philippa was starved for praise and companionship, James responded to a mild flirtation, and the daughters were too self involved to pay much attention to me. When I learned the day of their departure to Ireland, I secured identical passage, then allowed them to discover the marvelous coincidence the following evening. Philippa suggested that we travel together even before I thought to nudge her with the glamour.

The journey was tedious, uncomfortable, and fraught with delays and the two youngest daughters were particularly restless and annoying, but it provided ample time to work on the minds of each of them. By the time we embarked by sea for the final leg of our journey, it was already understood that I would be living with them, and upon arriving at our new home at number one on the Crescent, James was calling me his brightest daughter and the older girls were jealous and insisted I had been spoiled since the day I was born.

Dublin is smaller than London, but no less lively, and with no less unhealthy an underside. On the evening of our arrival, I found prey easily in a rundown quarter, a young vagrant with the sharp features of a gipsy who was sheltering from the cold in a dark alley. I crept up on him from behind and he died without seeing his death. Cautiously, I disposed of his body in the river.

December 2

I had not planned to remain more than a few months with the Balcombes, but I have given it much thought this past fortnight. The ease with which I have interposed myself among them is unprecedented. Lucy's mother suffered migraines whenever I touched her mind and her father would become absentminded and disoriented on those rare occasions when it was necessary to influence him. Lucy herself was an oddity; I believe that deep within herself she knew that I was false, but she was complicit in her own deception. She may have desired an element of scandalous rebellion as an antidote to the numbing pointlessness of her life. None of these complications apply to the Balcombes. Either the glamour has become even more effective, or more likely they simply lack the imagination to delve beneath the surface appearance of things. For whatever reason, they have accepted me completely; I have not noticed even the slightest hint of confusion or concern in any of them since our arrival in Dublin.

The contrary side to this is that they are a boring lot. Lucy's occasional outrages might have been childishly annoying, but at least she possessed the ability to surprise me. At number one on the Crescent, the individual days are almost indistinguishable from one another. I have been tempted to hunt more often than necessary just to escape that cloying conformity, but unfortunately that risk is not worth the small diversion it would offer. Almost I regret the loss of Vlad as my enemy. His animosity stirred my senses and forced me to be constantly aware of my purpose and my surroundings. Now that he has passed, there is little to challenge me, and I fear that I will descend into the same fog of monotony that already besets my new "sisters".

December 4

I attended the theater today and in the middle of a particularly mediocre performance before an unusually raucous audience, I realized that the action on the stage was no less artificial than that around me. The actors strike poses and occasionally improvise just as we all assume roles we wish people to perceive rather than just doing as we would wish. It is not I alone who leads a surface life false to my true being. James Balcombe plays the ardent military man, but in fact he lacks self confidence and has the soul of a clerk. Interpolating from his reminiscences, I suspect he never once saw battle personally and I know for a fact that he can barely managed to remain astride a horse. Philippa pretends to be the doting mother, but she secretly wishes her daughters would lead the more adventurous life she never dared aspire to, and she is quietly disappointed that they seem if anything even less spirited than she. This may explain the readiness with which she accepted me as a member of the family, sensing my wilder nature.

This revelation fascinated me and I spent the next day applying it to everyone I encountered, in each case confirming my theory. The butcher, Mr. O'Reilly, flirts with his lady customers, even though I have seen him in the small hours of the morning leaving the home of the young lad he romances under cover of darkness. Father Brennan appears the soul of rectitude, but when he welcomed us to his church I touched his mind and knew he had lost his faith. I believe I could accept communion from him without flinching. They are all actors in separate but related plays, improvising when they forget their lines, each striving to provide a convincing performance of the characters they wish to be rather than those which they really are.

Having recognized this fact, I have set myself a new challenge. The role of dutiful daughter in a modest home is too simple for one with my skills. I must embellish it somehow. If I were a man, I might try my hand at painting, or become a barrister. No, better yet, a physician. Imagine the convenience of having one's prey reward you for drawing some of their blood. But alas, I am a woman, and such professions are effectively closed to me unless perhaps I were to become a midwife, a solution I find completely unappealing.

So I have decided instead to build the kind of life I might have had with Jonathan, or rather a slightly more successful and imaginative Jonathan. Someone associated with the arts. A writer of plays perhaps. An actor would be too far beneath my station. Or a painter, an artist. I met Da Vinci once, but we disliked one another on sight. I thought then and now that his work was second rate, inferior to that of several of his own assistants. I must find a suitable man, induce him to marry me, and assume the role of a dutiful wife and a member of cultivated society. He must be susceptible to the glamour, of course, since it will be I who directs his career and charts our mutual course, but he must also possess an alert mind and high intelligence. It will be difficult.

Such an ambitious course entails some risk, but if it ends in disaster, Florence Balcombe will vanish and I will start again elsewhere. But I shall not fail. If this masquerade succeeds, and the emancipation of women continues into the next century, I might one day reign as a princess again, although the dust of my father's kingdom has been tracked to the far corners of the world by now.

December 9

I had a most interesting encounter this evening. James has decided that the theater is not suitable for young ladies and will no longer take us, and though he has not expressly forbidden it, my new sisters all interpret his disapproval as an absolute bar. I have sculpted my character as slightly rebellious, but open disobedience seems too extreme an act for Florence Balcombe. Fortunately, Florence has shown herself prone to sleep walking and nightmares, demonstrating such restless nocturnal habits that I have been awarded a room of my own, though in size it is barely more than a closet. A closet with a window, fortunately, which makes my moonlit excursions much more manageable.

Tonight we were all to dine with Sir William and Lady Jane Wilde, and the house was frantic with preparations because James and Philippa wanted us all to make a good impression. This was also the closing night of *The Handmaiden*, a comedic play of which I had heard a good report, so late in the afternoon I began complaining of a bad headache and with little difficulty found myself excused from the dinner party. I waited impatiently in my room for them to depart. James entertains some fanciful theory that it is more sophisticated to arrive late than to be punctual. Considering his career in the military, I usually find this conceit amusing. Perhaps he would have mustered his troops after the battle was lost in order to avoid being gauche? But tonight I fretted until they left, then raced from the house in an entirely unmaidenlike manner in order to arrive at the theater for the first curtain.

The play was disappointing, the humor relying more on innuendo than cleverness, the language coarse rather than witty, the actors buffoons rather than artists. If the evening was not bad enough already, I was suddenly struck by the hunger at the opening of the final act, and the press was so tight that I was forced to wait until the performance ended before leaving.

There were quite a large number of students from Trinity College attending, and they drifted off in that direction singly and in clusters. I had never chosen prey from among their number because it was more likely that questions would be raised if a student should be attacked or simply disappear, but I was driven by the hunger, disappointed and irritated by the play, and was having second thoughts about spending the next several years in my present guise. So I followed the scattering crowd at a discrete distance. Many of the audience had been or still were drinking, and it was quite possible that one might pause for a while and drift off into a stuporous sleep. I can satisfy my hunger without causing the death of my prey if I am careful, but there was always a chance that the inevitable wounds on the victim would raise curious eyebrows. So I rarely took the chance and tonight the hunger was so strong that I knew I would be unable to stop short under any circumstances.

I had taken shelter behind a tree in a small park, watching a handful of figures advancing through it in various states of insobriety when another young man lurched to a stop on the opposite side of the rough trunk. I hesitated; there remained more activity than I liked, and presently heard a low sound that I didn't at first recognize. My unknown companion was urinating at the base of our mutual shelter. It was impossible to resist the temptation to invoke Florence's playfulness, so I stepped out into his full view.

"Good evening to you, sir. A lovely night, is it not?"

He was solidly built but not remarkable in appearance except for a pair of lively eyes that flickered only slightly in surprise. His face otherwise betrayed no particular unease as he finished his task and adjusted his clothing.

"Your pardon, miss, but if you lurk in the shadows, you are likely to see a good many things best kept private."

"I was not lurking. I merely paused to let the riffraff pass through." I gestured toward another clot of students who had begun singing atonally in the distance. I took a step closer; I could smell the blood coursing in his veins.

"Then allow this riffraff to join its fellows." He half bowed and turned to go.

"Wait!" He hesitated, turned back. "Are you a gentleman, sir?"

His back straightened just slightly, a motion that would have been invisible to merely mortal eyes in the inky darkness. "George Shaw is as much a gentleman as any man, though I hold no title."

"A proper gentleman would not allow a lady to remain alone in such raucous and unpredictable company."

"Are you asking me to escort you home, miss?"

"No, that would be forward of me. But if you would but stay close by for a few minutes, until the worst of this unruly crowd has passed, I would be grateful."

Shaw shifted his feet nervously as though anxious to be gone and there was a note of impatience in his voice. "It would be churlish to do otherwise."

I waited silently as another threesome passed, one of whom clearly could not have remained standing had it not been for his two fellows. Shaw seemed uneasy with the silence. "I apologize again, madam. I did notice your shape in the darkness but I thought you were merely another statue. This park is littered with inadequate likenesses of unattractive people. I warrant they held a competition to find the most offensive faces to serve as models."

Despite the hunger, I laughed. There was a cruelty in the man's wit that I found attractive. "Perhaps that is indeed what I am, an ancient statue brought to life through the intervention of some goddess."

"An intriguing image, but it would be more likely a god. A goddess would be jealous of your beauty."

"How gallant. Perhaps after all you really are a gentleman." I closed the gap by another step. There were only a few stragglers within sight now. The glamour began to stir within me and I reached out with it, pressing with just enough force to slow his reactions, befuddled his mind. His will was strong and I hesitated, uncertain, and fate dealt me another card then because two young men sprung up out of nowhere, greeting Shaw by name and shouting loudly. I shrank back from him, prepared to bolt.

"Good evening to you, Sean. And is that Brian with you?"

They passed greetings back and forth and Shaw introduced me as an anonymous young lady in mild distress. Despite my protestations, the threesome then announced their firm intention to see me safely home and when it became clear that I could not dissuade them, I acquiesced just to be rid of their company. At my insistence, they did not accompany me to the door, although they watched from the corner until I was safely inside. Fortunately, the Balcombes were not yet home and I slipped out through a window at the rear of the house and finally assuaged my hunger in my usual fashion, a drunken street walker who had fallen asleep in an alley. When I returned, there was a carriage out front, and I managed to reach my room barely in time to respond to Philippa's knock.

James was in ill humor and remained awake for nearly another hour, haranguing poor Philippa about the moral decay of the aristocracy. Apparently he had been less than impressed by Sir William's household and even somewhat outraged by the behavior of "that woman", whom I took to be Lady Jane. I lay in bed, feeling the flow of fresh blood within my body. It was nourishing but not satisfying, sour with the effects of the dissipations of the whore from whom I had taken it. I would wager that young Mr. Shaw's would have had a sweeter taste.

February 2, 1876

    Philippa has surprised me by standing up to James, or rather, by slowly eroding his insistence upon having his own way. Despite James' low opinion of the Wilde family, Philippa seems to have been quite taken with Lady Jane, or perhaps it is simply that she enjoys consorting with the aristocracy rather than with the wives of other career officers. For whatever reason, she has convinced James that it would be impolite not to accept the invitation to attend another party so that they could meet the one daughter – myself - who was too ill to attend this past year. He refuses to accompany us, but tomorrow evening Philippa and I will be escorted by Mr. Nigel Nordsley, a friend of James who has an impeccable reputation and all the imagination and personality of a gatepost.

February 4, 1876

    I reluctantly confess to sharing James' aversion to Lady Jane Wilde, though for entirely different reasons. The woman has a touch of the glamour although I doubt she realizes it. Enough that she may have glimpsed something of what really lies beneath the mask that others know as Florence Balcombe.

    The evening began in an innocuous fashion. We arrived at Merrion Square by carriage and were escorted into a luxurious foyer and up a staircase to where Lady Jane was holding court. She is quite a large woman, much taller than her husband and with heavy bones and unladylike musculature. She was dressed as a gypsy, although this was no costume party, and insisted that we call her Esperanza. Although there were scatterings of other conversations in the room, it was more than evident that she was its central focus, and that most of the guests came to listen rather than converse.

    She's an ardent Irish nationalist, and if the average Londoner gave voice to half the sentiments she expressed that evening, he would be clapped in irons for treason without a second thought. The honored guest of the evening was a Mr. Sheridan LeFanu, publisher of the *Dublin Evening Mail,* and he spoke for a while about the dire influence of the Vatican among the Irish people, but Lady Jane overwhelmed him on more than one occasion with her insistence that his priorities were wrong. "You are losing sight of the true enemy,

Sheridan. It is the English who oppress us, not the College of Cardinals." To each assault, LeFanu responded calmly and measuredly, but I could tell his blood was up from halfway across the room.

Philippa pointed out several other lesser notables in the room. "Their son Oscar is not here this evening. He is a bit brash, but quite witty, and is about your age. That gentleman is Mr. Chadbourn, a painter, and next to him is Dennis Kilburnie, who composes music and works at the Shelbourne Hotel, and in the corner is Mr. Stoker, who writes for Mr. LeFanu's newsletter." Unfortunately, I was never actually introduced to any of these lesser notables, as they all accompanied Sir William downstairs to his den for brandy and cigars.

That was when Lady Jane finally deigned to notice me.

"You must be the missing daughter, Flora."

"Florence," I corrected mildly, with a short curtsy.

"Oh, none of that, dear. We are all equals in this house." I felt a flash of annoyance and suppressed it. If Lady Jane Wilde thought that she was eliminating class distinctions by wearing cheap jewelry while her more expensive necklaces and rings sat in a box in her room, she was fooling no one but herself. But when she took my hand, I sensed something else about her. This was a woman of great personal power, with a strength more than just physical, a fortitude of spirit I had encountered only a few times over the centuries. If Vlad had been born a woman, this might have been she. But there was more. I felt a growing uneasiness as though something unseen were touching me, and realized with considerable shock that she was reaching out with the glamour to sample my soul. Unconsciously, I am sure, but there was no question that she was fey. And the glamour responded to her and conveyed something of my true nature, because she flinched and her eyes narrowed, and she withdrew her hand a little too abruptly, although her expression was confused as well as displeased.

"It is a great pleasure to meet you at last, Florence." There was no longer any warmth in her voice, and when I responded with similarly feigned pleasure, she nodded and turned away.

She moved through the now diminished crowd of guests like a mother hen among her chicks, eventually seating herself in an overstuffed chair that more than slightly resembled a throne. Despite her fondness for inveighing against all royalty, she was holding court as regally as did Victoria herself. But there was no denying her passion for her homeland. Ireland might have been Eden in her eyes, and would be again if only the hated English could be forced to relinquish their control. From politics she moved to praise for the industriousness of the Irish people, to the brilliance of its artists, and to the richness of its history.

"We are a strong people, tempered by blood and iron and the passage of time. They can hold us down for a while, but sooner or later strong cream rises to the top of the churn." Through all of this, Philippa listened raptly, perhaps fascinated by a woman displaying the kind of strength she would never find in herself. It never even occurred to her that she was one of the people our hostess was demeaning.

Lady Jane's eyes strayed constantly among her audience, making certain that everyone was hanging on her every word, and when they fell upon me I made the mistake of meeting her gaze evenly. She paused in mid-sentence, caught herself, and then finished what she was saying, ending weakly.

"Have you ever heard an English fairy story?" she asked her audience. "Their fairies are pale, feeble creatures who fly around looking pretty, telling riddles, playing tricks, and occasionally granting wishes. Not so the Irish fairy. Ours are fearsome, magical creatures who dwell in their own world and brook no interference from the outside. An Irish child knows that a fairy is more likely to drink their blood than do them a good turn." As she said this last, she turned and met my eyes once more. Something passed between us at that moment, some mutual awareness that did not involve words but was no less real. It was neither hatred nor fear but rather wariness, a mutual recognition of each other's power. I doubted that I would ever be invited here again, but I resolved to watch over Lady Jane in some fashion. If there was a threat to me here in Dublin, then she is its agent if not its author.

Note by Edward Palmer, undated.

James,

I suggest you skip from here to the July 3 entry, although you may want to read the intervening pages later. They contain some fascinating anecdotes, but for the most part they relate details about the refinement of the Florence Balcombe persona. Mina or Florence or whatever we should be calling her by now seems to have thrown herself completely into the role of the pampered middle class daughter. She even avoids direct mention of her hunting habits most of the time, although there are allusions and hints that clearly indicate she was claiming a victim every fortnight or so, usually west of Castleknock or down the coast south of Blackrock. At no time does she express remorse for these deaths, and in a remarkable dichotomy of mind, she speaks sometimes with mild fondness about her new family, particularly Philippa, while referring to those she feeds upon in terms implying that they are somehow lesser beings whose fate is of no importance. I cannot help feeling that she thought of Philippa the way you or I might the well loved family dog.

During the spring of 1876, a number of young gentlemen came to court Florence. In fact, her two older sisters were apparently both quite jealous of her popularity. She particularly favored a Thomas Bradford for a time, but he apparently made unwanted advances of a particularly noxious variety and she banished him from her presence. There is a hint later on that she paid him an unexpected visit. I suspect that if we made inquiries in Dublin, we would discover that he either disappeared or had a fatal accident in May of 1876.

The only other item of possible interest is her uneasiness about the prospect of participating in a functioning marriage. She would be unable to give birth, of course, but childless marriages are hardly unknown. The greater difficulty from her perspective was the conjugal arrangements. For reasons she never states, sexual congress is apparently impossible for her. She was able to use this hypnotic power which she calls the glamour to delude poor Harker into believing they had a normal relationship, but apparently there were limits to how long she could maintain the illusion without permanently damaging his brain. But during the summer of 1876, she hit upon a possible solution.

Enheduanna's Journal

July 3, 1876

    I have finally met Oscar Wilde. We were introduced at Sir William's funeral in April, of course, but I don't believe his eyes ever really focused on me, and Lady Jane could not have whisked him away more quickly if she had seen my fangs poised above his throat. The Lady and I have met on only two occasions since I visited her home. We were both polite without being cordial. I have learned through a third party that she occasionally inquires about me, but her interest is diffuse and sporadic and I am confident that she can have heard nothing to sully my reputation or confirm her own formless suspicions.

    My curiosity about Oscar was initially quite minimal. I was interested to discover whether or not he shared his mother's fey power. I have now put that fear to rest. If anything, he is slightly more susceptible than most to the glamour and certainly possesses none of that ability in his own right. It has in fact been my experience that only the feminine gender can manifest this power to any great degree; although there have been tales of men mastering the art, I have yet to encounter one. Even Vlad had no more than a rudimentary awareness of the powers of the mind. He could sow confusion, sometimes impose a momentary paralysis, but he was never able to shape thoughts within another mind.

    I met Oscar at a party given by Kevin Chadbourn and his new wife, a waifishly thin girl with poor color and eyes that burn with an unhealthy fire. I sensed a disease in her blood as I have with others from time to time, and doubt she will live more than a year or two. It was a fine party, however. Oscar was home on vacation from Magdalen College and I talked him into posing as my escort for a while. He has a quick mind, a healthy disrespect for convention, and a gift for language. I told him he should become a playwright and he confessed he had thoughts along those lines. But the most important information I gleaned from our conversation was a secret which Oscar never realized he revealed, one which he may not consciously know himself. And it suggests a possible solution to one of the barriers that remains in my path.

    Oscar wishes to be seen as a bit of a rake. He enjoys the company of women, but more as badges of merit than as people. Where most men are at ease with their fellows and more or less excited in the presence of vivacious and attractive ladies of society, Oscar's reactions are quite the opposite. He is what my father's people called *drovna*, a man who is drawn to his own sex rather than to women. If it were not for his mother, I would consider binding him to me with the glamour and making him a ready companion. In fact, I may do so in any case, if only to keep her off balance.

July 4

I contrived to meet Oscar again today. I overheard him speak of an appointment with Dr. Gladwyn and loitered at a shop nearby so that I could keep a watchful eye on the physician's door. When he appeared and waited to hail a carriage, I stepped out from the opposite side of the street pretending to have the same intention. Happily he noticed me before I was forced to pretend the opposite, we talked briefly, and he offered to escort me home before returning to Merrion Square. We got along famously and my amusement at his quick wit was not even feigned.

July 10

Oscar has called upon me three times this past week, and has promised to take me to the theater tomorrow. I find him amusing, but he would not be flattered if he knew the true reason for my interest. Although he styles himself a bit of a rebel, he is very much a product of this new age in that he makes what should be very simple issues excessively complex. It is not enough for him that he desires a thing. He must always approach the object of that desire obliquely, creating rules for engagement and disengagement that have little to do with the matter at hand. Although it is the company of men that he prefers, he has begun to court me because that is what is expected of him, and because he deems me a suitable ornament. So much for his rebellion against society's expectations.

There are times when I am nostalgic for my old life. I can still remember how I felt as a young girl, watching the magnificent warriors preparing for battle, or returning with the trophies of their victory. Sometimes one would dare to look boldly at me, their ruler's daughter, and a flood of warmth would fill my body and I would fantasize about lying with them, of having them touch my body.

When it came time for my body to cease being that of a girl and become that of a woman, I expected these feelings to grow stronger, but my body stubbornly remained as it was and the desire that had seemed to burn my flesh slowly subsided and extinguished itself. At times I consider this the one greatest thing I have ever lost, but then I look around me, watch my simpering sisters molding themselves into mindless toys, or listen in dismay as Philippa constantly defers to James, whose intellect is inferior to hers. That is when I realize that I have sacrificed little and gained much. I have risen above the bonds of the flesh. The small losses I have endured by becoming who and what I am are of no consequence when measured against the freedom I have won in their place.

August 4, 1876

Oscar will return to Magdalen soon, and I must say it will be a relief to have him go. I considered severing our relationship but have refrained for the time being. Although he has obvious talent and promise as a writer, he lacks tenacity in his working habits. Perhaps more importantly, his lifestyle is a flamboyant one, no doubt a trait passed on by his mother, and I suspect that as his wife I would be subject to more scrutiny than would be welcome. It is a narrow path I must travel here if I am to achieve what I seek without attracting unwanted attention. My husband must be of sufficient stature to provide access to those elements of society with whom I wish to commune, but not so notorious that he, and more particularly I, would be forever in the public eye. It is difficult enough to satisfy my periodic hunger without dodging the representatives of the press or a crowd of admirers.

At our last meeting, Oscar pressed for some formal declaration of our attachment to one another. I put him off as gently as possible, insisting that such a thing would be premature, that we should discuss it again when he was no longer a student, when my older sisters were married and I was of a more suitable age to be making such commitments.

"Ah, my lovely Florrie, always practical. But in matters of the heart, reason and logic have no place."

"How can you say such a thing, Oscar? You have characterized religion, government, and fine manners as superstition, chaos, and mindless ritual, all lacking a rational raison d'etre, and now you insist that there is no place for measured thought between us?"

He had the grace to look somewhat abashed. "What can I say, dear Florrie? You have overwhelmed my senses and deprived me of the solace of orderly thought."

"Then perhaps it is more than time for you to return to your studies." I tempered the words with an arch look so that he would believe me only half serious, although in truth I would be glad to see the last of him, at least for the time being. Caution prevented me from severing the cord completely. It might well be that maturity would bring a more attractive calmness to his spirit. If not, I still believed that his talent was a prodigious one and it would be politic to remain at worst a lost love but an enduring friend.

There is also the matter of his mother, who is aware of our closeness and who clearly does not approve. I could remove that obstacle, of course, but for the time being it suits my purpose that she lives.

Note from Edward Palmer, undated

James,

Most of the remainder of this journal is illegible due to water staining. As I mentioned in my letter, a number of the volumes in this new cache of documents were exposed to fire and large segments of the history are missing. It is later revealed how this occurred, and I will refrain from distracting you by explaining here.

What fragments of the latter half of 1876 remain reveal little of consequence. Florence, as she now thought of herself, continued a mild flirtation with a number of gentlemen, but committed herself to none of them. There are occasional passages revealing frustration, even anger, about her inability to find a suitable partner. On at least one occasion, she killed a police constable who stumbled upon her while she was feeding on a street waif. She alludes to an increased sense of alarm in some parts of Dublin following this event, and the mention in the *Evening Mail* of a mysterious rise in the number of disappearances along the waterfront. Later on there is a fragment describing a farmhouse on the northern outskirts of the city, which may indicate that she changed her hunting grounds, at least for a time.

The first portion of 1877 is similarly damaged, as it was contained in the same volume. Fortunately the following one is in perfect condition, and while it contains a great deal of inconsequential material, the passages I have marked, beginning on April 24, are quite significant, although I didn't realize that until I had read further.

Enheduanna's Journal

April 24, 1877

I have given further thought to keeping a false diary for Florence Balcombe, just as I did as Mina Murray, but after several false starts I have discarded the idea. To put it bluntly, Florence leads an incredibly boring life and it would be too tedious a chore to chronicle it in any detail. I have spied upon the diaries of my sisters, in which they dutifully inscribe daily, and the shallowness of the prattle I found there was truly disheartening. They fall in and out of love as easily as they change their hairstyle, and with less thought.

We attended a small party at Mr. LeFanu's home last evening. The conversation turned to literary matters, and a gentleman whose name I never learned began extolling the virtues of something called *Melmoth the Wanderer*, apparently a gruesome but rather tedious tale. This led to mention of Mrs. Radcliffe's terrors, which I found laughable when I read them, and eventually to Polidori's book. I ventured the opinion that the author had romanticized the undead rather than portrayed them as the absolute evil that they must be, a conceit that I condescended to only because I was profoundly bored by the conversation. I did not expect to be taken seriously, and I could not of course tell them that I had once been known as Clair Clairmont, in which guise I had known Polidori himself and had firsthand knowledge of his inspiration.

But LeFanu turned and actually saw me, I think, for the first time. "You must admit though, Miss Balcombe, that there is an element of romanticism in the legend. If you will pardon the indelicacy, the vampire is in many ways a symbol for the male sexual act. He, um, penetrates his female victim, who subsequently undergoes a brief but rather traumatic condition, following which a new life, or unlife in this case, emerges. It is the power of creation, though perverted by his evil nature."

There was a smugness about the man that infuriated me. He spoke as though I were merely a child, and I confess that my color rose and I spoke without thinking. "You might construe it as such, Mr. LeFanu, but to do so would be to constrain your imagination. If there was really such a thing as vampires, then surely many of their number would be female. While they might well have seductive powers of their own, they could hardly be described as metaphors for masculine sexuality, now could they?"

His lips thinned but for a moment, but he hid his annoyance with a feigned cough, and replied reasonably. "Your argument is a valid one, Miss Balcombe. I am suitably admonished. I have for a time been contemplating a tale along the lines of Polidori's, but perhaps I should reconsider my premise. A female vampire offers interesting possibilities, the corruption of innocence, the presence of great power in an apparently weak vessel. Thank you, Miss Balcombe, you have given me fertile grounds for thought."

I was angry at myself for even such a small indiscretion and took myself to a seat elsewhere so that I might not be noticed until it was time to leave. My self-imposed exile was not to endure. A rather large man with brown hair and a short, rust red beard approached and stopped just out of reach as though waiting permission to approach closer.

"Pardon me, Miss Balcombe is it? We have never actually been introduced although I have seen you once or twice before. My name is Abraham, Abraham Stoker, although my friend call me Bram."

He did look familiar, although I could not precisely place his face or his name. I offered him my hand and asked him to call me Florence. A moment later he was seated beside me, and to my surprise he was quite charming.

"It was quite plucky of you to speak up to Sheridan like that. He is a good and fair man at heart, but he has a tendency to believe that his opinions are inscribed in stone."

"I was a bit rude though. My manners are not always quite as they should be."

"Nonsense. Serious thoughts are not confined to the minds of men. Sheridan shares what I fear is a Protestant myopia; he sees every issue in terms of black and white and never a shade of gray. Catholics are bad, Protestants good. Men are corrupt, women pure. He knows consciously that such absolutes rarely hold true, but always in the background the more simplistic prejudices impair his critical abilities."

"So you don't believe that all men are inherently sinful?"

"Only to the extent that I believe all women are inherently virtuous."

"Then is it bad of me to express myself on subjects normally the prerogative of men?"

"Not at all. It could only help our society if good women were more openly involved in shaping our civilization. Unfortunately, it is bad women who seem to know men best, and to be able to influence them the most."

I became rather curious about Mr. Stoker, particularly when he revealed that he was the author of the many theater reviews I had read in the *Evening Mail*. "Sheridan insists that they be unsigned, but I am indeed their author. Although that may not hold true for long. I have just received a promotion to Inspector of Petty Sessions and as such will be forced to travel a good deal. The theater will just have to manage without me for a time, and I without its pleasures." He also admitted, after minimal prodding, to having written a handful of short fictions for *London Society* and other periodicals.

"You are quite an accomplished artist, Mr. Stoker."

"Please, if we are to be friends, you must call me Bram. And I am no artist, Florence, but merely a wordsmith who occasionally manages a piece that strikes a chord with the reader. Writing is a craft, not an art. For the true art of our age, one must turn to the theater. Have you perchance ever had the opportunity to see Mr. Henry Irving perform?"

"I have never had the opportunity, although I have heard his name mentioned. Is he not the man who was accused of elevating his own senses above those of Shakespeare?"

Stoker made a dismissive gesture. "There are some individuals who interpret any innovation as error. Irving simply asserts that there is more to acting than reading the written words.

The actor must feel the part he is playing if he is to properly convey the desired emotional effect to the audience."

He went on in this vein for quite some time, and his praise of Irving became so effusive that I used the glamour to touch his mind and confirmed what I already suspected. Like Oscar, Bram is not truly interested in women, although he believes himself so. His admiration for Irving has a baser source than the man's theatrical talents. It is a shame that his aspirations are low. He seems content to remain a government functionary of no particular stature, even speaks of writing a manual governing the performance of his duties.

He asked about my family and I quickly turned the conversation to his own, learned that his father died only a few months ago in Switzerland, that one of his brothers was training to be a physician, that his mother and sisters lived abroad and had done so for some years. When Philippa finally decided it was time for us to depart, I took my leave somewhat reluctantly, for Bram is much better company than I am used to, and although I am reluctant to admit it, I sometimes miss the interplay of sharp minds. I have matched wits and traded words with Lord Byron and Mary Godwin on the shores of Lake Leman, and with Vlad Tepes and Ludovici Medici. I have whispered in the ears of the Maid of Orleans and manipulated the butchers of Paris and the arms of the Inquisition. I was once princess of a mighty empire. And now I live an almost cloistered life, surrounded by weak witted girls whose thoughts and speech are flat and stale. At times I am half resolved to abandon Florence Balcombe entirely and set out anew, but then I remember that to do so would necessarily thrust myself into the public eye and that is a level of scrutiny which I could not bear.

June 12, 1877

Bram Stoker came to call this afternoon, the first I have seen of him since the night of Mr. LeFanu's party. He has been traveling for much of the past few weeks and described himself as footsore and numbed in his senses. "I have not seen a play since April, and when I learned that Henry Irving would be in Dublin briefly, I remembered that you had never seen him perform and wondered if I might be honored with the right to escort you. I assure you that it will be a night you will never forget. His genius will instill in you a new vision of the theater."

Fortunately, James had previously met Bram and approved of him as an escort. These past few months he has been growing increasingly interested in what he calls my well being, but I have also seen him casting puzzled looks in my direction from time to time and I wonder if perhaps an old memory has slipped past the constraints of the glamour. I have noticed the same in Philippa but, oddly enough, she seems to wall off the memories she chooses to exclude without my intervention. At times I think she sees in my comparatively independent spirit something of the woman she might have been had she not subordinated herself in the role of dutiful wife and mother, and this acts as a censor suppressing what might otherwise be the acknowledgment of an alarming contradiction.

So I am to see this vaunted Mr. Irving tomorrow, on the arm of Bram Stoker, who promises to introduce me to the great man following the performance. Perhaps this shall be my escape. Irving seems suited to my purposes. He is a rising star with access to various levels of society, wealthy enough to suit me. Bram tells me that Irving is married, but that he and his wife have not spoken in several years. Apparently she disapproved of his career choice and insulted him so gravely that he abandoned her on the spot. She is also named Florence, a coincidence that I might have called fate where I not so certain that we each of us make our own futures.

June 13, 1877

My hopes are dashed. Irving cannot possibly play the role I had intended for him.

The performance was a relatively private affair, closed to the general public, consisting of a few scenes extracted from MacBeth, which Irving is currently performing in its entirety elsewhere. Irving's performance was in fact rather unsettling, but once I had adjusted to his agitated, effusive style, I realized that Bram was not entirely mistaken in his opinion. And there was no question at all that Irving cast almost a spell upon all who watched.

As promised, Bram arranged for me to meet the great man afterwards, but I don't believe his eyes ever rested on my face during the introduction, and my presence was forgotten almost instantly.

Bram's infatuation with the man was evident from the outset, confirming my suspicion about his inclinations. But there was another revelation awaiting me, one that brought with it a tiny thrill of apprehension.

Since arriving in Dublin I had only twice felt the force of the glamour – Lady Jane Wilde and, to a much lesser extent, an elderly woman I encountered on the street one day. But tonight I felt it again, strong, even surpassing Lady Jane's abilities, and for the first time in my experience it came from an untransformed male. Henry Irving, under other circumstances, might have been burned as a witch. I doubt that he is aware of his secret ability, or perhaps he has just rationalized it as an effect of his superior acting talents. But it was as obvious to me as if someone had struck a flame in a darkened room.

It would be impossible to superimpose my will over his or to affect his memories or perceptions. He is totally unsuited for the role I had intended. In any case, the man has a colossal ego and it would not be easy to suffer his company for any great length of time. If only he had Bram's personality! But then, if he did, he would not be such an outstanding performer on stage. Life is a tapestry of such contradictions.

June 27, 1877

Bram stopped by today to advise me he would be unable to call as he had planned next Wednesday. "Henry Irving has summoned me to London. I think that he wishes to further discuss some suggestions I made about stage management. It would be a great honor to support in even such a small way the career of a performer of his stature." He was quite excited and I confess to feeling a twinge of jealousy. The bond between these two men is extraordinary, although as far as I can see the admiration flows in only one direction. Bram may unknowingly love Henry Irving but Henry Irving loves only himself.

Note from Edward Palmer, undated

James,

I regret that from this point onward, you will have to jump from one journal to another in order to understand what was happening. I have inserted numbered slips of paper at appropriate points with directions wherever necessary.

In one of your previous letters, you indicated that Bram Stoker had left no journal of his own to explain the source of his inspiration for Dracula, and even remarked that it was odd for a man who wrote such an enormous body of work – literally thousands of letters on behalf of Henry Irving alone – to have committed so little of himself to paper. Well, the truth appears to be that he did in fact keep a journal, although only sporadically, because I have several volumes of them here and believe them to be authentic. The earliest entries are dated 1864 and were apparently written in Stoker's rooms on Harcourt Street. Those that follow are at irregular intervals, and most are tedious accounts of his fellow lodgers there and later at a house on Kildare.

The most interesting of these early ramblings – though they are unrelated to the matter that concerns us – are his notes on the poetry of Walt Whitman, to whom he had apparently written on at least one occasion. The most tedious are the accounts of his travels as Inspector of Petty Sessions, which are more concerned with the minutiae of his duties than the countryside he crossed. Much of this appears to have been notes he made in anticipation of the manual of operations he later wrote for that position.

There is only fleeting mention of Florence Balcombe prior to his trip to London to confer with Irving. He was in fact still keeping company with several other young women as well, and there is no evidence of a serious attachment in any of these cases. But you may be better served by reading his own words.

The Journal of Bram Stoker

July 1, 1877

It occurred to me to set down the general outline of my wonderful trip to London while it is still relatively fresh in my mind. Loveday, Irving's stage manager, personally met my train and kindly escorted me to the hotel and waited patiently while I freshened up. We met Henry at Corless's and discussed the staging of *Hamlet* over an excellent dinner. If all goes well, the production will come to Dublin in late September or early October. Oddly enough, Henry seemed only casually interested in the subject and interjected personal questions at odd moments. He has never previously expressed interest in my career or prospects and I was frankly quite flattered.

It was still early when we left and Henry suggested a visit to Phoenix Park, of which I had heard only in passing. We watched the wrestling matches for quite some time, a sport in which I had engaged from time to time during my student days. I must say that in many ways it is the epitome of manly sport. Chance has no role in the outcome, nor does it involve any implement to enhance the reach or strength or agility of the player. It is purely the body of one man pitted against that of another, directed by the mind, of course. Loveday claimed to be bored by the endless clinches and nearly motionless straining of arm against arm, leg against leg, but I must say I found the whole thing quite exciting.

I dared not ask why Henry requested my presence on such a subtle pretext. My presumption of the reason for his having summoned me was apparently misguided. There were a couple questions of staging upon which I thought I expressed myself to good account, but there was certainly nothing in our conversation so urgent that it could not have waited until his next visit to Dublin. Perhaps it is simply that Henry felt the need of a friend, someone from outside the theater community. He is such a prodigious, unorthodox talent that even those who admire his work feel that they must remain at arm's length from the man himself. Loveday defers to him constantly, and will only venture to disagree with him on inconsequential matters. I feel no such need for self censure, although in retrospect, our opinions rarely diverged significantly.

I have returned to Dublin with a growing discontent in my heart, however. The position of Inspector of Petty Sessions, once an object of considerable pride, now seems no more than that of glorified clerk. I cannot but recall how poorly my father was treated by the service to which he had dedicated his life, leaving him in his later years so low in funds that he was forced to live on the continent in order to maintain a satisfactory style of life. Is that to be my fate as well? I enjoyed my visit to Paris in 1874 greatly, but would I be as happy there as an economic exile? I am quite disturbed by these new thoughts and irritations as they have never troubled me before. It is almost as though another party had somehow reached into my brain and reshaped my attitudes so quietly that I never noticed the intrusion.

October 2, 1877

Saw *Hamlet* tonight. HI brilliant as always, the staging more than adequate, and I was pleased to note that some of my suggestions were incorporated into the production. Stopped backstage afterward but HI seemed preoccupied. Stared through me without a sign of recognition for several seconds and then dismissed me rather brusquely after only a few words. I fear I have done something to offend him.

October 3, 1877

There was a messenger at my door late this morning with a note from Henry, requesting that I stop by his rooms in the early afternoon. He apologized immediately for his coolness the night before. "Wasn't feeling at all well, Bram. Barely managed to get through the performance. A touch of fever, gone now. Sit down! Sit down!"

He questioned me quite closely about my career intentions for the next several minutes, and I confessed the doubts I had been having of late.

"Are you man enough to take a risk then?"

"That would depend on the nature of the risk. I have as much courage as the next man."

"Then how would you like to work for me?"

I was left speechless at first. This was so close to a conversation I had scripted in my mind that it was almost as though a part of my life was repeating itself. "I have little talent as an actor, Henry, and you already have an excellent stage manager."

"Yes, Loveday's as good as they come. But that is not exactly what I had in mind. In point of fact, I have no clear idea as yet just what I mean, but I feel a growing need to have someone to cull the distractions from my life. A personal manager of sorts. I cannot offer you anything at this time, but I felt I should broach the subject now." He leaned forward conspiratorially. "Can you keep a confidence?"

"Of course." I was a bit offended that he had thought it necessary to ask.

"I am involved in negotiations to lease a theater in London. It would provide a great platform for future productions, and a base from which to build a reputation, but I am not blind to the practical matters this would entail. There are questions of maintenance and staffing and advertising and probably scores of issues that have not yet occurred to me. I am an artist, Bram, not a businessman. I lack the kind of orderly mind that lends itself to commerce. I need someone who can shoulder these burdens for me, someone like you, a man I can trust. We might fail dismally and you would have given up your position for nothing, but we might also shine like a bright star in the sky."

To say that I was both honored and startled would be an understatement, even though the shade of my father seemed to loom above me, warning me against abandoning safety and security. But I listened to my own heart and told Henry that I would be honored to stand by his side. He settled back into his chair then, clearly satisfied with my response, then reiterated the need to be circumspect.

"Say nothing to anyone of this for the time being. The negotiations may fail, or a better prospect might offer itself. It will be at best several months before I can call upon you."

"You have merely to say the word," I responded.

The Journal of Florence Stoker

October 14, 1877

By chance I ran into Bram Stoker in the park today and remonstrated with him for not calling upon me recently. He apologized, apparently quite sincerely, and explained that he had been preoccupied with some personal matters with which he would not bore me. That only whetted my curiosity, of course, so I let myself be persuaded to accompany him for tea and conversation. To my surprise, he was extraordinarily tightlipped, although he did let slip that his inner turmoil was connected to Henry Irving in some fashion. I wondered if his secret attraction to the man had somehow been consummated and if this was the source of his uneasiness. That seemed the wrong answer, however, because I sensed elation as well as trepidation but not the slightest hint of guilt.

"You must call on me soon, Bram. I miss your good nature and sharp mind."

"I am certain you don't lack for admirers, Florence. Oscar Wilde mentioned you just the other day."

"Oscar is a casual friend and will never be more to me, Bram, although I beg you not to repeat that. His is a fragile nature despite his bravado and I would not hurt him unnecessarily."

Bram seemed quite uncomfortable. "He gave me to believe that the two of you were affianced."

I laughed, then covered my lips with my hand. "I am sorry, dear Bram, but Oscar's imagination sometimes colors his memories. I assure you that I am not committed to Oscar Wilde or any other man. Not at present."

"Well, then, I certainly will call upon you."

I am nearing the point where I must make a decision. If Florence Balcombe is to survive, she must take a husband soon. James grows increasingly inflexible and petulant, and even Philippa has taken to lecturing me on the need to find a future for myself. By which she means marrying above my station, of course. She has encouraged Oscar in his belief that I have deep affection for him, although she admits that Bram is a finer man. "He is more personable and stable, of course, but unless he carries through with his professed interest in becoming a barrister, he will always remain but a single step ahead of his debts. You would be far better off as the daughter in law of Lady Wilde. Their family fortune has dwindled but they are still comfortable, and would afford you legitimate entry among a higher class of people."

I am resolved to uncover Bram's secret. Trivial it may be, but it requires only a single feather to tip the scales to one side or the other.

The Journal of Bram Stoker

October 14, 1877

My life is suddenly rushing forward with such speed that I find myself searching for a handhold to steady myself. Had a letter from Henry yesterday indicating that plans in London were proceeding well. He has still not named the theater but based on his description, it can only be the Lyceum. The American, Hezekiah Bateman, seems to have abandoned hopes that any of his four daughters will prove themselves more than merely competent players, and the lease is due to lapse. I made some discrete inquiries and have learned that the building will require some renovation before it is presentable, but is essentially sound. This morning I found myself jotting down possible ideas for its redecoration, and by that act realized that I was emotionally committed already to throwing over my present position and casting my lot in London.

There is, after all, nothing to keep me here. None of my relatives remain in Dublin. My brother George lives just outside London and the rest are scattered across Europe at the moment. Most of my friends from Trinity have drifted away or married. It should not be such a great matter to dig up what remains of my roots and re-establish them elsewhere. Nevertheless, I feel the need to take with me a tangible reminder of my past. I am thirty years old, well past the age where I should have taken a wife and started a family.

I find I am not excited by the prospect. At one time I felt that my heart belonged to Genevieve Ward, but our time together in Paris convinced me that we could remain friends only if we remained apart. She has a talent second only to Henry in my experience, but she is willful, opinionated, and occasionally self indulgent, and would certainly never accept the limited role of wife and mother.

Of the unmarried ladies of Dublin, only Florence Balcombe evokes any real interest in me. I feel great affection for her, if not passionate love. She is sophisticated but demure, intelligent but proper. I know that she has some feelings for me as well, although I am not certain how deeply they run. Word that she was betrothed to Oscar Wilde had surprised but not dismayed me, and her insistence tonight that no such arrangement existed pleased but did not inspire me. A liaison between us has much to commend itself, however. We share many of the same interests and sensibilities. She is an intelligent young woman and dutiful daughter, but has not surrendered her lively spirit and has admitted to me that she looks forward to the day when she can manage her own household. I have no doubt she will do so ably. Her father is a respected if somewhat dull fellow, who has unfortunately passed on his narrow mindedness to Florence's sisters. Even the two older girls seem far less mature than Florence despite their impending marriages.

A fresh summons from Henry could come at any moment. I wish that I was better prepared to answer it.

The Journal of Florence Stoker

January 14, 1878

At last I have some inkling of the truth. Bram has been absent from Dublin with such regularity of late that it has proven even more difficult than I had expected to acquire intelligence of his plans. On those occasions when we have met, he has steadfastly avoided the subject, although I have managed to tease small crumbs from the outer crust. It was only when I realized that he was constantly finding small faults with the city, often trivialities barely worth mentioning, that I concluded he was summoning the nerve to leave. He had previously been so satisfied with his life here that I can only conclude he has been shown a better alternative, at least one that seems so.

He continues to prattle about Henry Irving, describing the man in such effusive terms that I sometimes lose patience with him. If only I could reveal to Bram that I sit before him as proof that no matter how prodigious a talent Irving might possess, he could never hope to play a role to rival my own. For a few hours, he stands upon a stage and spews forth lines already composed for him, in situations he can predict with absolute precision. My performance is nearly constant, the plot of the play as fluid as a river, and I create my own lines spontaneously and without the opportunity for revision or rehearsal. If he falters for a moment and reveals his true self, an adoring audience will overlook it. If I should do so, my audience would tear the head from my shoulders and the heart from my breast, and curse my name for generations.

We attended the theater recently and Bram spent a good deal of the evening commenting upon what he saw as infelicitous contrasts in color. "The theater itself is part of the experience of the play," he insisted. "A mediocre play in a fine setting will sometimes be more satisfying than a better effort staged in inferior quarters." This unusual interest leads me to suspect that Bram may have been asked to help design a new theater, perhaps hoping thereby to attract Irving and his company. Not in Dublin certainly, but in some other city. There is promise in this, if the plans are real and not some hopeless dream with which his mind has become infected. Nor do I have great confidence in any enterprise launched by Henry Irving.

February 1, 1878

I have been taken into Bram's confidence. My earlier suppositions were not far off the mark. Irving apparently has the financial backing to take up the lease on the Lyceum Theater, a much more ambitious plan than I had supposed. He has approached Bram with the offer of some as yet undefined position and, for various reasons, Bram is inclined to throw in his lot with this new endeavor. I had not planned to return to London for some years yet, allowing ample time for the deaths of those who knew me during my brief stay there as Mina Harker. As Bram Stoker's wife, I would move in very different social circles and the recent death of young Arthur, Lord Godalming, removes one remaining obstacle.

It would be an excellent match in many ways. Bram is an accommodating man who would be loyal but not entirely attentive to his wife, providing me sufficient freedom to satisfy the requirements of my secret life. He would feel duty bound to bed me but would derive no real pleasure from the act, so it would be unnecessary to employ the glamour more than occasionally to convince him that he was fulfilling his marital obligations. Toward the end, Jonathan Harker's mind began to fracture under the pressure; Bram would be largely unaffected.

I am still hesitant, however. On the very brink of making a choice, I find myself subject to an uncharacteristic anxiety. So much effort has been invested in this new life I have created for myself that I feel a strangely mortal reluctance to commit to a course of action that entails so great a risk. Oscar Wilde still writes, and I have not severed that cord either. As I suspected, he is making something of a name for himself, as much for his outrageous behavior as for his creative mind. The rest of the young men who have called upon me are unsuitable for one reason or another, and I have discouraged all but one or two quite successfully.

The Journal of Bram Stoker

February 21, 1878

Word of Henry's plans has slipped out, so I no longer need to be quite so circumspect. Florence seemed guardedly pleased at my prospects, although I sense sometimes that she resents Henry's place in my estimation. I have given serious consideration to asking for her hand, and might have done so this past week if James, her father, had not fallen ill with the gout. We share many common interests and values, and I enjoy our conversations. She is the only person I have taken into my confidence about my conversations with Henry, and I value her thoughtful, penetrating questions on the subject. Although she professes to have no interest in matters of business, her mind is first rate and she always has an eye on practicalities. I was surprised by these hidden depths, which she still conceals when we are not alone, and I feel certain that she would more than adequately fill the role of wife and mother.

My sole reservation now is that as my wife, she would be torn from her family. I am myself no longer emotionally tied to Dublin, in fact, sometimes chafe at the delay in taking up my new career. Florence, however, has never been parted from her loved ones. Would it be fair of me to ask her to abandon her life here and relocate to London? I have confided in her that my future lies in that direction, but have only hinted at the possibility that she might accompany me. When the day comes that Henry calls upon me to join him, will I have the courage to put her to the test?

The Journal of Florence Stoker

March 15, 1878

Oscar has written me again, pressing his suit after a fashion. I have composed a reply that neither acquiesces nor contradicts, but I suspect that anything short of an outright rebuff will be construed as agreement. I am more convinced than ever that Bram is the better choice, but as yet he has refrained from speaking of marriage, though I sense it in his mind. When last we met, he could talk of nothing but the prospect of adding Ellen Terry to the company at the Lyceum, an actress whom he believes "second only to Genevieve Ward" in her ability to seize the spirit of an audience. Oscar, on the other hand, regales me with an unceasing flow of anecdotes alternating between his own dissolute life and sneering portraits of the aristocracy.

The Journal of Bram Stoker

June 30, 1878

I have decided to ask for Florence's hand in marriage. The decision was made during the journey back from London, where I have been editing Vanderdecken's bloated prose down into manageable proportions. Henry was much more specific about his plans for me this time, and it appears that by the end of this year I will have a proper offer. Once that condition is met, I shall immediately call upon the Balcombes and state my intentions. There is little doubt in my mind that James will approve, and even his good wife seems to think more favorably of me of late, although she constantly hints that I would better serve myself by studying the law than by remaining in my current position. In truth, I cannot disagree, but neither can I divulge my more secret prospects.

During my visit, I managed a quick stop at the Lyceum and left a list of suggestions for its redecoration with Hawes Craven, the man Henry has hired to oversee set design. He found little fault and some merit and agreed to present them to Henry at the appropriate time. I feel that I have become a part of something greater than myself.

July 27, 1878

Terry has joined the Lyceum's company. At last Henry will have a leading lady with talent that approaches his own. The press is aflutter over this coup, and prospects for the theater seem brighter than ever. Any lingering doubts I might have had about the wisdom of linking myself to this rising star have been vanquished.

The Journal of Florence Stoker

September 14, 1878

Bram is gone to Glasgow to meet with Irving. He feels confident that a firm offer of employment will be forthcoming. Once again he suggested that we speak to James and Philippa and make our betrothal public, but I dissuaded him. Ostensibly this was because I wanted to make a clean break without a prolonged period during which my family and I would have to face each other daily knowing that separation was imminent. Philippa suspects something is up in any case, and I doubt James truly cares what I do so long as it does not reflect poorly upon my supposed upbringing. I still have some reservations about casting my lot with Bram, and will delay as long as possible.

I find myself oddly melancholy at the prospect of abandoning Philippa. She has formed a quite obvious attachment to me without being prodded by the glamour, a development which is unprecedented in my experience.

September 29, 1878

Bram returned from Glasgow disappointed but still enthusiastic. I believe Irving summons him on these minor errands just to exercise his power rather than because he finds any joy in Bram's company. If I were an ordinary woman, I would consider him a rival for my suitor's affections. As it happens, it would suit me well to marry a man whose attention was strongly diverted to another, but in such fashion that there would be not the slightest breath of scandal.

And speaking of scandal, I have received a present from Oscar, a gold cross of all things, with his name inscribed on the reverse. Religious icons can do me no harm in themselves, but it is bad enough that I must weekly accompany my family to church and pretend obeisance to this pale Christ figure. I once worshipped gods who could swallow him up in a single bite. What manner of god subjects himself to those who should be lying at his feet? I often wonder what these Christians would say if they knew that the god they worship was simply a man, and that his rise from the grave was only possible because on the night of the Last Supper he drank of my blood, not that of some god. And he rose and his disciples knew him for what he was and destroyed his body and buried it a second time.

I threw the cross into the sea. Its presence infuriated me for some reason.

November 15, 1878

The die is cast. I have agreed to marry Bram Stoker. He had word from Irving of a definite offer and has accepted. We have only a few days left before we must leave for Birmingham. Philippa is bustling about making preparations for a wedding at St. Ann's Church on Dawson Street. James sits in his study and smokes his nauseating cigars and occasionally forgets my name. I would be happy to forego the ceremony, which is meaningless to me, but I understand the importance of these petty rituals and have acquiesced, even made some specific requests to counterfeit enthusiasm.

December 1, 1878

Oscar has written requesting the return of the gold cross, professing to be hurt that I misled him into believing that he and I were betrothed. I would send back the bauble if I could despite his impertinence, but it is doubtless buried in the sand or lying in the belly of some great fish. I have responded that he should pick it up in person, that I would not trust to send it, and I am confident that he will not make the trip to Dublin for that sole purpose.

December 4, 1878

The wedding will take place shortly. Appropriately, this is the last blank page in this journal. When I start the next, I shall no longer be known as Florence Balcombe but as Florence Stoker, and I shall live in London, not Dublin. Although I cannot truly say that I am excited by the prospect, I will be relieved to leave Dublin behind. My normal prey here have grown more guarded this past year and it is increasingly difficult to satisfy my hunger without taking greater chances than I would like.

The Journal of Florence Stoker

December 29, 1878

      This is the first entry I have made since the day of my wedding to Bram Stoker. Our lives have been quite full of late and I have not had leisure to do so. By day I have helped my husband create our new household at 7 Southampton Street, and by night I have explored those parts of the city from whence I will cull those useless lives which I require to prolong my own. I was happy to see that the Seven Dials remains the squalid maze I remember, where no constable is likely to respond to a cry in the darkness. Even in the brief time that has passed since I was last a resident here, the city has changed enormously, spreading out to overwhelm the smaller communities along its borders. Most of the small commons have been absorbed, and only Wandsworth seems determined to preserve its quieter face.

      The day after our wedding, Bram and I set out for Birmingham, where we met with Henry Irving. To my surprise, Bram had made no mention of me to the "great man", and Irving was clearly startled and rather displeased to discover my existence. The mood passed quickly; the man's mind is so mercurial that it cannot retain any fact in which he is uninterested, so he simply ignored me throughout the evening at the Plough and Harrow. Shortly after dinner, I excused myself from the company, pleading fatigue from the journey, confident that Bram would remain with the others for at least several hours. In this I was not disappointed, and I satisfied my greater hunger at the expense of a thief who slipped into a darkened alley to examine a wallet he had plucked from the pocket of a passerby.

      Our accommodations on Southampton are adequate if a bit Spartan. We occupy a top floor flat of six rooms, which is ideally situated for Bram. He is only a few steps away from the Cadogan Steam Ferry, which carries him to Waterloo, a short walk from the Lyceum. The Covent Garden market is nearby, and the cobble stoned streets are filled with the coming and going of merchants and their customers, costermongers, chimney sweeps, stilt dancers, organ grinders, pickpockets, and the like. Bram has cautioned me against venturing out after dark without escort, as the mix is enriched at that time by muggers and other ruffians. Our building is in good repair, but many of those on neighboring streets have fallen into decay. The shops vary greatly in character, some attracting the aristocracy, some catering to darker souls. There are several taverns close at hand, which unfortunately means that the streets always reek of urine and occasionally blood. Even when I have recently fed, the coppery smell is a distraction. Carriage traffic is much heavier than in Dublin, and noticeably greater than when last I visited London. Broughams and hansoms pass under our windows constantly, and when those unwieldy growlers come by, the china rattles in the sideboard.

I have only hunted twice since reaching London, and on neither occasion was I forced to travel far from home, although in the future I shall vary my habits to avoid alarming the populace. Within a few blocks of Southampton, I encountered the kind of squalor that is perfect for my purposes. Men and women there will sell their own children for the right price. Cholera and other disease is common, and unexpected death is an everyday occurrence. If I remain circumspect and choose my victims with care, one from Whitechapel, another from Chelsea, the next from the Dials, and so forth, I believe the press of people in this great city is such that there will be nothing to lead the authorities to believe a single agent is responsible. The Thames tosses up dead bodies every morning, and the small number that I add to the mix will not likely be noted.

Note from Edward Palmer, undated

This is, unfortunately, almost the only page from the journals marked 1878-1879 to survive the fire. All of those that follow are damaged to some extent. Stoker's suffered the least, but unfortunately his are very incomplete and the entries are almost always weeks, even months, apart. In this particular case, I was unable to make out more than an occasional word or phrase from the remaining pages, which are largely charred completely beyond recognition, and which fall apart in my hands. There is one further legible excerpt which you will read shortly, and even that was so badly damaged that I have written in what I believe to be the correct bridges over a few inconsequential gaps in the account. It is particularly revealing. Stoker himself was so busy with the renovations and reorganization of the Lyceum that he was even less diligent with his journal than normal during 1879, and most of what he wrote concerned the details of the operation of the theater. He hardly even mentions Irving, in fact. I do recommend that you read his entry for March 10, however, as it provides some details about the conditions of their new life in London.

The Journal of Bram Stoker

March 10, 1879

We have settled into a comfortable routine and I am reassured once again that I have made the correct decision. Florence seems happy to be overseeing her own household and has done an extraordinary job of securing proper furnishings, although her tastes are a bit more somber than are my own. The neighborhood is not as good as I might wish, but the worst of it is hidden from our sight.

Each day I rise at mid-morning and Florence serves me a hearty breakfast. The 11:00 o'clock ferry delivers me to Waterloo and a brisk walk brings me to the theater, where I start my day by sorting through the previous day's incoming correspondence, deciding which should be ignored and discarded, which should be brought to Henry's attention, and which I might deal with myself, by far the largest portion. The renovations are largely done, although a few details remain to be completed.

I work until at least the early evening, sometimes later depending upon Henry's schedule, and on most days we have food brought in or on rare occasions dine out. Florence is most understanding about this and insists that I should continue with my devotion to my employer in order to bolster myself in his esteem. It is clear that she does not understand the mutual loyalty that arises between two men who have achieved true friendship and sees our relationship as purely mercantile.

Although she professes to be happy with our new circumstances, she sometimes seems restless and I know that she has occasional difficulty sleeping. On one occasion I wakened to hear her coming up the stairs in the small hours of the morning. Although she assured me that she had simply stepped outside to freshen the air in her lungs, there was an unusual furtiveness in her manner and I suspect that she walked about outdoors for some time, although it is hardly safe to do so at that hour, even for a man fully grown. I cautioned her against venturing out again and she acquiesced immediately.

Although she does not complain, I know that she continues to experience difficulty sleeping and often prowls the house at night, but she assures me that she naps during the afternoon while I am at the theater, and truthfully she shows no ill effects and is transparently happy to be free of her parents' house. Other than one brief mention of her mother, she seems to have forgotten her family entirely, and only wrote to them when I urged her to do so.

The Journal of Florence Stoker, damaged, undated but probably from early in the year 1879. Edited by Edward Palmer.

Tonight was the opening of *Hamlet*. Bram was very nervous and rose from bed while I was still preparing his breakfast. He paced the house constantly until it was time to meet the ferry. I have never seen him so agitated. Immediately he was gone, I resumed my rest until it was time to prepare for the evening. Bram's brother George arrived in a brougham at the appointed hour and was very proper and polite, although I think there is something in my appearance or carriage that disturbs him, because he is always uneasy in my presence.

We arrived <at the Lyceum> at precisely 7:30. I have not previously described the theater although <illegible passage>. The vestibule is quite handsomely appointed and a magnificent staircase leads upward, at the top of which I espied Bram, proudly greeting the inrushing crowd, many of them by name. Most of the interior has been redone in pale shades of green and blue, and the ceiling is of blue and gold. The moldings have all been <repaired> and restored to their original luster. From the box reserved for us, we looked down across <the audience> and the pit, which is marked by brass <railings>. Gaslights flicker all about, the light filtered through wine colored shades. Bram exerted much effort to influence the choice of color scheme and eventually prevailed only when he enlisted Hawes Craven to his cause.

As usual, I thought Irving's performance was overwrought and that he would have done better to have allowed Ellen Terry to more fully display her talents. At our first meeting, I sensed a power in her, not the glamour or any other of the fey arts, but a purely mortal strength of character that grows exceedingly rare in this modern age. She has the spirit of a queen, and I was surprised at her open association with Godwin, a weak and inconstant character about whom <illegible passage>.

Bram shares my high opinion <of Terry> whose close working relationship with him would give rise to jealousy in a mortal woman, although I am certain their behavior will not compromise my reputation. Like Bram she is mesmerized by <Irving's charm, or perhaps talent> and seems perfectly willing to subordinate her own career in service of his. Although perhaps we witnessed a moment of rebellion tonight, because when came the final curtain call, she was nowhere to be seen.

In the aftermath, George conducted me to Bram, who introduced me to a variety of notables including Lord Tennyson, whom I complimented dutifully although I find his poetry comically romantic and tediously long. His manners were impeccable, however, and despite his age I sensed a richness to his blood that set my senses aflame. At the same time, he seemed faintly disturbed by my presence, and I caught him looking back at me after he had moved on to greet another.   It was sufficiently unsettling that I watched for an opportunity to detach myself from the press, after informing George that I was feeling somewhat weary and needed to excuse myself for awhile. "You do look a bit pale, my dear," he said politely. I <illegible passage> and he became very awkward and assured me that he would make any necessary explanations if I wished to go sit by myself for a short while.

I slipped out of the theater unobserved and walked to the embankment, consumed by the uneasiness that Tennyson had aroused in me, which had also stimulated the hunger. If I chanced to find a solitary stroller, or perhaps stumbled upon some drunken lout lying in a pool of his own sour vomit, I planned to dispose of yet another body in the turgid waters beyond. To my surprise, the single lone figure I encountered was a woman standing with her back to a tree, staring down at the rushing waters. The woman was Ellen Terry.

There was no question of taking her blood. She was too prominent to meet with misfortune without a hue and cry being raised. And truthfully, I did not wish to end her life. She would be bones and dust all too soon, and she had an independence of spirit that nearly matched my own. But like me, she was of the fairer sex and must needs bind her spirit in the restraints of society just as we bound our bodies in these ridiculous corsets and bustles. I hesitated in the darkness, uncertain whether I should let myself be discovered. More than anything else at that moment, I wished to know what had drawn her there, when her star could be shining brightly inside the Lyceum. The need was so strong in me that even the cry of blood began to fade.

I should have turned away but I remained and eventually the weight of my gaze touched her because she turned and gave a little cry of surprise.

"I pray pardon. I didn't mean to startle you."

She had made as if to flee, but visibly relaxed. "Mrs. Stoker? Is that you? This is not a safe place to come alone at this time of the evening."

"Is it any safer for you?" I paused, but she made no answer. "And now neither of us is here alone."

There was a short, humorless laugh. "Sometimes it is possible to be alone even in the midst of a great crowd."

She did not, of course, have any idea how true that was in my particular case, and could not have realized how cruel that statement could sound. Nor was I prepared for the effect it had on me. I was the first and only of my kind and, since I had heard nothing indicating that Quincey Morris still walked the earth, I was even without surviving spiritual children until I chose to make another.

"If you don't mind my saying so, I find it strange that you would relinquish your moment of triumph. Mr. Irving will be looking for you."

Her laugh was louder this time. "Henry won't even notice that I have gone. As far as he is concerned, Henry is the only real actor on the stage. The rest of us are mere props. If he could contrive to play all the parts himself, he would do so."

"Do you regret your decision to join his company?"

"Sometimes. Sometimes not. For all his faults, Henry is a dynamic personality. His enthusiasm infects everyone around him.

His productions will attract great audiences and his performances will be the subject of argument, praise, and condemnation. I believe that he will transform the theater, that after him artists will no longer be viewed with suspicion and opprobrium, that he will lift us all to a higher plateau. With himself standing alone on the summit, of course."

"He certainly commands great respect. My husband speaks very highly of him."

"Oh, Ma is like putty in his hands." She looked uneasy for a second. "Many of us call him 'Ma', you see, because he mothers us so. You are very fortunate in having such a kind, thoughtful man as your husband." She looked wistful and I remembered my instinctive dislike of Godwin, her current paramour.

We talked a little more and eventually found our feet taking us back to the theater. Terry assured me that she was just somewhat overwhelmed by the crowd and had disappeared only to regain her composure. I pretended to believe her, but I knew even without touching her mind that the truth was different, that upon the stage this evening she had realized the truth, that she could never hope to be judged for her own efforts, but would ever be no more than an embellishment of Irving's career, and while she might resign herself to that fate, it was a decision that would never rest easy in her heart. We were both living the life of another person. The Ellen Terry who chose to become a satellite of Henry Irving was no more her true self than I was in fact Florence Balcombe Stoker.

Neither of us spoke as we walked back to the theater. I suspect that we were both preoccupied. Terry was struggling to come to terms with the new self of which she had just become aware, doomed to a lifetime of supporting roles. On the other hand, I was intrigued by the strong bond I was feeling to this talented, unhappy woman. I am not entirely bereft of emotion; at one time I felt a great affection for Vlad, for example, until he turned against me, and there have been others I have brought over of whom I have been fond. But this was the first time I had felt such a strong tie to an ordinary mortal. Philippa Balcombe and Bram were both entertaining company and I did take an interest in their successes and failures, but with Ellen Terry the sudden attachment was already far stronger, even though we had only spoken briefly twice before. Is this some new stage in my transformation from simple humanity, or a temporary aberration, a product of my attempt to loyally play the part I have chosen? The question requires further thought.

Upon my reunion with Bram I was forced to endure another conversation with Hall Caine, his writer friend. I cannot understand what Bram sees in him. The man's talent is meager, he talks incessantly about subjects of little merit, and complains constantly of his roommate, the foreigner Rosetti. I was tempted to inquire why he did not move to other lodgings if it bothered him to be perpetually tripping over paints and brushes and canvases, but I held my tongue. Fortunately, Tennyson and his party were gone and my bloodlust had faded as I stood on the embankment, although I would have to deal with it before the night was over.

Terry joined Irving at the center of attention, her face radiant, all trace of her earlier dismay concealed. It was perhaps an even more impressive performance than that she had delivered earlier upon the stage, although for that matter, all of us assembled there were playing one part or another.

Note from Edward Palmer, undated

The binding of Enhuedanna's second journal for 1879 and the first for 1880 were severely damaged in the fire. Fortunately, the majority of the internal pages survived and remain legible. Unfortunately, they were separated and scattered and reassembled in no apparent order. What's more, the top margin of each page is badly charred, and that is ordinarily where the dates were inscribed. I have selected a number of fragments and arranged them in what I think is more or less the order in which they were written. We should be able to assign approximate dates later by reference to verifiable events included in these accounts. There is a great deal of extraneous material as well, which you may want to peruse later.

The Journal of Florence Stoker, undated

Gilbert was very entertaining this evening, and he is certainly my favorite among the men Bram has found to escort me to the theater in his absence. His tongue is sour, his opinions crisp and sharply defined, and occasionally he is rather a bully, but at the same time he is witty and perceptive. He is currently hard at work putting the finishing touches on a new play, a pirate story involving a military officer of some sort..

"Your father made a career of the army, did he not?" he inquired of me.

"Indeed, although he is retired now, and was never promoted to the colonelcy he coveted. He remains Major Balcombe to his acquaintances even now."

"I have no doubt that he served his country well."

"Oh, yes. Had there been a war, he might have distinguished himself further. He was the very model of a modern major."

"To be sure. A nice turn of phrase, Mrs. Stoker. Might I borrow it?"

The conversation reminded me of James and Philippa. Philippa still wrote from time to time, and I answered occasionally, but as the months pass, the tone grows more like that one would use to an old friend than to a daughter. I sometimes wonder if my adopted mother has cast off the effects of the glamour, at least in part. If so, she seems content to maintain the pretense of our relationship. I always suspected she had depths that she concealed even from me.

The Journal of Florence Stoker

April 2, 1879

Bram has expressed continued concern that I am not with child. This is unforeseen as I had not thought Bram the fatherly type. Even now, I suspect it is more a question of the image he wants to project, and his perceived duties to me and to society, than the actual desire to raise a family. It may be more complex than that, however. For one such as I, immortality is a foregone conclusion. For these cringing Christians, it is a distant reward for having lived a good life, and I suspect more a desperate hope than a deeply held belief. The only tangible form of immortality available to them is through the creation of children, a poor substitute for the real thing.

I confess I am caught up in the role of Florence Stoker, however, and while childless marriages are not uncommon, the addition of a son or daughter would contribute to the image of normality I have sought to display to the world. It is not possible, of course, for me to actually bear a child, but I have an idea which I shall consider at some length before pursuing. Bram may yet have his way.

Loose Journal Pages, dates missing

Gilbert was my escort again this evening. Talked constantly during the production, which was rude no doubt, but his jibes were not unamusing, and he shares my unstated distaste for Irving. He is very pleased with the response to *The Pirates of Penzance* and suggests that Irving's heavy reliance on material which has already passed the test of time is misguided.

"Audiences want to see something new to them. They want to be surprised. Spectacular sets and enthusiastic actors will only divert them for a time."

. . .

James Whistler was here today with all of his papers. Bram is attempting to make some sense of them, but he shakes his head constantly. Given Whistler's evident lack of organization and thoughtless attitude, I wonder if all painters are inherently disorderly. Perhaps I did Hall Caine an injustice when I thought him petty in his remarks about Dante Rosetti, whose work is at least pleasing to the eye. Whistler seems to me a mere scribbler whose work is more suited for newspaper illustration than fine art. Out of respect for Bram's friendship with the man, I have not ventured my opinion, but I am firmly on the side of John Ruskin. Whistler still wears his one farthing settlement on a chain around his neck and claims victory, but it was a Pyrrhic one at best. Ruskin may have violated the letter of the law with his contention that Whistler's work is not truly art, but by granting Whistler only a pittance as compensation, the court has clearly sided with Ruskin's aesthetic stance.

I am working on a composition of my own at the moment, a far more complex one. Bram now believes me to be with child and is enthusiastically passing word to all and sundry. He suggested that George attend, but I have insisted upon a physician of my own choosing, a purely fictional character, of course, since I dare not risk an examination which would reveal the truth. The solution to the problem occurred to me but recently. In the past I have stolen many a child to satisfy my hunger, why not now steal one to raise as my own? It will need to be an infant, of course, and from a family who resemble Bram in appearance. It shall be a difficult time for me and I will remain in seclusion as much as possible, and augment my figure with suitable padding when it is not. A wet nurse will be required as well because of my "guarded" condition following the birth.

The mind of an infant is particularly susceptible to the glamour because it has yet to build its natural defenses. I believe that given time I will be able to shape the personality of the newborn as a sculptor molds his clay. From time to time I have made use of mortal servants, particularly in the early days when I could not suffer the sun for more than a few moments at a time without discomfort. Vlad was particularly skilled at securing the loyalty of his gypsy retainers despite his nature. If he could bend to his will such fiercely independent people, then surely I can manage one small child. There will be difficulties, of course, but if they become insurmountable, there is always the alternative of a terrible accident or childhood disease. A disease of the blood, no doubt. But I am determined not to let it come to that. At times I admit to myself that I am playing an elaborate game to which only I know the rules, some of which I construct along the way, but if it is a game, it is at times a glorious one, and it helps to pass the endless days.

. . .

Bram is full of ideas for this dining club or whatever it is that he and Irving are talking about. Calls it the Beefsteak Room. Another excuse for the long hours he spends attempting to please Irving. If I were a human, I would be heartily angry at being thus abandoned, and truthfully, there are times when Bram's slavish devotion to Irving troubles me. But his prolonged absences make my secretive excursions less difficult to conceal, although fresh difficulties will arise once the child is here.

I have located two likely candidates. Both women are with child, one quite obviously so. She is a bit too far along to coincide with my schedule, but her husband has both the size and general features of Bram, while the other is a much shorter, heavier man. It will be some time yet before I have to decide between the two.

. . .

Irving plans to accompany two of his admirers, the Baroness Burdet-Coutts and her shadow, Hannah Brown, on a Mediterranean cruise at the end of the season, while Bram remains behind to oversee the last of the restoration process at the Lyceum and make initial arrangements for the new season. Irving is less than enthusiastic about the proposed opening production, and Bram says that even Loveday and Hawes Craven have taken to avoiding his company because of his bad temper. The Baroness was introduced to Irving through the agency of Bram's brother Thornley, who prevailed upon him to perform this favor. Needless to say, Irving preened under her flattery.

I continue my clandestine meetings with Ellen Terry. We do not call them such to one another, but by mutual agreement neither of us has mentioned our friendship to anyone else. It is a new thing for me to use that term for another. I was raised a princess, kept separated from the other children of my father's empire, spent my life as a young woman and high priestess with no experience of men, and since the clock of my body has ceased to measure the time I have felt only a passing desire for companionship. For centuries I have existed in this fashion, and have never seriously missed the company of others. Those like Vlad whom I held close to me were not true friends, for they were compelled by the transformation to cling to the one who made them. The transition eventually passes and as each of them grew independent, they turned upon me as did Vlad, and each in turn I was forced to destroy, no matter how fond of them I had grown, and so I did not allow myself to feel any strong attachments that would have to be painfully severed.

It is different in this case. I have not even touched her mind with the glamour. Her friendship is freely given and seems genuine. Perhaps it is just that she wants someone to whom she can speak in confidence, for she has certainly told me far more than it is entirely proper for her to have done. Her marriage as a mere child to Wardell, her dissatisfaction with Godwin and his constant whining, her occasional indiscretions with Irving, who remains estranged from his own wife – she has described each in uncompromising terms. And beyond this, she has told me of her aspirations, of her love for the stage, for her children, the sense of fulfillment she achieves by losing herself in a part.

"The lives of these others, no matter how briefly touched, no matter how imaginary, enrich my own. On the stage, I can try on personalities that I would not dare otherwise. I can be kind or wicked or crazed or transformed with anger. The faults of my characters fade away when the play is done, and I learn about myself through them."

I contribute little to our conversation and she seems content to have it that way. But unlike Lucy Westenra, who prattled endlessly about trivial matters that held no inherent interest, Terry's words are invariably thoughtful and varied in subject. There are times when I wish that I could respond with similar frankness, but the parts of my existence which she would find most interesting are those I cannot share with her. She would recoil from me in horror if she did not believe me mad.

. . .

It will be the Wyndham child. Mary Christopher was overcome with a fever and died very suddenly, taking her baby with her. The woman is due in December, which is earlier than I had wanted, but it must serve.

Irving has cabled from Marseilles. All plans are to be thrown over as he has fixed upon Shylock as his next great role. Craven came by the house this past Saturday after hearing the news and rolled his eyes a great deal and insisted there was insufficient time to prepare sets adequate to the scope of the play, but Bram assured me afterward that this is a song he sings at the opening of every new campaign, and that the work will be completed to his usual high standards before opening night, which will be November 1.

...

Ever since Irving returned to London, Bram has been unusually late returning and on one occasion actually slept at the theater. He professes great enthusiasm for the new production but admits that Irving's plans for staging are ambitious even by his usual bloated standards and that time constraints are severely taxing the crew.

Bram is also unhappy about the appointment of Charles Howson to help keep accounts. In the past this has been Bram's exclusive domain and he has prided himself on his accuracy and timeliness. Irving has no cause for complaint, and I suspect this is merely another of his efforts to ensure that none of his retinue should be allowed pride in anything other than their association with the Great Man, or "guv'nor", as he has come to be called of late. I have met Howson only once, and briefly, and he struck me as a vile little oaf, small in spirit as well as in stature, another Renfield without the excuse of madness. It may come to pass that Mr. Howson shall be found floating in the Thames, the victim of some cutpurse or other rogue as far as the authorities may be concerned, although his blood is probably so thin that it will not properly satisfy me.

...

November 1, 1879.

Opening night for *The Merchant of Venice*. It is my favorite of Shakespeare's plays, as Shylock is in some ways a creature like myself, seeking his pound of flesh where I prefer a liter of blood. As Bram predicted, the sets are admirably dressed and do not look at all hurried. Bram clucks his tongue about Irving's insistence upon spending money at every turn and I nod sympathetically, but despite the man's many failings, he does know how to captivate an audience. Gilbert escorted me once again, and his wife accompanied us on this occasion. She is an insipid creature, full of petty complaints and so inattentive that she could not follow the story. It is no surprise to me that Gilbert prefers to keep his own company in the box, or squire the wife of some friend in place of his own. Only once was he at all forward, and seemed to take my mild rebuff in good humor, for he never referred to it again, nor repeated his affront.

As at the opening of *Hamlet*, Terry seemed quite low in spirits afterwards, although I think she managed to disguise her feelings from all but myself. We managed to exchange only a very few words because of the press of people, and I have promised to meet with her within the next few days, as it has been quite long since our last time alone together. I have in fact been avoiding appearing in public for the past fortnight and plan to continue this policy until year end, or at least until the Wyndham child is born. George Stoker has already commented that I seem underweight for so late in my term and asked pointed questions about the care I was receiving from my mysterious private physician. He later questioned Bram quite closely on the subject, but I have used the glamour to reinforce my husband's belief that he has met the man, who has forsworn public practice and insists on anonymity from those few clients whom he continues to see.

The Journal of Bram Stoker, undated entry from 1879

During my recent trip to Dublin, I met the most extraordinary fellow on the train. Sir Richard Burton was known to me by reputation, of course, but I had not thought him such a personable, voluble, and well informed fellow. His knowledge of the folk tales and legends of far lands is broad and deep, and he regaled me with some of the strangest to pass the time as we traveled.

One in particular struck an odd chord in me. I remember LeFanu's fascination with the undead but at the time it struck me as an unhealthy interest in a morbid subject. Burton described a legend he heard in Egypt of one such creature. It started life as a mortal human man, an Arab who became lost in the desert. Upon encountering another solitary traveler who was similarly bereft of water, the first struck his fellow down and drained the unconscious man's blood to assuage his own thirst. This heinous act caused him to be physically transformed and his skin blistered and peeled away when touched directly by the sunlight. As time passed the creature lost its hair, and then its limbs withered and disappeared until it was no more than a starveling serpent that lay buried in the sand by day. Eventually it took up residence beneath an oasis that was visited one night by a caravan, with predictable dire consequences for the unwary travelers, but although the creature's vigor was thereby restored, its limbs were permanently lost. Adapting to this new form, it dug for itself a deep burrow and remained there in a quiescent state for much of the time, emerging only under cover of darkness and only when unwary travelers took refuge at the oasis, killing them and draining the blood from their bodies.

I related this fanciful tale to Florence, hinting that I was thinking of using it as the basis for an adventure story. She seemed strangely affected by the concept and was silent for a surprisingly long time. She then expressed sympathy for the plight of what she called "your great white worm" and suggested that the story would have much more impact if I set it in England. "No one cares what happens to the inhabitants of some strange, far land, but if it might be one's neighbor or one's self in jeopardy, that is a far different matter."

I stopped to visit briefly with Florence's family. Her father appears to be suffering some mild dementia. He insisted that he has but four daughters and that none of them bore the name Florence. Philippa seemed a bit odd as well, told me that "it's almost as if we never knew her now that's she's gone." I made no mention of this upon my return, as Florence must gather all her strength and concentration for the next few months.

She continues to insist that she feels minimal discomfort despite her condition, and I see no reason to worry despite George's reservations. The babe is due in mid-January. Florence has suggested that we seek out a wet nurse, as her own mother was incapable of performing that maternal function and she fears she shares the same shortcoming. Both George and I have reassured her that this is not so great a fault that she should perturb herself unduly. I look forward to the event, although at the same time I must confess that the inevitable upset to our routine could not come at a worse time. Although *Merchant* goes well, Henry is constantly changing some detail or another and even Loveday is openly expressing exasperation. What cannot be helped must be dealt with.

The Journal of Florence Stoker

December 31, 1879

The deed is done, although the task did not go as I had planned it would. Dusk found me concealed in the shadows from whence I could watch the Wyndham's front door. The woman is punctual, if nothing else, for this was the very day the child was due. I have watched them for several months now, every few days initially, almost every night recently. It will be easier to impose my own will on the child's mind if it has not yet forged a bond with its mother, so I am resolved to steal it away at once.

The midwife was just leaving when I arrived and the commotion inside had largely subsided. I waited until the shadows had spread across the cobblestones and the sounds of distant carriages became so infrequent that each stood out individually. The Wyndhams lived on the second story of a decaying tenement building in Aldgate, sufficiently distant from Southampton Street that I was not worried about encountering them later by mischance. The adjacent building is unoccupied, and I was able to force my way inside and ascend to the second floor, where a narrow window faced the Wyndhams' bedroom. The shutters were secured but I forced the lock with little effort.

From my vantage point, I could see little. It was a particularly chilly night and the Wyndhams' lodgings were closed up tightly. The shutters were not locked, however, and I was able to leap across the gap and balance precariously on their window ledge. Silently, I eased the shutters open and successfully gained entry without having wakened anyone. The Wyndham woman lay in bed with the child beside her, and she moved restlessly as the cold air swirled around her body until I closed it off behind me.

I did not intend that the woman should forfeit her life. The hunger was several days distant, and I bore her no animosity. Indeed, as I stood over the bed, I felt what might almost have been envy. Immortality does not come without a price. Rather than create a new life, I am limited to transforming those that already exist. And even in that, I have never really succeeded, because all upon whom I have bestowed the gift of endlesss life have eventually attempted matricide, and so I have been forced to take back what I have given them.

The babe was asleep as well, and I reached out with the glamour and touched its mind. It was as I expected, unformed, undefended, undirected. I would rather that it had been a girl, but there was naught I could do about that. I reinforced its need to sleep so that it would not waken and take alarm while I was removing it, and all might have gone well if I had retained the presence of mind to wonder about the father.

Wyndham entered the room just as I was pressing the child to my bosom. He stopped in midstride and then bellowed loudly. "Here! What's this all about then? Who're you?"

Had I been quicker, I might have transfixed him with the glamour before he spoke, but I was concentrating all my attention on the child and its sleeping mother. His shouting wakened the wife as well, although the babe was completely under my influence. Wyndham came toward me with his massive arms upraised, and I pressed the child up against one shoulder and used my free hand to inflict a great wound to his throat and chest. I expected him to fall immediately and had already turned to deal with his wife, when he gave a roar of rage and struck me full in the back. The woman had already armed herself with a candlestick, but she could not strike me easily without endangering the child, so instead she rose to her feet on the bed and called encouragement to her husband, who had wrapped his massive arms around my shoulders. I was concerned for the child, who was caught in the vice of his arms, as well as the possibility that the uproar would bring curious neighbors to complicate matters.

I lowered my head and bit his left arm to the bone, and his grip loosened as he howled with this fresh pain. It was easy enough to shake him off after that. The infant stirred as I tore out its father's throat, and began to cry earnestly when I dropped it to the floor. Mrs. Wyndham had brought the candlestick down on my shoulder with such force that I could not retain my grip.

She died much more easily than her husband, and I used the glamour to force the child to sleep once more. There were stirrings and shouts from the lower floor of the house, and I knew I must leave quickly. Even though I was not feeling the hunger, I regretted the waste of so much blood. Its very smell confused my senses, and for a moment I thought to stand my ground and deal similarly with any who might come to investigate. But then I remembered my purpose and I was out the window and across to the empty house, from which I emerged with the infant so swaddled in my cloak that no one could tell without close inspection what burden it was that I bore. There was still shouting when I quitted that street, and I imagine tomorrow's papers will have embellished the night's events greatly.

I concealed the child where Bram would not stumble across it. The babe will not waken before sunrise unless I bid it to do so. After Bram has left for the theater in the morning, I will be overcome with early pains and will send for my phantom physician, who will have departed before my husband can be summoned home. I take a great chance with this, and it still may become necessary to sacrifice the child if I cannot trust the degree of control which I hope to exert over its personality. But it presents the most interesting challenge I have faced since leaving the Borgo Pass.

Later

All went well. The boy is to be named Noel. Bram seems quite genuinely pleased to be a father. I had feared that he might have second thoughts now that our life together is to be so fundamentally changed. A midwife has been engaged and all appears to be going as planned.

Note from Edward Palmer, undated

Both Stokers seem to have been quite heavily occupied during the next year. There is no journal for Bram at all, although I suppose it might have been one of those so completely destroyed in the fire that nothing remains by which it can be certainly identified. Florence/Enhuedanna did keep a journal, and it is not heavily damaged, but only a handful of pages are actually inscribed. It appears that she threw herself wholeheartedly into her role as wife and mother, presumably interrupting it only when her unwholesome hunger drove her to do so. There is a rather lengthy account of their holiday in Portsmouth, but other than a fleeting allusion to having found it more than usually difficult to locate her prey, the words could just as easily have come from an ordinary Englishwoman. I have marked only two brief passages for your attention.

The Journal of Florence Stoker

June 5, 1880

Had tea with Ellen again today. She is much improved in spirits recently, and I believe that my companionship has helped her by providing someone with whom she could talk without fear of criticism or indiscretion. Her enthusiasm for the stage astonishes me and I said so.

"It is a thrill quite beyond anything else you can possibly imagine, Florence."

"I will have to take your word for it. My talents certainly lie elsewhere."

"Don't belittle yourself, my dear. You are a remarkably intelligent woman, for all that you hide it from the world. It would not surprise me to discover that you had missed your calling."

"I am happy as wife and mother," I replied, then realized this might be construed as a criticism of her own behavior. "My energy and ambition are not equal to your own."

"Nonsense! That is what nurses and housekeepers are for. You must spread your wings a little, Florence. I insist upon it. It shall be my personal campaign to ensure that you perform upon the stage. I shall speak to Bram about it this very day."

"He will certainly tell you that I am unsuited for any such flamboyance." But I confess that the thought remained in my mind. It would be a play within a play within a play, of course, and there was a degree of risk, however slight, that I might be recognized by someone from my previous life who happened to sit among the audience. But I chafe at the necessity to constantly hide my face away, and the diversion might well be worth the risk.

October 14, 1880

I have begun to suspect that Bram is in some fashion aware of the presence of the glamour. His demeanor in my presence remains unchanged, but he has become increasingly interested in occult matters, speculates in my presence about the unknown powers of the human mind, and has even flirted with the idea of joining this secretive social club that calls itself the Hermetic Order of the Golden Dawn. They play at magic and pretend to possess secret knowledge, but at heart they are silly people who are deluding themselves. I could show them things which would leave them cowering in their closets or beneath their beds. I believe Bram knows them to be frauds, naughty children making outrageous claims to annoy the adults, but he is fumbling in the dark to explain an influence which he cannot even describe, and the suggestion that they may have access to mysteries unknown to the general public is tantalizing. Fortunately, I have not had to resort to the glamour to influence Bram for the past several months. Our relationship is stable and suits my peculiar needs. He has in fact seemed to grow even fonder of me than when we were first married, and I find myself actively enjoying his company at times. His skepticism about the group has grown recently and he seems to have turned his thoughts of the occult into an adventure story which he is confident will find praise from one publisher or another.

Noel is universally admired for his quiet nature. I have used the glamour to smooth the troubles from his mind, and to sense his discomforts and compensate for them. There is a clear bond between us; I suspect that he will be uniquely sensitive to the glamour as he grows older, and I am more confident than ever that he will prove an ally in his maturity. I have never played the mother before, and while I find many of the social obligations pointless and annoying, there is a certain charm to them that amuses me at times. These modern English feel so superior to the "savages" of the world, but they remain just as much enslaved to ritual and tradition as does the humblest blackamoor.

Bram has acquiesced to the suggestion that I might try a small part in a performance next season. He suggested that I portray one of the vestal virgins in some new play by Tennyson called "The Cup". I am more qualified for the role than he realizes, but it would not do to mention aloud that I am still a maiden.

Note from Edward Palmer, undated

Bram kept no journal for 1881, and there was once again substantial damage to the other materials from this period. A packet of letters from various individuals to Bram and/or Florence survived virtually intact, however, and I have marked passages from a few of these which you may find of interest. Both Stokers recorded moments from their lives irregularly for the next several years, but Florence was the most assiduous. She seems to have increasingly thrown herself into this new life she had created for herself, and on the few occasions when she alludes to or forthrightly records details of her secret existence, she seems to me almost to be embarrassed. I might venture to say that she immersed herself so thoroughly in the fantasy that it became more real to her than the truth.

The vast majority of her musings are therefore no more interesting than would be expected from a perfectly ordinary woman of the time. I have therefore marked only representative passages and the occasional extraordinary events henceforth.

Bram was occupied with several tours conducted by the Lyceum company in America. I have also marked a few interesting passages in his letters to Florence, but they are generally not relevant to her career.

The Journal of Florence Stoker

Undated, but some time in 1881

 The closing of *The Cup* most decidedly did not distress me as I thought the play thoroughly insipid. My curiosity has been satisfied; it is not an experiment I will repeat. Ellen and Bram characterized my distress as stage fright, and perhaps it was some close cousin of that disorder. More likely it is that concealment has grown to be such a central part of my very being that performing publicly, standing with the eyes of hundreds of people focused upon me, was too great a strain. I only managed to control my panic by convincing myself that running from the stage or refusing to go on would have attracted even more attention. And it would have been a great shame to have disappointed Ellen. Fortunately, the count of one fewer virgins following opening night was not remarked upon by the steadily thinning audience. Ellen has finally confessed to the origin of the flowers which I received following my first and last performance. I knew from the outset that she had not sent them despite her claim to the contrary. She is so used to telling me her secrets now that it was only a matter of time until this intelligence slipped out as well. So Oscar Wilde has not forgotten me. I sometimes wonder what might have chanced if I had accepted his hand other than Bram's. It would surely have been a more colorful, if less secure life.

 Gilbert has invited Bram and I to see *Patience*, which draws enormous crowds. Ellen has been already and reports that it neatly skewers our mutual friend Oscar Wilde, of whom Gilbert disapproves almost as much as he does Irving. Upon reflection, however, I can think of few public figures of whom he does not disapprove to at least some degree.

 Under the Sunset has finally appeared and Bram is very pleased with the result. I found the tale a bit tedious, but if it has provided an outlet for Bram's preoccupations with the occult, I will be pleased. He is expressing more interest in Noel as well, now that the child does more than merely sleep and eat.

Letter from George Stoker to Bram and Florence Stoker, dated July 11, 1881

I will be happy to accept your kind invitation to join you in residing at Cheyne Walk. It is very convenient to my practice, which I confess is a much more compelling argument than your assurance that our neighbors will include Oscar Wilde and other notables. I visited Chelsea earlier today by carriage and noted that it affords a wonderful view of the Albert Bridge, and that the class of people I observed on the streets is a considerable improvement over those disposed around your previous lodgings. The embankment area seems also a pleasant place to walk and think.

I also wish to thank you again, Bram, for your efforts in securing me the position of medical consultant to the Lyceum. Many of my patients are in serious arrears on their payments, but I lack the heart to cut them off even though I remain out of pocket for their treatment. The stipend from the theater will offset some of this.

Arrangements for the movement of my belongings are in progress. I shall be with you soon.

As ever,

George

Excerpt from Letter from Florence Stoker to Ellen Terry, dated July 31, 1881

I hope that your holiday was as refreshing as you had hoped it would be. We have been quite busy with our new home. Noel settled in quite easily but Bram still prowls restlessly about, a great bear uncertain of his new cave.

Our social life is no less frantic now that the season is over. Lady Jane Wilde has rediscovered us and if we were to accept every invitation she proffered, we would have no time to visit with any of our other acquaintances. She remains as astringent as ever, but she does attract the most interesting people. Bram had quite an interesting conversation with an American writer named Harte recently and I was entertained by a charming young man named Dexter who aspires to be a poet.

The only petty misfortune in our lives of late is the unfortunate decision by our neighbor, the artist Rosetti, to take a new roommate. The new man is a drunkard and a debaucher and staggers home at odd hours singing lewd songs at the top of his lungs. Bram has promised to speak to him about his behavior.

The Journal of Florence Stoker

July 31, 1881

I had expected to find Lady Jane much changed with the passage of time. Since the death of her husband, she has moved about considerably, and her anti-English sentiments have gone out of fashion again. When her invitation arrived, I was of two minds about accepting, but curiosity finally mastered my reservations.

To my surprise, she seemed little changed, other than the additional lines in her face and a slight easing of the rough tones of her voice. Her words remained as coarse as ever, and I sensed her wariness even as she greeted us and thanked us for coming. Bram was oblivious, of course, and drifted off to discover what strange assortment of people she had assembled this time. He finally fell into company with an American writer and they spent most of the evening huddled in a corner.

I chatted with several people whose names escaped me within minutes. There was a goodly assortment of cakes and other small treats, but none of the heartier food I remembered from Dublin. Rumor has it that she has squandered much of her husband's estate, refusing to relinquish her prominent and overstated lifestyle.

We were among the last to leave, as Bram was reluctant to abandon his new friend, and on the way home our peace was intruded upon by the voices of an obviously drunken duet, a song replete with sexual innuendo and scatological humor. Bram grew quite stiff necked and pretended not to hear the words, and I humored him. The voices remained quite clear even after we arrived at, and to our dismay, they grew louder while Bram was paying the driver. The serenaders turned the corner before we were inside, and Bram slammed the door irritably to shut off the sound.

"It's Swinburne," he informed me. "Rosetti's new roommate. The man's an ass. Brilliant, but an ass. In his sober moments, he can be quite entertaining, but they are all too infrequent of late. I can't imagine what inspired Rosetti to take him in."

Mrs. Nelson was still up and she assured me quite unnecessarily that Noel had been no trouble at all. The singing finally abated, but Bram remained upset and insisted that he needed to sit up for awhile. I found him dozing off in his chair half an hour later, and left quietly, as the need to feed was upon me.

Cheyne Walk was nearly abandoned now, although I could hear carriages moving in the direction of Oakley Street. Caution made me keep to the shadows as I proceeded, but even so I was taken unawares when a grotesque little man lurched out from behind a lamp post, his features unnaturally pale in the flickering gaslit glow. His feet were unsteady and he reached out toward me, apparently for support. Startled and disgusted, I flinched away and he almost lost his footing.

"Your pardon, m'lady. My limbs are not presently in agreement with my mind." Those were the words he spoke, but his voice was slurred so that they were nearly unintelligible.

"Away with you, sir. You are drunk and I will have nothing to do with you."

"Drunk, am I? Well, maybe t'is so. The spirit takes me when I take the spirits, you see. When I put pen to paper, I often find the muse has deserted me for the land of spirits so it is among the spirits that I seek her." And he launched into a mercifully brief chorus of the same rude song which we had heard earlier in the evening.

"You must be Mr. Swinburne."

"Must I? Well, if you insist, then I am indeed Swinburne. Algernon to my friends. Are you one of my friends?" He narrowed his eyes and tried to focus on my face. "No, I don't believe so. Women generally don't like me, you know, and I return the compliment with full vigor." He took another step in my direction, raising one fist in what may have been mock anger, or perhaps was genuine. In either case, I was startled and enraged, and the hunger had lessened my self control.

I can only see the shadow of my face in mirrors and other reflections although others observe nothing untoward under those circumstances. Through portraits I have a clearer appreciation of my features, and through long habit I have learned to apply powders and rouge and to properly arrange my hair. All this is false, for my true face is terrible to behold. It first came upon me the day my father died. The slave who watched its emergence was the first to die by my hand and the first whose blood I tasted. I know only that it is terrible to behold and I have learned to control it. But that evening, I was careless.

When Swinburne lunged toward me, I caught him by one wrist and lifted him from his feet as my true face emerged. He was a small man, reaching only to my shoulder, and even an innocent Florence Stoker might well have been his physical match. I drew him close, intending to solve two problems with a single act, satisfying my hunger and ridding the neighborhood of an unwelcome resident. The man stared directly into my eyes, his face twisted with terror, and suddenly went limp, apparently having swooned. His life would have ended at that very moment if I had not been distracted by the sound of a gate opening.

Our neighbor, Rosetti, stepped out into the street, not looking in our direction. Angrily, I tossed Swinburne into the gutter and retreated into darker shadows, watched as the artist belatedly noticed his friend's recumbent form and carried him inside, remonstrating uselessly with the unconscious man about his unseemly behavior. My wrath was so great that I took an unnecessary risk moments later, claiming as my prey a drunken lout almost within view of his friends. My temper has been shorter these past few weeks, and I am convinced it is a result of Ellen Terry's departure. Our infrequent but invariably pleasant encounters have a calming influence which I greatly miss.

August 1, 1881

A most distressing encounter today. Bram visited Rosetti to complain about the behavior of Swinburne. He returned somewhat mollified but still indignant, and I thought that would be the end of it. Ever since the Savoy opened with its electrical lighting, Bram has been moody and preoccupied. He is convinced that the Lyceum will have to follow suit, and is uncertain about whether or not the financial resources can be found for both that and the expansion of the seating which is already planned. At the same time, he reports that the effects of the new illumination at the Savoy were not entirely congenial, describing the shadows as very sharp and distinct and lacking the soft textures to be found at the Lyceum and elsewhere. Several hours later he went for a walk and Noel and I were both napping when someone rapped on the door. Mrs. Nelson was out, so I roused myself and answered it, found myself facing Rosetti and the now sober self styled poet, Swinburne, who looked more dreadful alive than some of my prey did while dead.

"Pardon us for disturbing you, Florence, but Mr. Swinburne has something to say to you." Rosetti stepped aside and the smaller man looked up at my face for the first time. Only the words "I am dreadfully sorry..." emerged from his lips before his eyes went wide and the pupils contracted and he fell to the ground, his limbs flailing about purposelessly, his spine rigid, spittle spraying from his open mouth. I have seen others subject to fits of this nature, but Rosetti seemed quite horrified. He insisted that I go inside and shut the door while he enlisted the aid of a passing organ grinder to carry Swinburne back to his room. The latter's monkey trailed behind, tethered to the man's waist, displaying more dignity than had Swinburne.

I feel certain that the man's fit was caused by his recognition of my face. My first impulse is to take his life this very night, but upon reflection I am reluctant to strike so close to home. The man is so strongly under the influence of drink and other debaucheries that his mind should have few defenses against the glamour. Tonight I shall visit him and attempt to blur his memories of yester evening. If I am not satisfied with the result, he shall not see the morning sun.

Later

Swinburne is reprieved. His mind was all a-scramble even before I entered it, and it was not difficult to accomplish my purpose. I should probably have left an injunction against late night serenades as well, but I would be just as happy if his propensity to drink should hasten his decline.

Letter from Oscar Wilde to Florence Stoker, dated January 28, 1882

My Dearest Florrie,

I know that your request that I write more often was mere politeness, and I pray that you will pardon me for taking up your time. Back in our Dublin days, I always found you inordinately easy to talk to, and as I write these words I imagine that I am speaking them to you as you sit across the table from me.

There are two subjects I wish to share with you, the first of which is, I confess, a boast of sorts. I have finally met Walt Whitman, of whose work you have heard me speak far too often, I venture. Nevertheless, he is in person every bit as daunting and inspiring as are the words he commits to paper, and although I was unable to convince him to take a public stance on a subject of concern to me, he declined in such a well mannered fashion that it was not the great blow it might have been.

The second subject is one which I should never trouble you with if it were not for the high esteem in which I hold you. I have been bothered for this past month by disturbing dreams in which you are a participant. The first occurred three weeks past, the night of one of Mother's parties. There were several new faces there, including a droll little man named Swinburne who was quite amusing at first, but quite coarse as the evening progressed. For some reason he fastened upon me like a leech even when I became quite openly insulting, and I finally fetched his jacket and prepared to expel him from the house.

"Might I hail a carriage for you, Mr. Swinburne, or do you drag your own behind you?"

He accepted his cloak, and fell suddenly quiet as he had been wont to do several times previously. "If you would be so kind, young man. I confess that my legs are a bit unsteady."

I accompanied him outside and prepared to bundle him into a brougham cab that was just passing. "And what address should I give to the driver?"

"Cheyne Walk. Number 16 if you would, sir."

You can imagine my surprise. I immediately asked if he was acquainted with his neighbor, my good friend Florence Stoker. But at that precise moment, his mood seemed to shift again. His eyes grew wide and I fancy he was seeing some demon of the bottle because he shook as though with fever and clutched my hands so tightly that I protested.

"There's a demon haunts that woman," he whispered. "Mark my words, she'll come to a bad end." There was more to that effect, much of it incoherent, and I shall spare you the telling. It was no doubt the effect of the wine upon his brain, but it disturbed me, and that evening I dreamt of you standing in a darkened street, with a great cloak of blackness all about you. And standing a short distance away stood an even darker figure, an enormous man with eyes like cooling embers. There was some great tension between the two of you and I knew he meant you great harm, but the tableau held until my sleeping mind moved to other subjects.

I would not have brought this to your attention except that I have had the same dream several times since that night, and Mother always told me that it was important to pay attention to dreams, that they are messages sent to us by other worldly forces, the fairies no doubt, who are otherwise unable to interfere in our conscious world. More practically, I wonder about the rationality of the man Swinburne, and hope you will be cautious. I fear that madness is reaching out for him and once in its grip, he might become a danger to himself and others. I would hope that you would not be among those others. Please convey my warmest regards to your husband, and my fond wishes to Noel, whom I have not yet had the opportunity of meeting. Perhaps you are best to shield him from reprobates like myself.

I remain,

Oscar Wilde

The Journal of Florence Stoker

January 30, 1882

Gladstone came to dinner this evening. Bram was quite puffed up about having the Prime Minister in our home. They discussed the Irish question interminably, and Gladstone seemed to genuinely value Bram's opinion. His manners were beyond reproach and I overheard him refer to me as "the beauty", which I suppose was meant to be complimentary, but there is something about the man I find unsettling and I felt a great relief at his departure.

I had a letter today from Oscar which causes me to believe he has in fact inherited some fey ability from Lady Jane after all. This is further evidence that I was right to choose Bram over him, as it might have hindered my ability to use the glamour to conceal my secrets.

Swinburne continues to pose a problem. I shall give the matter further thought.

September 14, 1882

A terrible coincidence has left me shaken and full of self doubt. After all these centuries, I had believed myself no longer prey to sudden panic, but this day I nearly revealed myself to Bram and George. Let me set this down as it happened, first summarizing the reason for Bram's startling homecoming.

He left as always for the ferry, which cast off as scheduled. It was an unusually gray day and he was anxious to reach the theater and immerse himself in his work. His rivalry with Howson has grown quite bitter of late, and even Bram admits that Irving has undoubtedly elevated the man to his present position because he enjoys seeing his subordinates at odds with one another.

Shortly after setting off, Bram noticed an elderly man who was a stranger to him. Most of the other passengers were regulars whom he knew by sight if not by name, and this interloper attracted his attention. No sooner were they well away than the man sprang to the rail, shouted something to the effect that he was no longer master of his own mind, then leaped into the river with the apparent intention of ending his life. When it was apparent that no other would go to the man's aid, Bram divested himself of his coat and plunged in himself.

Eventually others lent their hands to pull Bram and the stranger back onto dry land, but the latter was unconscious. Knowing that George was still at home, Bram flagged down a carriage and brought him to the house, calling loudly for George. The tumult upset Noel, and I quieted him before descending, only to find a waterlogged body lying on my new mahogany table, bleeding from several small cuts and abrasions. George exerted himself heroically to restore the man, whose eyes fluttered from time to time, but who did not regain consciousness. He and Bram were so intent upon the recumbent form that they failed to notice me, fortuitously since I imagine my shock was not well concealed.

The man lying on my table was none other than John Murray, the supposed father of Mina Murray. I had thought the couple long since dead, counting on the briefness of mortal lives, or at least safely retired to Cornwall. If he were to revive and recognize me, the consequences would be unpleasant to say the least.

"His pulse is quickening," reported George.

"I'll fetch some blankets," replied Bram nervously. "We must get him out of those sodden garments." He fairly raced from the room.

"Might a stimulant help?" I suggested in a small voice, not exactly feigning shock.

"A bit of brandy perhaps."

I took a step, then deliberately stumbled and reached out to the wall for support. "I am sorry, George, but I suddenly feel faint."

"The stress, of course. Here, sit quietly. I'll fetch the spirits."

I acted the second he left the room. There was not time to drink fully of the man, and his blood was thin and sour in any case, but I took enough through a tear on his wrist to ensure that he would never open his eyes. George returned more quickly than I had expected, but I was turned away from him and he saw nothing untoward. After explaining that I thought I heard the man speak, I withdrew to let him continue his fruitless efforts. Murray died within a few minutes.

It was pure happenstance, I feel certain, but it served nevertheless to remind me not to become too complacent.

October 12, 1882

A chance encounter this evening has proven quite enlightening. I was in Whitechapel, which is so populated by whores, drunkards, halfwits, and cutpurses that I fancy I am performing something of a public service in thinning the population from time to time. It was an unusually warm evening and there was no lack of suitable prey. A young man with handsome features marred by evidence of chronic dissipation wandered into an alley to relieve himself in private, and I descended upon him swiftly, ending his life with merciful speed and satisfying my needs. I emptied his purse and bludgeoned him repeatedly about the head and throat to disguise the manner of his death and left him there; another such corpse in this vicinity would be dismissed almost without remark.

I was about to return home when a familiar voice gave me pause. Keeping to the shadows, I moved to the head of the alley and spotted two figures, one a whore named Daisy whom I had nearly taken a month or two ago. She was a full figured woman whose bosom threatened at any moment to burst free of her garments. The man facing her was heavily cloaked and his face was half turned away from me, but I recognized him instantly. It was Gladstone!

He was exhorting her to change her lifestyle, to embrace religion and find a more virtuous calling. Spirited persuasion was his chosen weapon; he did not upbraid her at all. To all this she stood listening politely, but her posture betrayed her hostility. Gladstone was betrayed as well, in his case by his voice, which was so filled with the rasp of lust that I was certain Daisy could sense it as well as I. Fascinated, I listened to the balance of his admonishment, saw him hand her some small sum of money with which to "start your new life", and then faded back as he turned in my direction and hastened off.

Impulsively, I decided to follow him.

He hailed a carriage a few moments later, so I ascended to the rooftops and followed where I was less likely to be observed. In due course we reached his home, and I sat perched in a tree while he let himself into his house and closed the door behind him. A moment later, there was a light at an upper chamber window, which was promptly thrown open to the warm night air. As it appeared that the PM was about to retire for the evening, I told myself that it was time to return to my own bed, but at that moment I became aware of a strange, repetitive sound that was probably inaudible to ears less sensitive than my own. It appeared to originate from within Gladstone's bedroom.

There was still considerable traffic, both foot and carriage, but I found a sheltered corner and ascended the exterior wall of the house, made my way across the roof, and then circumspectly descended to the window and peered inside. The sight was quite astonishing. The honorable William Gladstone stood facing a full length mirror, entirely naked and sporting a raging member, his back smeared with ribbons of blood. In one hand he held a scourge with which he was systematically flogging himself in penance for some mysterious sin.

When Vlad decided to renounce human prey, he told me that our kind was a perversion of humanity. I wish that he could have been with me this evening to find the depth of perversion of which simple humanity is itself capable.

Letter from Ellen Terry to Florence Stoker, dated September 30, 1883

I have been very remiss in writing, but in truth there has been little to say. This holiday was intended to be boring as an antidote to the excitement of London, and in that it has to a large extent succeeded admirably. The only exception was our time aboard *The Lady Torfrida*. We were touring the Scottish coast and admiring the wild, tortured seashore when an unexpected storm rose from nowhere and buffeted us relentlessly. Many aboard were made ill by the violent movements, including my daughter Edith, but I found the whole thing rather exhilarating. Almost as good as an extra curtain call.

But I have missed your company, even though we meet less frequently than we once did. While in London, I always know that if the need should come upon me, I could send you a note and we would arrange another of our clandestine assignations so that I could once more sweep the cobwebs out of my soul. When I am away, that reassuring knowledge is denied me, and I feel your absence more gravely. I don't know how I shall ever manage the long tour in America, and I wish you would reconsider and come along. I know it is selfish of me, that you plan to take Noel for a protracted visit with his grandparents, and I don't seriously expect you to reconsider, but I feel better merely for having asked, so that you will know how much you mean to me.

Say hello to Ma for me. I miss him as well.
With Love,

Ellen

Note from Edward Palmer, undated

x

I'm sure your sharp eye has noticed this already, but from 1882 onward Enheduanna seems to have thought of herself as Florence Stoker and labeled even her secret journals as such. This seems quite significant to me, an indication that she had grown so absorbed in her secret identity that she identified with her own fictional character.

The Journal of Florence Stoker

October 11, 1883

We went down to see Irving off today. Most of the members of the company are traveling aboard *The Britannic*, although Bram and the remainder must follow on the *City of Rome* to watch over the sets and other properties. Ellen's terrier Fussie has finally learned to tolerate me, and no longer rumbles in my presence, though he will not approach nor allow me to touch him. Irving's beast Charlie is another matter entirely, a foul little creature. Perhaps he will jump overboard during the voyage.

Oscar Wilde was there as well, appearing quite prosperous and happy, although I felt his eyes on me constantly even though he was supposed to be escorting a young actress named Langtry. She seemed a slip of a girl, but then I reminded myself how much older I am than any of those around me. I wonder if Oscar will ever marry. There have been rumors about his relationship with Miles, the artist with whom he shares lodgings on Tite Street, but he made light of it at the time and the fickle public moved quickly to other gossip.

October 20, 1883

The trip to Dublin was less tedious than I had expected, the rail service having improved dramatically. Philippa met us at the station with a servant, who saw to our bags while we found ourselves a carriage. She fussed over Noel incessantly, which gave me the opportunity to use the glamour. As I suspected, there are doubts in her mind about me, but she has driven them into a dark cabinet and locked the door, more pleased with illusion than reality. I felt a moment of what might almost have been gratitude to the woman. It will not be necessary to compel her to support my legitimacy after all.

James suffers from dementia and is frequently confined to his bed. His condition seems to have arisen naturally and is not a result of my interference. His moodiness and temper tantrums cast a dark cloud over the house, however, and I have considered ending his life as a gift to Philippa. The only thought restraining me is the trace of genuine affection she still feels for him, so unless the situation demands otherwise, I will spare him for her sake. His mental decline adequately explains his continued refusal to acknowledge me as his daughter.

My sisters have all stopped to visit and meet Noel. They each seem to have some difficulty remembering me, but their minds are so shallow that the anomaly left nary a ripple. Not one of them has inherited their mother's sharp but well concealed mind.

I had mixed feelings about this return to Dublin, but I could no longer put it off without distressing Bram, who professes to have a guilty conscience about taking me so far from my family. And it has soothed my concern to find no apparent threat to the story of my origin. The encounter with James Murray has left a taste of uncertainty that I feel will never leave my tongue. As this human civilization grows more complex, the world has begun to shrink, and the chance of encountering some acquaintance from a previous identity grows ever stronger. The more frequently I change surroundings, the higher the risk, but there is also risk on the opposite side, for I have already begun to hear remarks about my continued youthful appearance. I shall have to find new ways to counterfeit the appearance of age. As time passes from one feeding to the next, my features apparently do show some decline, but my youthfulness is immediately restored when I take my prey, and it is impractical to spend this time in seclusion on a regular basis.

Letter from Bram Stoker to Florence Stoker, dated November 11, 1883

I hope my earlier letter was less boring than the trip it described. I was rather hoping for a storm during the crossing, but the weather was unrelentingly calm. This will be hastily written so as to make today's post, but I promise a more detailed missive in the near future.

New York City is at one time very like and very unlike London. The buildings are all much more modern, of course, and rather less imposing, but the lifeblood of the city, its inhabitants, is very different. They move with an enthusiasm and energy that is quite palpably different from that of Londoners.

We are staying at the Hotel Brunswick, which is quite modern in all important aspects but without sacrificing comforts. Indeed there is a surprisingly high number of baths for an establishment of this size, and other amenities as yet missing from similar accommodations in England. Everyone has settled in quite well although Henry's dog is a source of constant irritation. We, the Unholy Trinity as you call us, dined last evening at an establishment in Long Acre Square known as Delmonico's, and I must say the fare there is superior to anything London has to offer. Henry didn't care for it particularly, or at least would not admit that he was enjoying himself, but Loveday was quite effusive and made a point of complimenting the owner personally.

There have been many little last minute details to see to, particularly with regard to transportation of the company properties, but things seem well in hand at the moment. We have also received a letter from President Arthur inviting us to dine with him at the White House, and even Henry was somewhat startled at the honor, though obviously pleased.

Please give my warmest regards to your family, whom I have rather neglected of late, and convey my affection to Noel, who must be wondering at the long absence of his father. I remain your loving husband,

Bram

Excerpt from Letter by Bram Stoker to Florence Stoker, dated February 14, 1884

Charlie died while we were in Detroit. Henry professed to be devastated by the loss, but Ellen Terry has "loaned" him the companionship of Fussie for the balance of the trip, and Henry's recuperation from grief has been spectacular. I know that in the past you have charged that he is so full of himself that he leaves no room for others, and perhaps that is the case. Great men function by rules different from those that govern the rest of us.

I confess that at times he does irritate me, however. Howson's employment is quite unnecessary as I have never had any difficulty keeping track of the company's finances, and this division of labor poses needless hindrances because neither of us is in possession of all the facts when we disagree. Even more annoying of late is the elevation of Louis Austin, whom you have not met. Only Walter Collinson, his personal dresser, spends more time in Henry's presence. Austin has some skill with the written word, but the speeches he has prepared for Henry are unnecessarily flowery and circumlocutious, lacking in real content. To date I have been able to convince Henry to use my more sober prose, but the very fact that he continues to encourage Austin is disconcerting.

Mention of Walter reminds me of a tale I almost decided not to pass on, although upon reflection I realized that would be dishonest of me. I am afraid it shall reinforce your opinion of Henry's character, but it is too good a story not to repeat, and in any case you would no doubt learn of it once we return home.

Contrary to my expectations, the hotel in Detroit refused to allow Fussie to stay in our rooms. Henry was quite colorfully irate, and I argued heatedly that no such condition was mentioned in any of our correspondence, but the manager was adamant and Fussie was exiled to the stables. Irving was devastated that such an indignity should be heaped upon his new best friend and prevailed upon Walter to spend the night there as well to keep the animal company. Walter is so firmly enwrapped in the man's shadow that he acquiesced cheerfully, while the rest of us shook our heads in wonderment.

Remind me upon my return to describe in detail our meeting with Henry Ward Beecher. Although as you know I have no patience for these newly fashioned evangelical movements, they are quite popular here in America, and I confess that Beecher is of such sober demeanor and reasonable nature that my natural distaste for the breed was somewhat tempered. It is perhaps another significant cultural difference between our two nations. I have been keeping notes throughout our trip, and will perhaps prepare a small pamphlet on the subject upon our return.

The Journal of Florence Stoker

June 14, 1884

We had dinner with a Mr. Louis Stevenson the day before his departure from Bournemouth, a young man whose travel accounts Bram has found most entertaining. The pleasant coincidence of meeting him while on our brief holiday here has distracted his mind from the incessant feuding at the Lyceum. It was a most animated conversation. We were speaking of Hamlet and his ability to be both base and noble at the same time. Stevenson expressed great perplexity in understanding how the human mind could tolerate such contradictory positions.

I had been somewhat reticent throughout the discussion, but offered the suggestion that each of us harbors more than one personality, that we display to the world a compromise among our warring impulses, and that if we could simply refine out the impurities, we might create a stronger, more admirable character. I further speculated that angels and devils were two halves of the same original, a human soul split into Good and Evil and continuing under those guises. The conceit seemed quite clever to me, although I may have strayed a bit out of character, for I noticed Bram considering me quite thoughtfully.

Stevenson found the concept quite thought provoking and thanked me for posing such a stimulating line of thought. He does not travel much any longer because of his health, but promised that if he should ever return to London, he would make a point of visiting us there.

September 9, 1884

I have finally met the new Mrs. Wilde. Constance is a rather plain girl, but she entertains very unconventional ideas, which makes her a suitable wife for Oscar. She can hardly criticize him for being a gadfly given her own inclinations. At one point she suggested that I join her as a member of the Society for Rational Dress, and while I admit that I would much prefer to abandon these irritating corsets and the other devices of self torture that modern women are forced to wear, the notoriety involved in a controversial organization is such that I was forced to decline. Such a position would clash with the image of Florence Stoker that I have created and might lead to questions I do not want posed, let alone answered. The Wildes have taken up lodgings in Chelsea, to which they will be moving as soon as they leave Dublin.

I had a bad moment when first we met. Shortly after introducing Constance, Oscar remarked that I appeared quite unchanged since he had first met me during his time at university. "It is positively uncanny. You don't appear to be a day older."

I acted as though it were a great but unwarranted compliment. "It's magic. You see, I have this portrait of myself hidden away in the attic, and I have charmed it so that all the signs of age appear within its frame rather than on my face."

The couple both laughed and the subject of our conversation changed but I remained ill at ease throughout. It is time that I take more serious steps to alter my features. A wig perhaps. Bram would certainly have access to the proper tools, though I must be circumspect in this regard. It may be necessary once again to employ the glamour to influence my husband. I have not done so since Noel was an infant and feel an unusual reluctance to do so. Something of a bond has grown between us quite naturally and I am curious to see how it might develop on its own.

Bram has written again, most enthusiastically, about his meeting with Mr. Walt Whitman, an American poet of whose work he is fond, and whom Wilde also admires. All verse seems doggerel to me. I do not share the human fondness for narrative prose, but at least I understand the appeal of such entertainments. The construction of poetry, in whatever form, seems more an intellectual game than a form of art and, like music, it depends upon a pre-existing disposition rather than an acquired taste. Lacking this precondition, I pretend to an appreciation I do not feel.

Excerpt from Letter by Bram Stoker to Florence Stoker, dated October 5, 1884

I beg pardon for the intemperate language in my last letter. The rigors of this second protracted trip to America are no doubt playing havoc with my nerves. Louis Austin's promotion as Henry's private secretary did nothing to soothe them, and I have also entertained doubts about the competence of Austin Brereton, our newly acquired press agent. I have spoken in private to Henry about both these men, and he acknowledges their shortcomings and asks that I exercise restraint. "They are flawed men, perhaps, but you cannot do everything yourself, Bram. It would not be fair for me to ask that much of you."

These soft words make it very difficult for me to press the issue without seeming thankless.

The American writer I spoke of, Mr. Mark Twain, has shown up again now that we have returned to New York. He is quite an entertaining fellow, and I know that you would take to him as quickly as have I. At one moment he is the colorful rustic, full of homespun humor and occasional crude remarks, and at the very next he is a sophisticated intellectual impaling poorly constructed arguments on the head of his rhetorical spear. One remark of his struck me as particularly perspicacious. "Every man is a moon and has a dark side which he never shows to anybody." When he spoke those words, I instantly accepted their truth. It was as though some secret mystery had been lurking unseen within my head, and with that single sentence he focused a beam of light on the blackness and dispersed it.

We will be in Canada next month. Christmas should see us in Pittsburgh for the last leg of our trip before the long voyage home. I regret missing the holiday, but then you have never set great store by Christmas so perhaps it is not that serious a loss.

Excerpt from Letter by Bram Stoker to Florence Stoker, dated April 3, 1885

Henry addressed an assembly of Harvard students at Sanders Memorial Theater last week. He chose to use Austin's speech in place of the one I prepared for him. As usual, it lacked substance and elevated rhetoric above intellect, but I am resigned to the fact that Henry is ever the showman, and if this is the part he chooses to play, then I must submit.

I was delighted to hear that Oscar is a father at last. I trust that young Cyril will bedevil his life as much as Oscar no doubt did his late father.

One evening recently we were at loose ends and decided to attend a local production, purportedly based on Polidori's *The Vampyre*. It was a ghastly play, ill written, poorly staged, and ineptly acted, but I must admit the imagery remained with me for some time afterward. The possibility of doing something in the Grand Guignol style has been discussed with Henry from time to time, but he has always insisted that no unearthly role short of the devil himself would be appropriate for an actor of his stature. This evening he brought the subject up without provocation, and I believe that he too noticed that spell cast upon the audience by the staged manifestation of evil.

The Journal of Florence Stoker

June 1, 1885

My husband has broached an unusual request in his roundabout fashion. Irving has suggested that Bram accompany him on a protracted vacation on the continent this summer. Because of his long absence for this past American tour, he was uncertain about my reaction. Once I had nudged him into speaking his mind, I set about reassuring him that I recognized how important it was that he remain close to his employer. Brereton, Howson, and Austin have not been invited, and it would be foolish of Bram not to take advantage of the situation to shore up what remains of his former influence.

What I could not say was that it would make life much simpler for me if Bram were elsewhere for the next few months. Noel has matured to the point where he is asking questions, sometimes unsettling ones, about the nature of our relationship. He is sometimes aware of the glamour now, has even resisted it once or twice, although never successfully. He is too young to be brought fully into my confidence, but some small steps in that direction must be taken or I risk having to sacrifice all the effort I have exerted in shaping him to the tasks I have in mind.

Excerpt from Letter by Bram Stoker to Florence Stoker, dated August 4, 1885

Rothenberg was quite stimulating. We visited an ancient castle which has been kept in quite good repair. The torture chamber has been recently restored to its original condition, and the atmosphere was quite chilling. I could almost hear the cries of its victims echoing from the walls, and the musty smell had the coppery undertone of old blood. Henry was unusually attentive to details and I think he has already made a firm decision that *Faust* shall be the main production of the new season. With himself as the devil, of course. While we were in Paris, he even insisted that we visit the city morgue.

My mind remains filled with strange images and the threads of a story and I have made several notes for a tale I shall write following our return. You will be disappointed to learn that its subject is once again the morbid, but I have become fascinated with these hints of unnatural evil forces lying in wait for the unwary, and I believe the form is sufficiently novel that it will be received favorably by one editor or another. And hopefully with the public at large.

The Journal of Florence Stoker

November 14, 1885

That infuriating woman senses something about me! I am sorely tempted to pay her a visit this very evening and bring an end to her veiled challenges. I speak of Lady Jane Wilde, of course, who has been wary of me since our first meeting and who was undoubtedly greatly relieved when I broke off with her son to marry Bram.

Her latest gambit has been to send me a present. It was a book of fairy tales drawn from Irish legends. Accompanying it was a brief note indicating that she came across the volume quite recently and thought of me immediately, drawing my particular attention to the fifth story. Although I have no interest at all in such childish nonsense, I sensed a deeper meaning in those few scrawled words and turned immediately to the tale in question and read it through.

The story is about an impudent child who calls upon the fairies to carry him away to their land because his parents will not let him have his way at all times. In due course, his entreaty is heard and answered, and a beautiful young fairy girl appears to him as he lies in bed and invites him to accompany her to the land of Faerie. Of course he agrees, but as soon as he crosses over, she falls upon him and drinks his blood. The moral apparently is to be grateful for what you have, or perhaps to be careful what you wish for. Lady Jane's purpose in drawing my attention to this tale is less clear. She cannot know what I am, but obviously she senses something of my nature.

I have done nothing to harm her or those she holds dear. Why cannot the woman leave me in peace?

December 20, 1885

Went with George yesterday to the opening of *Faust*. The play is shallow and Irving is as overblown as always, and looked absolutely ridiculous in that vermilion costume he insisted upon wearing. I must confess that the staging was quite spectacular, particularly the ladder of angels and some of the apparitions. Bram is concerned that the production will generate insufficient revenue to cover the extremely high costs, but the Walpurgisnacht scene left the audience stunned and will surely draw unprecedented crowds. The limelights provided a suitably eerie glow, and when we went back stage afterward, the smell of lime pervaded everything.

I must return to Dublin to retrieve Noel soon. Although I am confident that he is incapable of betraying our confidence despite his youthfulness, I find that I miss the secret understanding that exists between us. Bram would like to accompany me but cannot because of his duties at the theater, and he is particularly loathe to leave while Howson and the others are free to continue their campaign of influence with Irving. He has also been invited to lecture at the London Institution, and is quite puffed up about the honor.

I will have to visit with Bram's sisters while I am there. Fortunately, Matilda continues to study painting in Paris and has announced her engagement to Charles Petitjean, a minor bureaucrat of some sort. She is the only one of Bram's siblings whom I have never been able to win over, although I have no idea what caused her immediate and continuing animosity. Charlotte and Margaret are both back in Dublin now, and Margaret is married to a surgeon named William Thomson, whom George says is a very fine man as well as an excellent physician.

Ellen and I had tea together earlier today. We have not been as close recently as I would like, and she seemed quite distracted, even secretive. I know that there have been efforts to lure her away from the Lyceum and perhaps she is torn by the necessity to make a decision. She has also been saddened by the death of Godwin, although I cannot see what value she found in her relationship with him. Following so soon upon the death of Charles Kelly, her first husband, it may simply have reminded her of her own mortality. It is difficult for me to appreciate the stress that the prospect of death must inflict upon mortals. From the moment of their birth, they are already dying. They comfort each other with fairy tales of another life following death, unaware that I walk among them as proof that there can be a continuation, but not in the form they imagine.

Mrs. Cassan Simpson visited last week. She has quite a sharp wit and was most entertaining. At times she reminds me of Ellen, or at least Ellen before her recent bouts of melancholy. She has invited me to come along with her to the continent in the spring and I am of a mind to accompany her. It might be possible to retrieve some of my earlier journals and bring them back to England.

March 12, 1886

I had a most distressing experience this evening. Bram prevailed upon me to attend *Faust* again because he wanted to introduce me to the Lessinghams. The play seemed interminable this time and not even the elaborate staging could hold my attention, so I turned instead to a study of the audience. No sooner had I started to survey the other boxes than I spotted a figure who reminded me distinctly of Vlad Tepes. The piercing eyes, heavily chiseled nose, and the mane of white hair were all as I remembered them, and my hands began to tremble uncontrollably. I know now how mortals feel when they believe they have seen a ghost.

Hawes Dawson sat next to me and he apprehended something of my alarm and asked if anything was wrong. I reassured him but then indicated the figure in question. "That white haired gentleman. He looks familiar to me."

Dawson craned his head about, then turned back to me. "Perhaps you have seen him at one of his concerts. I believe that is Mr. Franz Liszt, the composer."

"Are you certain? I am quite sure I've encountered the gentleman previously."

Dawson summoned one of the pages and asked him to confirm the names of the occupants of Box 12. A few minutes later he was back, and Dawson read the card quickly. "As I said, it is Liszt himself."

I felt easier afterward, but could not stop my eyes from straying in his direction from time to time thereafter. Oddly enough, I felt what could only be described as disappointment at learning the truth. There is no question that the world is a far less interesting place now that Vlad is no longer a part of it.

March 15, 1886

Dined with the Gilberts today. I was amused to learn that he has just finished reading Polidori's story and was considering including a vampire in his newest project. Gilbert was lamenting the fact that he could not come up with a novel idea for the staging. "In order for an actor to properly dominate the stage, he must first make an entrance which will capture the audience's attention." I suggested that he pose an actor motionlessly behind a frame so that the audience believed him part of the scenery, and then have him step out into the "real" world at an opportune moment. He thought this idea had considerable merit and complimented me on my quick wit. Some moments later he asked if I had any suggestions for a clever means by which a vampire's identity could be discovered and I suggested that he be identified by a similarity of signatures, one in the present, one perhaps thirty years old, both obviously by the same hand although the vampire was in appearance quite young. Again Gilbert praised my inventiveness, unaware of the fact that I had once almost suffered discovery by these very means.

Letter from Ellen Terry to Florence Stoker, dated June 28, 1886

I was happy to hear from you again and indeed we must get together some time soon. It has been months since I last saw you except in passing at the theater. I certainly should like to see your new place at St. Leonard's Terrace. It must seem enormous in comparison to the old, particularly now that your brother-in-law has married and moved out on his own. Bram complains of late that he no longer has time for his afternoon walks, so it is probably good for him that he has been further removed from the ferry.

So Oscar has finally begotten a child! I would never have expected such a thing. Constance is a good wife to him, no doubt, but I always thought her a badge of office, or perhaps a prize in his collection, rather than a lover. We both know where Oscar's real inclinations lie.

We will be off to America again this year. Faust requires an inordinate amount of work for minimal artistic achievement, but it is unquestionably a crowd pleaser. Bram has volunteered to go with the advance party this time, as you no doubt already know. It must be a great hardship for you to be parted from him for such extended periods. I know that it was very difficult for the late Mr. Godwin and it certainly contributed to the uneasiness of our relationship.

My daughter Edith is turning into quite the young woman. You will scarcely recognize her when we return to London. And her brother Edward has become much more sober of late and is beginning to take a strong interest in his studies. I am quite proud of both of them.

We must get together as soon as I am back. Until then, I remain...

Your friend,

Ellen

The Journal of Bram Stoker

December 1886

The voyage home was largely uneventful but blessedly swift compared to the trip out. The *Etruria* was plagued with mechanical problems and rough seas. I am reasonably satisfied with the

preparations for our coming tour, but was dismayed by my visit to
Whitman in New Jersey. He has aged a very great deal since our first
meeting, and is noticeably infirm.

I occupied my free time by reading law, for I have decided to
finally take the bit between my teeth. If father were alive, he would
probably have mixed feelings, glad on the one hand to see me
embracing a more exalted profession, but disappointed because of
his lifelong abhorrence of barristers, whom he believed were
parasites on the body politic.

Aboard ship as well was an American touring company,
Buffalo Bill's Wild West Show. Theirs is a less structured, brash
form of entertainment, but the novelty of it will certainly draw
enthusiastic crowds. I shall endeavor to attend myself if time
permits. The man is a bit of a charlatan, but a marvelous one. He
performed mind reading tricks in the ship's salon one evening and
was quite droll, and covered his frequent errors with some agility,
but I fancy my Florence could pick thoughts out of his mind far
more easily. She has certainly demonstrated an almost magical
ability to anticipate my thoughts in the past.

The Journal of Florence Stoker

April 15, 1887

It has been easy for me to forget that immortality does not
mean I am not at risk. I have become complacent at times, and the
events of the last two days have reminded me that even I might one
day perish. When I see those around me grow older, stumble and die,
it is hard for me to feel any great sense of tragedy on their behalf.
Their flames burn for such a short time, what does it matter if they
are blown out a few years earlier than they might have been? On the
other hand, I have all of eternity before me, and if some mischance
should lead to my end, what an enormous loss that would be.

We set out on April 13 from Newhaven on the steamship
Victoria. Cassan Simpson was almost unsettling in her joyous
anticipation of our holiday, and her enthusiasm infected Noel as
well, who was unusually playful. We were to land at Dieppe the
following day but in the middle of the night, there was a terrible roar

and shuddering, and it was obvious within a very few minutes that the ship was in serious trouble.

Noel's thoughts were almost as turbulent as the water, and my own composure had slipped sufficiently that I did not trust myself to try to calm his troubled mind. Fortunately one of the sailors took him in hand and led us all to a lifeboat. We had barely reached the water when the *Victoria* heaved itself up at an impossible angle and began to subside under the waves. The jagged rocks which had breached its hull were thus exposed, and the crewman were able to maneuver us safely around them.

We were left adrift and soon lost sight of the other boats. There was only one sailor aboard, and he told us that he was quite confident we were not too distant from the coast and that we would be picked up shortly, but I could tell by the tremor in his voice that he was far less certain than he claimed. In the event, we drifted for most of the day and tempers were quite short by the early evening when a steam tug spotted us and we were rescued. It was only later that we learned that the light at Cape D'Ailly had failed, misleading our captain into believing himself in safe waters.

Although there was a happy outcome to our adventure, it left me pensive. What might have happened if I had been closer to the time when I needed to feed, and if our rescue had been further delayed? I might have claimed a victim during the night and dropped the body overboard without detection, but in such a small boat, the odds were strong that I would have been discovered. I might even find myself overmatched by ten adult males.

I have agreed to travel with Bram on the tour this fall, which means crossing the ocean for the first time. It was an adventure I was looking forward to, but now I have serious reservations. It will be a much larger vessel, of course, and the chances of a second shipwreck in the same year are reassuringly small, but one does not live as long as I have without realizing that even the most unlikely events will take place if one waits long enough.

Note from Edward Palmer, undated

The remainder of the journal for 1887 was completely destroyed, which is of particular consequence since Florence and Noel traveled to America on the *City of Richmond* and spent several months there. Bram made sporadic attempts to keep up his journal for that period, which survives, but the press of events left him little time to write. The only information I have gleaned from his accounts is that Florence spent most of the trip in her cabin, and was apparently quite upset whenever the weather worsened, probably a reaction to the earlier shipwreck. He also mentions the loss of one of the steerage passengers overboard midway through the trip. The body was never found, and I suspect that we have Florence to blame for the "accident", although no record survives to prove the case.

The Journal of Florence Stoker

March 15, 1888

This damnable snow has finally ceased to fall. Bram may enjoy the liveliness of New York City, but I cannot wait to return to London, although the voyage back will be another ordeal. We have been penned up in the hotel for three days and two nights ago the hunger came upon me again. The streets were deserted and I despaired of finding suitable prey until I noticed the flicker of flame from a large drainpipe and found two mendicants huddled over a small fire. It was necessary to dispatch both of them, of course, and I disguised the wounds as animal bites. With luck the rats will be at them before they are discovered.

May 12, 1888

Coincidence, or fate, or whatever unseen hand provides stage directions to the world has taunted me again. Joseph Harker, Jonathan's younger brother, is now employed by the Lyceum as a scene painter. Bram is attempting to secure studio space for him at Her Majesty's Theater as well. He invited Harker to supper this evening, and even though I had met him only once before, when he was only nineteen, I was uneasy throughout the evening and quitted their company as soon as I was able. He gave no indication of recognizing me, and my anxiety was no doubt unnecessary, but I have felt for some time that my past is attempting to catch up with me.

Oddly enough I find the idea rather exciting. Although I am pleased with my performance as Florence Stoker and derive considerable pleasure from the ease with which I am now able to mimic those around me, I sometimes miss the thrill of uncertainty that prevailed when I was more vulnerable. Perhaps the ultimate price of immortality is endless boredom.

Bram was well pleased by his recent walking tour in Scotland. Apparently he was particularly impressed with the Cruden Bay area, and talked at great length about the ruins of Slains Castle. He is once again contemplating writing an adventure story, although the ideas he has proposed in my presence seem pale and uninteresting compared to what I have experienced. Perhaps someday I shall write my own history. But no, that is a dream I can never realize, for to reveal myself even anonymously would be to jeopardize my future.

Whistler came to dinner today. He has been employed by D'Oyly Carte on a redecoration project at his new home. I cannot imagine a less appropriate choice. No doubt he will choose dismal, bucolic colors designed to lull the occupants into lethargy.

August 5, 1888

Tonight has been a string of disasters. I am seriously considering abandoning everything and fleeing at once to Scotland or Cornwall, or perhaps even further. Once again chance has played me foul, and my efforts to mend the situation have gone doubly wrong.

Let me set my thoughts down coolly and in the proper order so that I can consider them more rationally.

The day was pleasantly overcast and I hired a carriage to take me to the Strand for an afternoon of shopping. I found a nice piece of imported silk near Somerset House and some fancy lacework not far from Drury Lane, and took tea at one of the new shops across from King's College. I was about to hail a carriage for the return trip when I happened upon a small group of gentlemen who were in such deep conversation as they walked that they did not notice me. I heard one say that he had recently taken a position at the asylum in Southwark when his companion jostled me unintentionally and stopped, apologizing profusely.

I hardly heard his words, however, because the man who had just spoken turned his head in my direction and I recognized Jack Seward. Even worse, it was quite apparent that he knew me as well. We stared at each other in stunned silence for a few seconds, and one of his companions inquired if something was wrong.

"No, nothing, Leslie. But I believe I know this woman." Seward's voice was guarded, and confused.

I found my voice at last. "Might I speak to you a moment, sir, in confidence?"

The others excused themselves and withdrew a few steps, although they were obviously curious. "Mina? But I thought you dead!"

I needed time to think. "I can explain everything, Jack, but not at this moment. Please, say nothing to anyone about me. Trust me for awhile."

"But I must know." He shook his head. "I must understand."

"And you shall. Meet me tonight at Mitre Square and I will tell you everything. At nine precisely."

His look of consternation remained, but he nodded. "Certainly. I am your servant, as always. But are you well?"

"I am fine, Jack. But your discretion is essential if I am to remain so," I told him truthfully.

And so we parted.

I returned home in such tumult of mind that I left my packages in the carriage. Noel sensed my uneasiness but I had no time to deal with him gently and instead resorted to thinly veiled threats. He sulked but subsided. Fortunately Bram will be away for another two nights, so I did not have to consider him in formulating my plans.

I chose Mitre Square because it is normally abandoned in the evening. The occasional whore passes through, but none stay, and if things went well, I would not require a great deal of time. I was resolved to correct an old error. Tonight Jack Seward must die as he would have long before had he not disappeared overnight.

Would that things had gone so simply.

I arrived twenty minutes early and watched for Seward from the roof of Kearney & Yonge. Predictably he came in advance of our appointment as well, stood leaning against the lamp just below me and lit a pipe. A police constable had passed through just moments earlier, but I knew from my previous visits that his rounds would take him well away before he returned to this vicinity.

Thieves' Kitchen has long been one of my favored hunting grounds. Encompassing Whitechapel, Spitalfields, and Aldgate, it is filled with people among whom sudden death and disappearance are so ordinary that such incidents are rarely even remarked. The lodging houses are crammed with humanity, including many weak in the mind, or enslaved to the bottle or worse vice, or impoverished and unable or unwilling to find gainful employment. Every second woman styles herself a seamstress, and earns her four pence per night doss money by offering favors to the men who frequent these streets for just that purpose. Occasionally an encounter would go wrong, and although it was usually the woman who ended up dead or in hospital, sometimes things went the other way. I planned to remove all of Seward's papers from his body, and with luck he might not even be recognized.

I descended surreptitiously and then entered Mitre Square. Seward saw me almost immediately and stood away from the lamppost. "Good evening, Mina." He glanced around. "Surely we could have met in a less unpleasant place than this."

"I must not be seen with you, Jack." My voice was low and I reached out with the glamour, hoping to lull him even further. Only a few steps separated us.

"Why ever not? What is this great mystery, Mina? Why have you pretended death for all these years?" The years had treated him well and I felt as though I had been thrown back in time. I was curious about his disappearance, but too anxious to delay the inevitable long enough to inquire about it.

"I will explain everything, but come closer, I must whisper my secrets where none but you can hear." He stepped out of the pool of light and I came to him as he leaned forward to hear what I had to say. "Oh Jack, I must confess that I regret this necessity." And so saying, I lunged for his unprotected throat.

Over the centuries, I have killed so often that I can anticipate every defense. Jack was taken by such great surprise that he was quickly stunned, and offered no resistance as I lowered him to the ground and fell upon him to finish my task. But then the second mischance of the day was to occur.

His mind snapped.

It has happened before, infrequently, but often enough that I understood immediately what was happening. Sometimes the mortal consciousness is so strained by the outrage to the body that it reverts completely to the irrational animal nature of its distant past. Seward was suddenly a dervish, twisting violently within my arms, throwing himself about with such vigor that I lost my hold and tumbled to one side. I raised myself on one arm and sought to restrain him with the other, and he lunged forward and bit my wrist. Instantly my plan to leave his body in the semblance of a mugging victim for the constable to discover was rendered useless. Having tasted my blood, Seward would rise from his own grave. Even worse, he would not be mentally capable of adjusting to his new existence as, hopefully, Quincey Morris had done years earlier. His mind would never recover now that it had broken, and he would be a ravening, thoughtless creature who would make little attempt to conceal his nature.

I knew I would have to destroy him completely.

My strength was far greater than his. I tore his jaws from my arm and raked his face and throat. The smell of his blood excited me even though I had no need to feed this soon. Although he tried to escape, I was more than his match, and the battle would have ended within seconds if we had not been interrupted.

For some reason, the constable had altered his route this evening, doubling back upon his own path. He entered from the opposite corner of Mitre Square, near the row of vacant houses, and was blowing his whistle and walking briskly in our direction.

I experienced an uncharacteristic moment of indecision, and Seward rolled to his feet and ran off in the direction of Duke Street. Briefly I considered dispatching the constable before pursuing, but already there were distant shouts and another whistle, and I decided instead to make a discrete exit. I ran toward St. James Place and, as soon as I had turned a corner so that I was concealed from the constable, I ascended to the rooftops and made my way toward Duke.

There was no difficulty remaining hidden until the uproar had subsided. I tried to follow Seward by the scent of his blood, but my clothing was so soaked with it that the effort proved fruitless. Although I am quite sure that his wounds are mortal, I am equally certain that he will not remain long in the ground, and that he will emerge as a nearly mindless creature whom I must destroy.

August 6, 1888

Spent the night in the East End. No sign of Seward. Bram returns tomorrow. I am low in spirits. I may have to abandon Florence Stoker just as she has grown comfortable.

August 7, 1888

Still no indication that Seward has survived. The newspapers report a woman brutally stabbed to death in Whitechapel, but that is hardly so unusual that I give it much thought. Is it possible that Seward has crawled off into some lair and quietly expired? More likely, his wounds have not yet proven fatal. The days, or rather the nights to come will tell the tale.

August 14, 1888

There was a small notice in the *Times* today. The friends of Dr. Jack Seward are requesting that anyone with knowledge of the man's present whereabouts or activities since August 5 write to a postal box. It appears from the notice that Jack went off to India after we returned from the continent. I knew at the time that he had become disillusioned about his work at the madhouse and was considering throwing it over for some other area of medicine.

September 1, 1888

Just when I had begun to grow easy about Jack Seward, fresh intelligence brings new alarms. Another woman has been found murdered and mutilated in the evil quarter mile of the East End. Her name wais Mary Ann Nichols, likely a whore, and her murder is being linked to two previous ones. One of these took place before my encounter with Seward, but the other, the Tabram woman, might also be Seward's work.

I cannot be positive, of course, but it seems likely. In both cases the throats were savagely cut, almost severing the head. The thirst must be burning intensely in Seward to inspire such frenzy. The second woman was greatly mutilated, which might well be Seward's maddened desire for vengeance against me. Her body was taken to the workhouse mortuary on Eagle Street, which I will visit secretly tonight to confirm what I suspect already, and to ensure that she will not rise herself.

The inquest was held today, and the newspapers report that the police believe the killer to be left handed and to have received some surgical training. Dr. Jack Seward was left handed.

September 2, 1888

It proved all too easy to enter the mortuary, somewhat more difficult to find the body. I cannot be absolutely sure of my conclusions. The body was drained of blood, of course, but I could not ascertain at what point that was accomplished. If this is the work of Seward, he may feel repelled by his own urges. Such a perverse reaction is not unknown to me.

I also visited Buck's Row, searched the basements on Thrawl and George Streets, and watched the whores with their gentlemen on Flower and Dean. There was no disturbance. Spitalfields alone offers several hundred potential lairs, abandoned buildings, boarded basements and suchlike. I could search for a year and not find him.

September 4, 1888

The *Times* today insisted the Whitechapel killer must be a madman. If they only knew.

September 8, 1888

Bram was away again this evening, so I made another lengthy search, starting in Aldgate and working my way back. I lost track of the time and the sun was threatening to rise when I passed the Black Eagle Brewery in Spitalfields. I was crossing Hanbury Street on my way home when the unmistakable smell of freshly spilled blood led me to a shadowy backyard.

There I found a street urchin stripping the rings from the body of a woman. She had been savagely attacked, and once again the throat was cut so deeply that her head was nearly detached. Her assailant had also gutted her and the intestines and some internal organs lay nearby. The child heard my footstep and bolted, and I made no effort to follow. It was quite certain that he was not the killer, although the wounds were so recent that they steamed in the morning air. It seemed to me that the removal of the internal organs had been interrupted, and that I attributed to the rise of the sun. Like all those who are recently transformed, he will be incapable of withstanding its withering influence for at least several years, and only with moderation for centuries thereafter.

Concerned lest I be discovered there, I quitted the yard, convinced that Seward still lurked in the area.

September 10, 1888

The *Times* reports the latest victim to be one Annie Chapman and the *Star* insists that all of London lies beneath the weight of a "nameless terror". Well, I could put a name to that terror, but I doubt these modern gentlemen would credit what I told them. Police Commissioner Warren promises Herculean efforts to identify and arrest the party responsible. It would be amusing to see what they would make of Seward if they should somehow capture him.

September 12, 1888

There are handbills everywhere announcing a reward for the capture of the Whitechapel killer. As I feared, Seward has attracted far too much attention to himself. I am spending as much of each evening as possible searching for his resting place, and have been forced to use the glamour to ensure that Bram sleeps undisturbed during my prolonged absences. Fortunately, he is so exhausted by the preparations for *Macbeth* that it takes little effort to push him into the deepest of slumbers.

The newspapers report an increased conviction on the part of the police that the killer has been trained in the surgical arts. George has mentioned that even he has noticed that many among his patients are unwilling to visit him unaccompanied of late. The city is caught in the grip of hysteria.

September 20, 1888

Nothing new from Whitechapel. I wish that I believed Seward had somehow perished, but it is more likely that he is disposing of recent victims in a less public manner. The river hides many secrets. Perhaps some animal cunning has made him more discrete.

September 27, 1888

The papers report today that a letter has been received from the killer, who styles himself Jack the Ripper. I would not have thought it possible that Seward would retain sufficient faculties to compose and dispatch a letter. Either something very strange has taken place, or I am utterly mistaken and these killings have nothing to do with the man I seek.

September 28, 1888

I visited the Central News Agency on Bridge Street tonight, waiting in the shadows and using the glamour to touch the minds of those who came and went. Eventually I found one susceptible to my influence, a reporter named Best who awkwardly agreed to escort a young lady to a more respectable neighborhood, unaware of the fact that I had loosened the restraints in his mind so that he would speak of things he had promised not to divulge. Apparently the purported letter from the killer was in fact penned by a fellow reporter named Tom Bulling. I was so relieved to hear so that I spared Best's life. That Bulling accurately guessed the familiar name of the killer amused me.

September 29, 1888

It is dark and stormy tonight and I would far rather remain indoors. This seemingly endless search has become an albatross slung round my neck. I have more than once been accosted by men believing me to be another of the local whores, and my efforts have been hampered by the large numbers of police, as well as the patrols mounted by the various vigilance committees.

September 30, 1888

It is over at last. Seward will walk no more.

I was near Berner Street just before midnight when I heard a loud commotion from the International Workingmen's Educational Club. Thinking that perhaps another body had been discovered, I cautiously approached, and discovered only that a large meeting had just ended. Several score men were dispersing from the building, some talking loudly amongst themselves. The building has a very large basement which I had not yet checked, so I waited for the streets to grow silent and approached.

There were still as many as a dozen people active inside and the lights remained lit, but it was not difficult to slip past them and find the staircase to the lower level. Although the door stood open, the stairs were encumbered with so much debris that passage was nearly impossible. That was no bar to me, however, and I descended into the blackness, my eyes quickly adjusting to the gloom. I found myself in a veritable warren of small rooms. The floors were earthen and there were no exterior windows. It seemed to me the perfect place for Seward to be hiding, and I expended nearly an hour before concluding that my search must continue elsewhere.

The activity upstairs had almost entirely ceased when I exited through an open window into the unlighted yard behind the building. I was somewhat discouraged, and was therefore taken quite aback when I realized that the dark figure facing me was Jack Seward, and that he was crouched over the supine body of a woman.

He was not the man I remembered. I had done more damage to his face that I realized, and the wounds had still not healed themselves, although they would eventually. One cheek was laid open to the bone and his nose was partially torn away. The punctures in his throat had closed but the flesh remained heavily scarred. More striking, however, was the filth that clung to his body. His clothes and hair were matted with mud and dried blood, and some not so dry. He wore an apron tied around his waist, as though some small part of his mind retained a hint of the fastidiousness Seward had shown in life. His latest victim lay with her throat cut from ear to ear, although her clothing was as yet undisturbed.

"Hello, Jack." I reached out with the glamour but was not surprised to discover I could not touch him with it. His madness was an effective shield to outside influence. He remained motionless and did not answer; indeed, I am not sure he was any longer capable of speech. The flawed transformation had reduced him to the intelligence of a wild animal, an animal I currently held at bay.

He raised an arm and I saw that he held a large blade in his hand. It made me cautious. There was no question that I was physically superior to him, but with the desperation of the insane he might well do me some grievous hurt that would be troublesome to heal. Nor was it entirely impossible that he might by lucky chance win the day. I have shaken off more than one mortal injury in the past, but if my head were severed from my body, or my heart torn from my bosom, I would perish just as certainly as would a mortal.

Our brief standoff was interrupted before I could act. There was a commotion at one end of the yard and I turned to see a pony cart halted at the entrance. The smell of freshly spilled blood must have alarmed the animal, which refused to enter, and the increasingly loud exhortations of the driver would likely draw unwanted attention to the area very quickly.

I turned back toward Seward, wondering if I could dispatch him quickly, seize the body and flee, but during that brief moment of distraction, he had taken himself away. With a curse that would have shocked poor Bram if he heard it from the lips of his darling wife, I slipped off into the darkness as well.

All was not lost, however. The scent of freshly spilled blood lingered in the air. I followed Seward westward, more than half a mile, though I was forced to shelter in concealment several times along the way. The Mile End Vigilance Committee was out in force despite the bad weather, and it seemed that every constable in London was arrayed along my path. Even now I marvel that Seward was able to follow this same course without being discovered.

I never realized where he was leading me until I saw Church Passage ahead. He was returning to Mitre Square. Once again I was forced to remain in hiding while a constable passed by, but then I hastened forward, confident that I knew where I would find my prey.

I was almost correct.

He had been there before me, perhaps waiting for me, but he had found someone else instead. The woman lay motionless, her body mutilated far worse than the previous ones. Her throat was cut, of course, and he had probably drunk her blood from that gaping wound as he had the others. But then Seward had cut her from breastbone to thigh, removing her internal organs and arranging them on the ground and across her body. The nose was completely severed.

There was no sign of him, but once again I was able to smell the blood in which he was drenched.

It soon became easier to travel the streets. The alarm had been raised back at Mitre Square, most of the police in the area hastened in that direction, and it was not difficult to avoid being seen. Unfortunately, the same was true for Seward, who led me ever onward until we reached Whitehall. There I almost lost the trail, but soon found it again at the entrance to a construction site. He had descended into the bowels of what would soon be the new Metropolitan Police Headquarters, almost as if daring them to capture him.

I followed Seward into his lair. He had chosen a dark underground room in which to hide from the sun. When I entered, he lunged at me with the knife, but I snapped his arm with a single blow. The rest did not take long. I used his own weapon to ensure that he would never rise again.

The remains of another body were in a corner, wrapped in cloth, the head and limbs removed and missing. There was also an odd collection of items Seward must have accumulated in response to lingering memories of his former existence – a newspaper, several knives, a large piece of moldy cheese, a bottle of wine, an umbrella, several glass bottles, two of which contained what appeared to be human organs. I disposed of his body in the Thames after destroying what remained of his face and removing all forms of identification from his person. The nameless victim I left where she lay, but I removed all of the other items and disposed of them except for one of the bottled trophies, which I retained on impulse.

To further confuse the police, I left Seward's bloody apron near the Wentworth Dwellings, a largely Jewish district, and for good measure scrawled a cryptic message, "The Juwes are the men that will not be blamed for nothing" on a wall nearby. With luck, the crimes will be blamed on the Jews, who seem the scapegoat of choice lately.

Perhaps things will return to normal now.

October 1, 1888

Catherine Eddowes and Elizabeth Stride have both been added to the list of the Ripper's atrocities. The city is in an uproar, and only I know that the autumn of terror is finally over.

October 2, 1888

The police have found Seward's lair and the body that lies therein, although they have not as yet connected it with the other murders.

Ellen visited briefly today. She seems less than pleased with the role of Lady MacBeth, but I sense that it is not the specific play that bothers her so much as it is the role to which she has been relegated in the company in general. She no longer talks of Irving much, and I suspect that their uneasy love affair has once more struck rough water.

October 12, 1888

An arm has been discovered near the Southwark asylum, and it is probable that it originally belonged to the torso found at New Scotland Yard. Apparently Seward wandered far during the weeks I sought him, and may well have had more than one lair.

I have surrendered to impulse after reading a particularly irritating interview with that insufferably conceited George Lusk, self styled chairman of the Mile End Vigilance Committee. Today I posted to him the trophy I saved from Seward's collection. I only wish that I could see the expression on his face when he opens the parcel and finds himself regarding a human kidney.

November 9, 1888

The hunger came upon me with unusual strength this evening, and since much of the activity in the East End has died down now that the Ripper killings have stopped, I decided to venture back there. I followed two prospective victims separately, but in neither case did an opportunity arise to strike. One was a woman who staggered under the weight of heavy drink, but who nonetheless kept to public ways and well lighted areas, perhaps having adopted new habits so deeply engrained that they drove her body independently of her brain. The second was a man even more obviously gone over to wine or ale, but he was joined by two companions just as I was about to strike and the opportunity was lost.

My third choice was a woman who stood motionless under the brick archway that leads from Dorset Street to Miller's Court. I had crept quite close to her but was once again thwarted when she turned abruptly and entered the shop adjacent. Angry and frustrated, I entered Miller's Court, wondering if I might fall upon one of the lodgers there, but all the doors were barred and the windows locked or shuttered.

As I was about to quit the area, I heard a door open and concealed myself behind a wooden crate that stood in a darkened corner. A largish man emerged, walking briskly, and turned away before I could react. For a moment I thought of following him, but then I noticed that he had left the door ajar behind him. I entered a small, crudely furnished room and saw a woman lying on a bed in the far corner. Her eyes opened as I approached and she raised her hand, holding in it a large carving knife, and lunged toward me.

The blade penetrated my left shoulder and ripped downward through my clothing. I felt a flash of pain and then rage overwhelmed me. How dare the woman! Not even Vlad had given me such a grave wounding. I quenched my thirst a second later, giving her no time to cry for help, but my rage burned ever hotter and I finally turned upon her with her own blade and slashed and hacked until I felt almost faint. When I recovered my composure, I looked down upon the wreck of what had once been a woman and realized at least in part the unbearable rage which must have fueled the engine of Jack Seward's maimed body.

There was nothing for it now but to complete the job. I slashed the throat repeatedly to conceal the nature of my initial attack, and then removed several of the internal organs. The knife disappeared into the roiling waters of the Thames. The police will almost certainly conclude that the Ripper has been active again, and I see no reason to disabuse them of that notion. Now that there is no chance that Seward's unnatural condition can be discovered, the belief in a crazed Whitechapel killer is not necessarily contrary to my purposes.

November 17, 1888

I shall not repeat my addition to the saga of Jack the Ripper. There is such renewed turmoil in the East End that I am forced to hunt elsewhere, in less convenient and sometimes riskier environs. There is a virtual state of insurrection during the day, and the streets are barely less crowded at night. New lamps have been placed on the streets and it is unusual to find anyone walking unaccompanied. More often they are in groups of three or more.

William Prescott has once again invited Bram to join his occult society. Bram has politely declined, despite his continuing interest in the subject. He feels that Prescott and most of his friends are dilettantes with no authentic grasp of the powers they purport to study. Personally I find Prescott himself morbidly offensive. The man is a coroner, and something of the death he deals with every day has rubbed off on him both mentally and physically. He wreaks of decay and mortality and corruption and his presence disturbs me. Constance Wilde has joined, but she has ever been inclined to throw herself into groups with contrary goals.

MacBeth is to open December 29. Ellen has responded to my note and says she looks forward to the season, but there is little enthusiasm in her words. I sense some brooding unease in her, or perhaps it is just a reflection of my own restlessness. This business with Jack Seward has upset me greatly for some reason, and even Bram has remarked that I seem preoccupied and melancholy.

Note from Edward Palmer, undated

Florence's 1889 journal survived intact, but she filled barely a third of its pages, and most of that consists of detailed accounts of their tour on the continent. The Stokers visited Paris, Amsterdam, and Germany. She must have hunted from time to time during their travels, but there is no mention of such activity, and from this point on she rarely even eludes to her victims. It is almost as if she grew ashamed, or at least embarrassed.

I have marked a few brief passages that reflect something of her state of mind, but for the most part, this year is of little interest.

The Journal of Florence Stoker

June 5, 1889

The *Times* reports that portions of a dismembered body were found floating in the Thames yesterday. I had almost put Jack Seward out of my mind but now I wonder if before his death he passed on his madness to some other creature. If one of his victims tasted Seward's blood before dying, the power might have been passed on.

June 7, 1889

More body parts have been discovered, this time concealed in a park. I find that these reports continue to unsettle me, but at the same time I am unable to avoid reading them and in fact share somewhat in the morbid excitement of the city. If Jack did pass on his life within death, it will be difficult to contain it and I feel that events are moving beyond my control.

June 25, 1889

Still more parts. The papers are referring to the case as the Thames Torso Murder, and rumor has it that police have identified the victim, although the head is as yet undiscovered.

July 16, 1889

Another woman has been murdered and some of the papers have linked her to the Ripper. This is quite impossible, of course, but I continue to entertain the possibility that Seward somehow infected another before I dealt with him. I will invade the mortuary tonight to see what the cadaver will tell me.

Later. False alarm. Alice McKenzie no doubt died brutally, but the stab wounds to her throat were quite distinct and were not made by one of my kind.

July 18, 1889

Finally met Ellen again. The gaps between our meetings grow longer each year, and I sense that she no longer finds great solace in our conversations. She did, however, confirm what I already expected. Gilbert and Sullivan have spoken to her about coming to the Savoy, an offer which she finds flattering but not greatly tempting, and now Bernard Shaw is also trying to woo her away from the Lyceum.

I am once again considering revealing something of my history to the world, although it would have to be well disguised as a fiction. Since Bram seems determined to infuse his writing with elements of the supernatural, I might as well use his inclinations for my own purposes. I must be the heroine rather than the villain, of course. It would be a small revenge on Vlad to cast him as the great villain of the piece. I am surprised to realize that I still resent him strongly for turning against me, even though he has already paid the ultimate price of perfidy.

August 6, 1889

Bram took me to the Savoy Hotel today for its grand opening. The appointments are quite impressive. Each suite has its own terraced balcony and there are speaking tubes connecting to room service so that one may order a meal with great ease. The courtyard and fountain are also quite impressive. We spoke with Lillie Langtry briefly, and the Doyly Cartes. Sir Arthur Sullivan was there as well, but he was speaking to Whistler and I did not suggest we join them.

April 30, 1890

Bram is now a barrister and rightly proud of his achievement, although I frankly cannot imagine him finding the time to practice his new vocation. Despite the division of labor that he claims to resent, he remains thoroughly occupied and away from home until all hours of the night. And when he is at home, he writes. *The Snake's Pass* has found a publisher, and I have suggested to him a vampire tale along the lines of Polidori, but with a more modern setting, and he seems enthused.

I have suggested that we take a holiday in Whitby this year. This will afford me the opportunity to retrieve some documents I have concealed there and add them to those stored at the theater in London. It will also help me to convince Bram that Vlad's landing must be in Whitby rather than elsewhere as he has planned. He has already agreed with my suggestion that his "fiction" should make use of as many actual historical facts and settings as possible to enhance its credibility, and once he hears the story of the wreck of the *Demeter* and other convenient events, he should be even more amenable.

August 5, 1890

We leave tomorrow for Whitby. It will take eight hours by train. Bram has rented a cottage at 6 Royal Crescent, which I remember as being in a pleasant neighborhood. I must remember not to show familiarity with the area, since I am not supposed to have been there before.

I have discovered that with sufficient powders and hair colorings, I can now see myself as others do, or at least close enough to serve the purpose. I have progressively lightened my hair and made other alterations which should sufficiently modify my appearance so that if perchance I meet someone who remembers Mina Murray from her brief residence there, they will see only a strong resemblance and not guess my secret. I have also taken pains to appear older, although I have necessarily introduced these modifications slowly.

August 19, 1890

Whitby is charming and restful. I have so far encountered only a single familiar face, the painter Francis Aytown, who gave no indication that he recognized me. There have been some changes, the docks have been modernized and are in better repair, and the oiled paper shacks have all been torn down. The Westenra house is at present unoccupied and in considerable disrepair but it is out of the way and well concealed by the surrounding gardens, which have for the most part gone wild.

We had a most entertaining dinner tonight with a writer whom Bram chanced to meet while out walking. His name is George DuMaurier. He was most charming, even mildly flirtatious, and made a rare and welcome effort to include Noel in the conversation as an equal. DuMaurier mentioned that he had traveled with a mesmerist on the trip to Whitby. Bram believes mesmerism to be a trick of charlatans. "A man's mind is solely his own." DuMaurier thought otherwise, and although it was somewhat out of character for me to speak up in contradiction of my husband, I could not resist.

"Surely not all minds are of equal strength and character."

Bram conceded that they were not. "But I believe we are all born with the same potential. It is only through experience, education, and strength of character that the superior personality rises above his baser fellows."

"Well then," said I, "perhaps some minds can rise high enough that they can exert influence upon others. Great orators do so through the power of persuasion, great soldiers do so through force of arms, and perhaps great thinkers do so through the power of thought."

Bram was perhaps impressed as much by my unusual temerity as by the force of my argument. "If such a power existed, why would we not have seen evidence of it?"

"But mesmerists have demonstrated some extraordinary feats," interposed DuMaurier.

I could so easily have proven my point by manipulating Bram's mind at that very moment, but of course I dared not do so. Realizing that, I lost interest in the conversation, but invented a tall tale so that I would not be seen as having struck my colors without a fight.

"When I was a child in India, my father told me of a local wise man named Svengali who took an orphaned child and turned her into a great musician through the power of his mind. Without ever having taken a lesson, she was able to produce wondrously beautiful music."

DuMaurier nodded enthusiastically. "It would be a marvelous talent to possess." His brow lowered. "But I fear it would ultimately corrupt its user. A man with such power would be a threat to us all."

"Undoubtedly that is what the sheep think about the shepherd," I replied.

August 21, 1890

I have found an old friend. The time had come for me to attend to my private needs, and Bram was conveniently out for the evening with DuMaurier. Whitby has no equivalent of Whitechapel. It has become something of a resort and the townspeople assume that tourists have no interest in being reminded of those less fortunate, so the latter have largely been moved out of sight.

The cluster of small holdings inland were much as I remembered them. On more than one occasion I had snatched a child from its sleeping chamber, or found an unlucky traveler camped in the woods. Many of these people were illegal squatters, and I judged them unlikely to appeal to the authorities or raise any kind of public alarm. They had grown wary by the time I quitted Whitby as Mina Murray, but the passage of so many years free of my unique form of taxation should have lulled them by now. And so it was, for I found a young couple lying naked in a shallow hollow. They were deeply asleep and I could have killed them both easily, but I hesitated for I abhor waste and there was no reason to take two lives when one would suffice.

But there was another, less fastidious, pair of eyes watching.

I had no warning of his presence until he fell upon the couple, a dark shape that erupted from the foliage. Something must have alerted the boy, because he half rose onto an elbow, but it was too late to do him any good. The rich smell of blood filled the air as he fell back, clutching at his throat. The girl sat up, her expression confused, and the night was dark enough that she may not have seen their attacker. But she must have sensed the danger for she sprang to her feet and tried to escape, running directly toward the bush behind which I waited.

Her blood was fresh and strong and sweet and I drank deeply before allowing her limp form to fall at my feet. My unexpected accomplice was standing just beyond reach, motionless, watching me.

"Hello, Quincey. I am pleased to see you are well." It was Quincey Morris, of course. Like all those whom I have made like unto me, he was drawn back to his creator, but I had left him no clue as to my present whereabouts, so he had come to the only place he connected with me. Whitby, where he had known me as Mina Murray.

It required some urging before he would relate his history. He had survived, barely, those days of confusion that inevitably followed the change, had nearly perished one morning when he had unwisely tempted the sunlight. Even now he could tolerate only the briefest of exposures; it would be a decade before he dared move about in the day for limited periods. Even I must still be circumspect. I was no more vulnerable than most fair skinned mortals, but a mild burn was much more troublesome than for mortals, requiring weeks to heal.

Initially Quincey was wary, even slightly hostile. He felt abandoned, justifiably, and resentful that I had brought about the change against his will. "The alternative was to let you die, Quincey. The wound would have stolen your life. If it is such a burden to you, simply wait for the sun to rise and end it yourself."

I gave him a guarded account of my recent history, for I am not yet certain that I can trust him. His old mortal affection for me survives, albeit somewhat changed, but he is still suffering feelings of guilt about the means he must employ to survive. He has brought with him the soil in which he was buried, but he changed the subject when I asked where it was hidden. I have advised him to remove himself to London and to post a notice in the *London Times* once he has found a suitable lair.

"I will be in touch with you when the time is right, and we shall make further plans together."

I am hopeful that Quincey will prove a valuable asset. Although Noel is now almost fully cognizant of my true nature, he will always be subordinated to me because of the extensive use I have made of the glamour to channel his mind in the direction I intended. Quincey can never be my equal, of course, and only Vlad ever had a real chance to be my rival, but he might yet prove equally useful. I hope that he might serve to some degree as a confidant, someone with whom I can safely speak of those things I cannot share with Bram or Ellen Terry. There are times when the pressure to speak freely is almost unbearable.

December 11, 1890

I have finally read Oscar's story of *Dorian Gray*. The note that accompanied the issues of Lippincott's Magazine which he sent states that the idea came to him during a conversation with me some time past. I have no such recollection, but after reading this fanciful tale, I wonder how often I may have been indiscrete.

Note from Edward Palmer, undated

There is nothing in Florence's 1891 journal of consequence, and no further mention of Quincey Morris. I was amused to learn that Florence became rather a fan of Conan Doyle's Sherlock Holmes stories, and she and Bram met Doyle on at least one occasion. The following year was much the same with one startling exception, which I have marked.

The Journal of Florence Stoker

September 25, 1892.

I accompanied Bram on his visit to Tennyson today. Although I remain opaque to the appeal of verse and find his works in that area so much sentimental drivel, I was very favorably impressed with *Becket*, even if Bram does feel it is not well suited to the stage as written. Curious to meet again the mind that could craft such an excellent work, I maneuvered Bram into having me included in the invitation, even though our first encounter had been troublesome.

It was a dreadful mistake. Tennyson is an aging, infirm man, but his mind remains sharp and quick, and with the approach of death he has developed fey talents more intense than I have ever found in a male. His eyes clouded the moment he touched my hand, and he avoided my gaze for the remainder of the visit, although I caught him regarding me out of the corner of his eye on more than one occasion. Even more unsettling is that when I attempted to confirm my suspicion by touching him with the glamour, I felt a contrary motion. Although I doubt that he has conscious control of the ability, Tennyson was quite definitely using a touch of his own to investigate me.

As we were about to depart, Bram went to call the servants and I was left alone with him for a moment.

"You must pardon me if I do not rise." His tone did not match the polite words.

"Don't disturb yourself. I know that your health is fragile."

"Yes, I'll be in my grave soon enough." For the first time since our arrival, he met my eyes directly. "I will rest comfortably there, though not like some I could name."

If I had been mortal, my heart might have stopped at that moment. I could not think how to answer, and was spared the necessity when Bram returned.

Did Tennyson somehow divine my true nature, or was it just the raving of a dying man?

October 3, 1892

I have not been able to find peace of mind since our visit to Tennyson. Bram began speaking this evening of the adverse consequences of the recent Franco-Russian rapprochement and I wanted to reach across the table, take him by the throat, and shake the meaningless words from his mouth. I have been brooding about the visit to Tennyson for several days and cannot concentrate on anything else.

I must do something to remedy things.

October 6, 1892

It is done. I entered Tennyson's bedchamber without incident and found him snoring wheezily in his four poster. It took but a slight touch on his shoulder to waken him, and to his credit, he collected his wits quickly enough.

"Who's there?" I waited in the shadows while he fumbled to light the lamp beside his bed, moving only when he reached for the bell rope to summon a servant, drawing it beyond his reach.

"Good evening, Sir Alfred."

His eyes widened a bit, but he showed no great alarm, for which I give him credit. "Mrs. Stoker? Is that you indeed? I had thought myself an old fool, dreaming even while awake, but perhaps I should have trusted my feelings."

I said nothing, but moved closer to the bed.

"What would you have of me, then?" His voice was steady, resigned perhaps, even welcoming. I think he was profoundly weary of life. "I'm too near death to fear you, I think."

His blood would not have been nourishing even if I had had need of it, nor did I intend to leave any such obvious evidence of my actions. His last words proved inaccurate. I revealed to him my true face and his eyes went wide and the breath caught in his throat and he fell back against the pillows and expired.

I doused the lamp and left as I had entered.

Note from Edward Palmer, undated

It appears that Bram Stoker made no effort to keep a journal for the remainder of his life, or if he did so, it was lost or destroyed. Florence made entries almost daily during this period, but they tend to be quite short and pedestrian in nature, detailing her social life, Noel's accomplishments – of which she seemed quite genuinely proud, occasional references to the political infighting at the Lyceum or Bram's growing concern over the company's finances, and sometimes brief mention of the international political situation. She mentions receiving letters from Oscar Wilde on two occasions in 1893, but these are not among the papers in my possession.

Not entirely to my surprise, I discovered that Bram visited Cruden Bay again in 1893, and that the entire family spent part of the summer here during the following year. Florence took singing lessons for a while, but with apparently dismal results. There is nothing of real interest until the following entry.

The Journal of Florence Stoker

March 25, 1895

Although I have never regretted choosing Bram over Oscar, I still feel a lingering interest in the latter, and his present difficulties have aroused my sympathy. I doubt that he ever realized how completely separate from society he would place himself by admitting his preference in lovers. Society condones such tastes so long as they can avoid acknowledging them, but Oscar was always one to flaunt his differences, and now he rots in gaol for having the audacity to be different. He is only fortunate in the sense that he might at another time have been put to death immediately, as would no doubt be my fate if ever my true nature were revealed.

Nevertheless, today I grew angry over the imbalance of justice in this world. Irving, the posturing, pompous manipulator, was knighted today, along with Bram's more deserving brother Thornley. He posed in a place of honor while Oscar stood in the dock awaiting word of his inevitable conviction. I could bear it no longer without making at least a gesture, so I disguised myself with heavy veils and delivered a bouquet of violets to him in the courthouse. Noel helped me to escape without being identified and I felt better for having tweaked the collective noses of these self important fools.

This evening we attended a party celebrating Irving's ascension, a tedious affair that further tried my fraying temper. At one point I found myself on the periphery of a conversation about the primacy of mankind in the universe. Florence Farr was there, although Bernard Shaw had sent his regrets as expected. William Heinemann was standing next to Louis Austin, who was pontificating rather drunkenly about God's plan.

Herbert Wells was listening politely, but was clearly disdainful. When Austin finally paused for breath, Wells shook his head. "I don't wish to dispute the matter with you, Mr. Austin, but I am not as convinced as you that the universe in all its breadth and wonder was created solely for the amusement of the human race. Although it is self evident that we are alone in this, our own little corner of creation, I cannot be so certain that nowhere else in the vast reaches of the universe are there minds capable of reason."

I had been in a foul mood all day, and for a moment I was drawn beyond my self imposed limits. "You lack imagination, Mr. Wells. For all we know, a vast and inhuman intelligence greater than man's is keenly and closely watching us even now. It may lurk among us unobserved, or dwell within the depths of the ocean, or hover in the sky beyond the range of our vision, all without our knowing of it."

"Nonsense!" Austin's voice was unusually shrill and uncomfortably loud. "For what reason would God have created us in his own image if he were then to award equal or higher intelligence to some other form. The very idea is ridiculous."

My temper began to rise again, but this time I had the sense to take myself away from the source.

After Bram retired for the evening, I went through the latest draft of his manuscript. I regret to say that I agree with Mrs. Miniter's opinion that it is unpublishable as written, perhaps because the story is not born of his own imagination and fits him poorly. If I truly wish to see this part of my history in printed form – altered to conceal my true role, of course – then another means must be found. I am considering using the actual documents, deleting the damning content first, and simply employing Bram's talents to smooth over the transitions. Although I have no creative ability myself, I believe I can assemble a largely coherent narrative.

Walter Osborne arrives from Dublin tomorrow to begin my portrait. I have taken great pains to ensure that my features will reflect my pretended maturity, and a painting will provide an unchanging base from which to plan future alterations. Inevitably I will be forced to assume a new identity, but with each passing decade, the process becomes more difficult.

Note from Edward Palmer, undated

1896 was similarly uneventful. Florence betrayed a rather excessive glee when Lady Jane Wilde passed away, and implies that she had something to do with Henry Irving's accident, which led to three weeks of cancelled performances, although this might be wishful thinking on her part. Noel went off to school at Winchester. The Stokers spent another holiday in Whitby, and Florence took an increased interest in painting and painters, although there is no indication she ever attempted work of her own. Walter Osborne apparently introduced her to several London artists, including Philip Burne-Jones, and this was to lead to some interesting events in the year that followed.

The Journal of Florence Stoker

January 30, 1897

Had dinner this evening with Twain and his two daughters at Chelsea House in Tedworth Square. Clara was quite hospitable and outgoing, but Jean remains withdrawn and just slightly unfriendly. I feel just the faintest touch of the glamour from her. She is no threat to me but probably senses that there is something unusual in the air. Twain and Bram have become quite friendly, and I have been badgered into reading some of Twain's work. I find it of reasonable quality and varying interest, at its best when his bitterness about fatuous pride and social position show through.

March 13, 1897

The Osborne portrait is quite handsomely done, but I find myself dissatisfied with it. What he has achieved is a faithful reproduction of the likeness of Florence Stoker, which is what was intended. What the painting does not reflect is even the faintest hint of my true self. That is a face I have not seen since I thought my years were numbered and I was but a girl in a country that is no longer even remembered except by dusty historians. No, even that is not true, for my true face has also changed over the course of centuries. It is my hope that I will one day recapture the ability to see my own reflection instead of the façade that is my human disguise, but I fear I am lost to myself forever.

May 18, 1897

In order to protect the stage rights to *Dracula*, Bram arranged a staged reading of the play today at the Lyceum. Edith Craig did a creditable job playing Mina, although she lacks the talent of her mother. The performance was closed to the public, but Ellen attended, although we did not have a chance to speak more than a few words to one another. Whitworth Jones was totally inadequate as Vlad. I persuaded Bram to enlist an "old friend" of mine to portray Quincey Morris. I was amused to observe Quincey (although he uses another name now) reading his own words as though they'd been written by another hand.

The book is to appear within a fortnight. I look forward to it with quite unusual eagerness. Even though I did not write most of the words, it is to a great extent my creation, for it was I who shaped most of the events, and it was certainly my hand that directed the structure of the narrative.

We have decided to return to Cruden Bay this summer. Bram's fascination for the place serves me well, for I hope to make arrangements there and eventually move at least a portion of my scattered caches of documents to that vicinity. Many are currently stored under the false bottom of a trunk in the Lyceum prop room, and although they should remain there undisturbed, the possibility of a chance discovery remains.

June 22, 1897

Just when I had begun to despair of a solution, one has offered itself. Through Osborne's good efforts, I have been introduced to one Philip Burne-Jones, an indifferent artist who produces flattering fantasies and calls them portraits. The number of people of both sexes who succumb to this little conceit are sufficient to keep him in quite a comfortable living, and he moves among the aristocracy as a near equal. What makes him ideal for my purposes is his high susceptibility to the glamour. I believe that I can lull his mind into believing that he is drawing the product of his imagination rather than reality, and I may even be able to suppress his memory of the entire incident afterward. I must experiment further before taking such a chance.

June 30, 1897

Burne-Jones is ideal. I am able to shape the contents of his mind almost at will. I have discovered, for example, that he is hopelessly infatuated with Mrs. Patrick Campbell, even though she has shown him no favor and is, of course, quite contentedly married. I have met her more than once and she seems to me a woman of unremarkable appearance and demeanor, but men often superimpose virtues upon women that are otherwise not in evidence. I have broached the subject of a portrait to him in confidence, under the pretense that it is meant as a surprise for my husband. He has quoted an exorbitant price, but since I have no intention of paying him, I made only a token objection.

July 4, 1897

My first sitting with Burne-Jones is over. At first I feared that I had misjudged his malleability and that I would be forced to dispose of him in his own studio. He continued to complain that he could not do the subject justice when seen only by lamplight, but since I cannot reveal my true face in the day, this is a point upon which I cannot compromise. Before leaving, I reinforced the imperative in his mind to keep my identity secret. I shall allow him to exhibit the painting, of course, though it shall never be connected in any way to Florence Stoker. It may well be that I am helping his career, for the subject matter will certainly mark this as a radical departure from his previous monotonous work.

Although it is inconvenient, I must make haste on this, as we are to leave for Cruden Bay next month.

July 24, 1897

Burne-Jones assures me that only minor work needs to be done to complete the portrait. I have finally been able to examine my true face in some detail, and I am quite pleased. I have impressed upon his mind that no one should see the painting before our return to London, but that he should complete the finishing touches during my absence so that all is in readiness. He has from time to time grown confused about my role in all this, because he has seen both my faces now. Fortunately, his vanity is such that I have convinced him that the more melodramatic elements spring from his own imagination, and that I have altered the cast of my features to disguise myself and avoid a scandal.

I am drawn crouched over the body of a man who, through my influence, vaguely resembles a reclining Vlad Tepes. It is a petty revenge, but I am unrepentant. My hair is unencumbered and falls freely about my shoulders, my eyes are bright with a flame that burns brighter and truer than that of mortals. My dress is a bit daring for even these modern times. I am confident that it will cause a considerable stir when the public sees it, and I shall secretly glory in the notoriety I cannot risk in person.

August 29, 1897

I have received word that Oscar Wilde has gone into exile in France. After my own fashion, I shall miss him. Life in London will be more predictable in his absence.

Cruden Bay is even more suitable than I had realized, and I have already found a woman who might serve as caretaker for my journals. She has a daughter, a strange girl with no likely prospects for marriage, a potential successor to the task. I must convince Bram to return next year so that the final arrangements can be made.

September 16, 1897

The work of more than twenty years was almost wiped out in an instant. The day after our return to London, Ellen Terry called. We spoke for a while, but the closeness of our earlier meetings was almost completely absent. Although she rarely speaks of it any longer, Ellen has grown bitter these past few years, and has turned within herself, holding her old acquaintances at bay. She blames Irving, of course, although not consciously, and everyone associated with him. Through Bram, I am also guilty, I suppose.

Just before departing, she mentioned casually that Philip Burne-Jones was about to display a painting about which he had been hinting for weeks. "It is supposed to be something quite extraordinary. He has been very close mouthed about it. I imagine we will all be very disappointed when he unveils it."

I was sure that I knew the nature of the painting. Somehow my admonition to await my return had slipped. I was preoccupied for the remainder of Ellen's visit and as soon as she was out of sight, I summoned a carriage and went to his flat. There was no answer to my knock, and his landlady told me she had not seen him since the previous morning, so I took myself home in no good humor. After darkness, I returned in my own fashion and entered through an upper floor window, but Burne-Jones had not returned, and a thorough search revealed that the painting was gone as well.

The following day I made discrete inquiries, but his whereabouts remained unknown. "He will be at the Victoria tomorrow, though. That's where he plan to reveal this masterpiece he's been prattling about."

It was not as I had intended, but I was more annoyed than alarmed. There was no way that the face in the painting could be linked to Florence Stoker. Even if Burne-Jones stated that claim publicly, it would be dismissed as nonsense. And if necessary, I would arrange a rather serious accident for him in the near future. After all, his work was done.

If I had only known.

I was among the crowd at the Victoria the following morning, unannounced and as anonymous as possible. The time of the unveiling approached with no sign of the artist or his work, but at the last minute he entered the foyer, followed by four lumbering workmen who carried a heavily veiled canvas and a folded easel. Burne-Jones gave a little speech of which I heard not a word as I moved through the crowd, searching for a vantage point from which I could see the portrait (which I had yet to observe in natural light) and the reactions of the onlookers.

And then the moment came and the cloth fell away, and my true face was to be revealed to a curious if not particularly attentive public.

Except that it was no longer my portrait.

That wretched man had painted out my features and superimposed upon it a caricature of Mrs. Patrick Campbell!

Had it not been day, I would have been lost in that moment, revealed in my full fury. As it was, I made a sound so full of wrath that the people around me retreated a step. By the time I had another reasoned thought, I had crossed half the distance separating me from the painting and its creator, intending to tear out his throat in full view of several score onlookers, some of whom might know Florence Stoker by sight.

With a great effort of will, I turned away. I have too much invested in this life to abandon it because of the perfidy of a small minded man or for the satisfaction of a brief moment of righteous anger.

But I can taste his blood in my thoughts, and one day soon, once the inevitable furor dies away, I shall reveal my true face to Mr. Burne-Jones one more time.

February 19, 1898

I suppose it was inevitable that eventually some harm would come to at least part of the record of my existence. It has still come as a terrible blow. A fire raged through the storage room at the Lyceum yesterday, destroying much of the company's property, including over two hundred scenes from various productions. Bram was distraught.

Because of the efforts to salvage whatever was possible, I was not able to locate my trunk until this evening, and as I had feared, it did not survive intact. Many letters and some journals are completely destroyed, others badly damaged. I feel as though parts of my life are gone forever because eventually I shall lose the memories, and will not have the records to refresh them. This disaster has made me more anxious than ever to move what remains to Cruden Bay, although in truth, there is no place where I could store them that will be entirely beyond the reach of mischance.

That infernal dog of Irving's happened upon me as I was searching the wreckage. Like all its kind, the beast cannot tolerate my presence. I opened a trap door and managed to catch hold of the creature and cast him down, and his neck was quite efficiently broken by the fall.

We have had financial difficulties as well. The Lyceum is on the brink of bankruptcy and Bram fears that Irving will be forced to sell control to outside investors, which will further diminish his own authority. The only bright spot this spring has been Noel's engagement to Nellie Sweeting, who seems likely to make him a suitable wife. She is quite proper and somewhat awkward around me, but I find no trace of the glamour about her and have no fears on that account.

March 14, 1899

Had lunch today with Ellen Terry, who has grown darker and more distant than ever. Although it was she who broke off the affair with Irving, she is incensed by his recent carryings on with Eliza Aria, a fashion writer and shop owner whom even Bram describes in quite uncomplimentary terms. It has become the final straw in a veritable whisk broom of complaints, however, and Ellen has admitted to me in confidence that she is leaving the Lyceum to join another company. She also said something very unsettling before we parted.

She had just confessed to feeling guilty about her growing hostility, and I was reassuring her as best I could. "We all have our dark sides, Ellen. You must not worry yourself about a failing common to every mortal."

She gave me a very peculiar look before answering. "You have never shown your dark side to me, Florence, but I know it is there. I can feel it hovering around us sometimes when we talk, waiting to spring out of the shadows."

"My dark side is hardly that impressive. You have always valued me as a friend because my life is so much simpler and safer than your own."

"No, I don't think so. I believe you are far more complex than you seem, and sometimes when we are together, I feel as though I am a child trying to converse with an adult. Ever since we first met on the embankment, I have sensed your power, and sometimes it has even frightened me. I imagine that must sound rather silly."

Despite those last few words, I knew that Ellen was absolutely serious, and that she had somehow glimpsed some aspect of my true self. She had no trace of the glamour and must have done so purely through thought and observation. I wondered that I did not feel threatened, but somehow I understood that Ellen was revealing this secret knowledge to me and to me alone, and that it was in a sense her parting gift. We might see each other again after this, but it would never again be as close friends.

She was growing old, I realized, and as I measured things, nearing the end of her life. I would miss her.

Note from Edward Palmer, undated

The Stokers were a bit embattled for the next three years. The Lyceum was sold, Irving's health remained precarious, and the income from Bram's writing while steady was not enough to support the family. There are some minor allusions to a project in which she had enlisted Noel's aid, but nothing specific is said about this until some years later, and I will leave that for you to find as I did.

Florence was rather perturbed when Bram wrote a new introduction to a foreign edition of *Dracula* in which he implied that there was some connection between the book and the Jack the Ripper killings, although he was vague on the subject and did not have any certain knowledge of the link. She theorizes that after so many years in close proximity that he might sometimes be aware of the glamour that surrounded her even when she was not consciously using it, and that he might somehow have access to her thoughts or memories.

The Stokers nonetheless returned to Cruden Bay in 1902. At that time, the documents which are now in my possession were transferred to the care of Augustina Dobbit and her daughter, and periodically updated.

The Journal of Florence Stoker

August 30, 1902

We have rented the Crooked Lum in Whinnyfold, which overlooks the North Sea. Bram finds the view acts as a restorative, and he has resumed his long morning walks along the coast. His spirits remain low, however, and he has aged visibly these last few months. Or perhaps it is just that my eyes grow more sensitive to what had already been obvious to others.

Noel reports no progress on my behalf, but promises to continue his efforts. Nellie is somewhat puzzled by his behavior at times, and probably none too pleased, but she remains loyal. His judgment was sound when he chose her to be his fiancé.

I am content with my choice of the Dobbits. Mother and daughter share a near total lack of curiosity or imagination, and the prospect of financial independence, if not prosperity, should hold them to my purpose. The funds I have taken from my victims over the years are more than sufficient to cover their allowance, and I have quietly supplemented Bram's income from time to time when it was possible to do so without his knowledge. I have recently begun to contemplate the final days of Florence Stoker and find that I shall regret her departure.

Note from Edward Palmer, undated

Florence had planned to bring each year's journals and such other papers as she accumulated during an annual trip to Cruden Bay. They could not afford to do so during the next two years so she posted a parcel which never arrived. The period of September 1902 through the spring of 1904 is therefore missing. The next entry of interest is a detailed account of Noel's marriage to Nellie Sweeting, which includes this interesting passage.

The Journal of Florence Stoker

August 1, 1904.

Noel is married at last. Although the bond between us is the stronger, he feels a genuine affection for the girl, and through him, so do I, though somewhat removed, even though she has never warmed to me.

He has made me promise that when the time comes to share with him the gift of immortality that I will not object if he in turn passes it on to Nellie. It is a complication I had not thought of, and will need to ponder more, but there are years to pass before that event, and the situation may be quite different when the subject next arises.

I have been introduced as well to Mary Whitlow. She is a good enough actress to have worked at many of London's theaters, but not good enough to have joined any company on a permanent basis. Noel brought her circumspectly and she sat in front of the Osborne portrait so that I could judge for myself. My surrogate son has succeeded beyond my expectations. With her hair colored and cut differently, she could pass for me among close friends so long as she remained silent; her voice is close but her accent is unacceptable. Her profession makes her no stranger to training in speech, so that is not likely to be a serious impediment. It will be necessary to take some risks to test her suitability, but Noel has been discrete and, if necessary, Mary Whitlow will disappear even more permanently than is already intended.

August 10, 1904.

The Whitlow girl has proven to be an excellent choice. Noel has done extraordinarily well. She is intelligent but unimaginative, ambitious but indolent, patient but occasionally petulant. She is only moderately amenable to manipulation by the glamour, but it was never my intention to secure her loyalty in that fashion. Burne-Jones has shown me the foolishness of relying on its influence in my absence, and if Whitlow is to properly impersonate me in the years to come, she must do so of her own volition, by conviction rather than compulsion.

As might be expected, she reacted with skepticism when I offered her eternal life in return for a few years of service. It didn't require the glamour to recognize that she thought Noel and I had gone mad. A demonstration was required. I might have shown her my true face, but not even Noel has seen that, and in any event, I did not wish to frighten her. As far as she is concerned, I have discovered a far more mundane form of immortality, the secret of which I am willing to pass on to a chosen few. She does not and will not know my true nature. I have no present intention of honoring my word although that decision is far in the future, and I might well choose to reward her as promised when the time comes.

It was not difficult to be convincing, although Noel had to deal with her hysterics when I tied a rope around my throat and dangled from the ceiling for several minutes. I stopped my heart and my breathing and feigned unconsciousness until Noel cut me down and Whitlow assured herself there were no remaining signs of life. I then restored the semblance and sat up, at which point the woman swooned. When she was recovered, I drank a cup of poison as though it were tea to emphasize the point.

"If you serve me favorably for ten years, the gift shall be yours as well."

As I had previously noticed, she was quick witted. "What would I have to do?"

"Refine your manner of speaking, make some minor alterations to your appearance, and act in my place from time to time. You will attend the theater, socialize with the better elements of London, and oversee my household. When your presence is not required, you shall reside at a flat nearby but will disguise yourself at all times so that the masquerade is not revealed. If you are discovered, our bargain is broken and you shall die in your time."

"But your husband? How could he be fooled?" And she blushed and I knew the cause immediately.

"Do not fear on that account. My husband is no longer interested in matters of the flesh and we have separate bed chambers. Any assignations on your part would pose far too great a risk, I regret to say."

"I have no great use for men," she answered stiffly, and I saw that it was true and was pleased.

"Then I believe we have struck a bargain, Mary Whitlow. Welcome to my family."

Note from Edward Palmer, undated

Florence's entries for the next several months are very terse and uninformative. She mentions meeting with Quincey Morris on two occasions, but the entries are completely innocuous, stating merely that he is "getting on well" in his new situation. Similarly Mary Whitlow's name rarely appears. I have speculated that this is because she wished to leave no evidence in her home that Whitlow might stumble across which could reveal her secrets. It is clear that the impersonation became more frequent with the passage of time.

There are several detailed entries about Noel's marriage and career. Florence expresses a maternal pride that is either startlingly genuine or a masterpiece of artful deception. I am inclined to believe the former. Her darker nature only emerges once in 1905, following the death of Henry Irving.

The Journal of Florence Stoker

October 15, 1905

A letter came today from Bram confirming the news. Irving died in Collinson's arms after collapsing on stage. Bram arrived before the end and was quite shaken by the experience. He has had little experience with death. I have replied sympathetically, although the news displeased me only because I have more than once hoped for the opportunity to silence Irving myself. The only thing which stopped me was the adverse effect this would have, will have, on Bram's career. It is fortunate that he has continued his writing, although nothing of his own has enjoyed half the success of *Dracula*, a fact from which I derive a good deal of secret satisfaction.

Note from Edward Palmer, undated

I am going to rush you along through the next few journals. Bram's health began to decline in 1906. He suffered a stroke that impaired his eyesight and left him with a pronounced limp. Although he worked for a time with a smaller theater, he seems to have lost much of his enthusiasm for drama and turned instead to his own writing and occasional lectures. The Stokers moved to Durham Place, the very house once tenanted by the notorious Captain Bligh, which seemed to amuse Florence immensely. She was even more pleased to be invited to Conan Doyle's wedding to Jean Leckie, as she continued to be an avid fan of Sherlock Holmes.

In 1907, Mark Twain returned to London and he and Bram took up their old acquaintance. Stoker left a brief account of one of their meetings, the pages of which were torn from their original binding, folded, and inserted inside the back cover of Florence's 1908 journal, which is otherwise unremarkable. In April, there is a brief reference to Quincey Morris, who had apparently quitted London some months previously for an unstated destination. There are only the briefest and most inconsequential mentions of Mary Whitlow.

Notes written by Bram Stoker, undated

Twain and I met with some friends at the Cheshire Cheese Pub this evening. The conversation turned to the subject of witchcraft, and I found it all oddly unsettling. Field started it off by telling us one of his acquaintances insisted that he had nearly thrown himself off a cliff after an argument with a neighbor and felt that he had been unnaturally compelled.

"He insisted the old woman invaded his thoughts and urged him to destroy himself."

"More likely he felt guilty for badgering the lady." Stern, ever the rationalist, dismissed the possibility of supernormal intervention, but Twain was less certain.

"Let us not rule it out so quickly. I have had experiences in my life that make me wonder if there might be an unseen world wrapped around the one we know. Perhaps some individuals are sensitive to that other realm and can manipulate it in ways the rest of us cannot perceive." He turned to me at that point. "Your wife, for example, seems to read my very thoughts at times. I have but to think that I might be thirsty and she offers a drink, my stomach prepares to rumble and she hands me a piece of cake."

I nodded proudly. "Perhaps she is a bit fey at that. She has always been able to anticipate my needs."

But Field would not be put off. "One can be a gracious hostess without resorting to witchcraft, but to will another to take his own life is a far more serious matter."

Stern shook his head. "What evidence can you offer other than this person's unsupported and rather incredible claim?"

"A lack of evidence does not disprove the assertion. One should keep an open mind. There are many strange and unexplained things in this world, are there not, Stoker? Perhaps there really is a Dracula and you are just his historian, not his creator."

"It sometimes seems that way to me as well," I said lightly, attempting to make a joke of it. But his jibe disturbed me. I think I am rather meticulous in my writing methods, and I can remember every step in the creation of my various efforts. Except in this single instance. For months I struggled with the basic idea, but the story never seemed within my control, and I was not happy with the way events unfolded, almost as if independently of my efforts. Then, when I had thought to put it away as a bad job, I found myself making final revisions to a completed manuscript, with only patches of recollection of the intervening process. There were entire passages I could not remember composing.

It is unquestionably my most popular work, so why is it that it often seems to me that I have plagiarized someone else?

The Journal of Florence Stoker

May 12, 1909

Bram's second stroke has been much more severe than the first. Dr. Browne assures us that he will recover, although he will never be as robust as before. He has prescribed arsenic and strong soup, but has forbidden meat except as a seasoning.

It is time for me to prepare for the next chapter of my life. Bram has only a few years left to him, and to my utter astonishment, I have realized these past few days that I will miss him greatly. I have even considered making him one such as I, but it would be cruel to do so now. He might never die, but he would face eternity with his present infirmities, and I believe that he would really prefer death. I sense a great weariness in him. It would also mean revealing to him that our life together has been something of a lie, and that I cannot bear to do.

There is no need for haste, but I can put things off for only a little while longer. Possibly I shall repair to the continent; Paris seems a good choice. Or America, perhaps. The ocean crossings are quick enough to be manageable now if I plan properly, and the newer vessels are reportedly quite safe, even in the face of great storms. The *Adriatic* has been called "unsinkable", and while I recognize that as the hopeless vanity of mortals, it is nonetheless somewhat reassuring.

The Dugdale woman has offered to recommend a nurse for us. She has served Thornley's wife Emily well and I respect her judgment, but this is too critical a time for me to allow another person to reside beneath our roof. Our finances are not good in any case, and this will provide a reasonable excuse for our move to other lodgings. Bram's eyesight has declined so much that he has difficulty writing, and Mary has already passed muster by impersonating me in his presence. In our new home, hers will be the face seem by the public while I prepare for a new life. If I am successful, she and Noel will watch over Bram during his final days before joining me, if they so choose, although Noel seems quite content with the life he has made for himself. If not, I can return to my old identity and plan anew.

August 2, 1911

I am a ghost in my own home now. Even Bram accepts Mary in my place, and I confess to feeling moments of jealousy even though this is all my doing. I am also greatly saddened by Bram's decline. I think he knows that the end is near. The dogged determination with which he wrote *The Lair* in less than a season has dissipated and now he merely drifts from day to day.

It will be America for me. There I will find no familiar places or faces to haunt my memories and remind me of what I have lost. I need a fresh start. I have already secured identification papers under a false name. Provision has been made through a solicitor to support the Dobbits and the other caretakers of my history and I have set other safeguards in place as well. All that remains is to secure passage on a seaworthy vessel and give final instructions to Noel and Mary.

April 5, 1912

In a few days, I shall leave Florence Stoker behind me forever. This will be my final entry in this journal, which I shall post to Cruden Bay on the morrow. Bram is rapidly failing and I must be gone before his passing. I had believed myself forever safe from the weak human emotion of grief, but I find that either I was mistaken or that I have rediscovered it. From a distance, it shall not be so hard to bear.

My trunk is packed and has been sent on ahead. Five days from now I set out for my new life on the maiden voyage of the proudest ship ever to put to sea, the *Titanic*. I anticipate that it will be a voyage to remember.

Note from Edward Palmer, undated

That is the end of it, apparently. Bram Stoker died just a few days after the *Titanic* went down. Could our elusive lady have been one of the survivors, or did her story end off the coast of Newfoundland? There is nothing here to tell us.

"Florence Stoker" is still alive, officially, although I don't know her present whereabouts. I hope that you can assist me in that matter. We must discover whether it is in fact she, or whether this Mary Whitlow continues the impersonation, living off the proceeds of Stoker's literary estate, waiting for her mistress to return with the gift of immortality.

I would pursue these matters personally, but there is still the matter of Shirley Appleton to be resolved, and I am bound and determined not to fail her.

Edward Palmer's Travel Diary

July 7, 1920

I spoke to a police detective this morning and was not happy with what little he was willing to tell me. Although he insisted that the investigation was ongoing, I had heard elsewhere that the searches were being discontinued. The absence of blood has apparently convinced them that the actual crime was committed elsewhere, perhaps far from Cruden Bay. Inspector Gladdings even suggested that the other bodies may have been "thrown from the cliffs and taken out to sea where we'll never find them".

Frustrated, I cycled to the village and knocked up Moore, or rather Lembic. Moore seems never to be in his office. Lembic must have made a late night of it as well, because he appeared quite disheveled and visibly fatigued. Not to mention unwashed, although he had masked the latter by liberal application of a cloyingly sweet scent. I asked if he thought Moore might be willing to look into a matter of missing persons.

"What persons in particular?" He stood firmly in the doorway and did not invite me in.

"Miss Shirley Appleton and her cousin."

"Ah, the young ladies from the motor car."

"Yes, precisely. The authorities seem disinclined to pursue the matter vigorously, and I thought perhaps a private party might do better."

"Yes, well, under ordinary circumstances Mr. Moore might be interested, but as it is, I am afraid we shall have to decline. You see, we have become quite busy of late, and I am not even certain when next I will see Mr. Moore, as he left yesterday for Glenolden."

I was quite convinced that the man was lying to me, but there was nothing to be gained from a protest. "Very well then, I shall employ other means. Good day, Mr. Lembic."

"Good day, sir." He didn't sound as though he meant it.

Later

I returned to the hotel and arranged to hire a car, which was ready for me promptly after lunch. I spent the remainder of the daylight, and a great deal of petrol, driving aimlessly around the countryside. With the aid of a map grudgingly provided by Waverly, I explored all of the public ways that were marked, and quite a few that were not. It was only with the coming of dusk that I realized the hopelessness of my effort. It is possible that I unknowingly passed within shouting distance of my quarry. Shirley could be lying dead or injured in the high grass, in the basement of one of the cottages I passed, in one of the many caves that lined the shore, or perhaps Inspector Gladdings was right and she and her cousin had both been thrown to the waves.

Disconsolate, I drove back to the hotel, avoided the dining room and attempted to drown my sorrows in the bar. As you no doubt remember from our school days, I should never drink on an empty stomach. When a waiter gently suggested that I retire for the evening, I discovered that my legs were not entirely under my control, and the contents of my stomach rumbled rather threateningly. With exaggerated deliberation, I made my way through the lobby and up the stairs to my room, fumbled with my key for several seconds before discovering that the door was already unlocked. I assumed that the maid had been neglectful and slipped inside, closing the door behind me.

The lights were out and the moon was hidden behind clouds, but I knew the way to my bed and staggered in that direction, not even bothering to undress. It was the purest chance that saved me. A finger of cloud lifted away from tonight's singularly bright moon, and a sharp reflection caught my attention just as a figure rushed from the darkness and thrust itself at me.

I tripped over my own legs and reached out for support, caught hold of the arm that had swooped toward my chest. My assailant was not nearly as large as I, and quite unintentionally I pulled him off balance as I fell. There was a bit of a confused struggle and then a sharp, biting pain along my left side that provided a saving stimulus. I bent one knee and kicked out, caught the man on his hip and drove him back. When I tried to rise, I realized how unsteady I was, so rather than close with him, I scooped the water jug off my dresser, threw it in his general direction, and heard it shatter loudly against the wall.

The occupant of the next room shouted angrily and I raised my own voice. "Help! I'm being attacked!"

The intruder hesitated only an instant, then bolted for the door and passed through into the corridor. I could hear his footsteps as he ran for the exterior staircase. If I had reached the door quickly enough, I might have been able to recognize him by the corridor lighting, but it would have been superfluous.

The man's scent was unmistakable. It was Lembic who had tried to kill me.

July 8, 1920

The police have decided that last night's attack was a bungled burglary, and I said nothing to discourage them from that conclusion. I could have named Lembic, and they would certainly have questioned him, but even though I was quite certain of his identity, the evidence would probably not be adequately convincing for Inspector Gladdings and his associates. It would have also have warned Lembic that he had been recognized and I have in any case resolved to take matters into my own hands.

There is a woodlot near Moore's office, beyond which is a small car park for the Laird's Inn. I shall conceal myself there this afternoon and see what there is to be seen.

July 10, 1920

So much has happened these last two days, I grow weary at the very thought of writing it all down. But I must do so now, while the details are fresh in my memory, because I am quite certain that in the years to come, I will look back on all this as just a fever dream. I must organize my thoughts.

As I had planned, I found a vantage point from which I could watch Quentin Moore's office with little fear of discovery. I had brought a popular novel with me and pretended to read it, to avoid attracting unwanted attention from anyone who chanced to pass by. It was relentlessly boring. Moore might have a superfluity of clients at the moment, but if so they were conspicuous by their absence. Not one of them visited that day, and if I had not seen Lembic accept a parcel from a letter carrier, I might have thought the building empty.

At dusk, Lembic appeared abruptly, locked the door behind him, and retrieved his bicycle from the alley beside the building. My legs protested as I stood up, but I was able to move briskly enough to see Lembic turn along a narrow path that ran toward the coast.

Fortunately, I had placed my own bicycle in the backseat of the motorcar and I retrieved it, pedaling furiously through the village streets until I reached the path and set out in pursuit.

Several minutes passed and I grew distraught. There was no sign of the man ahead of me. We had reached no diverging paths, but he could have ridden off through one of several meadows. The darkness was coming quickly now, and shadows crowded all about, any of which could have concealed him. I quickened my pace until I was hurtling along quite recklessly, and gave a great sigh of relief when an oncoming lorry's headlamps washed across the path ahead and illuminated a spindly bicyclist moving at almost as heedless a pace as my own.

It was Lembic.

I slowed in order to maintain some distance, convinced that he could not take a divergent path without my knowing of it even if I was unable to keep him under constant surveillance. Not wanting to warn him with the sound of my own passage, I stopped for a moment or two whenever it looked like I might overtake him.

We left this path some time later, crossed a gently rolling field, and took up a narrower track that wound among trees and rocks. At this point we were quite close to the ocean, and I could hear the waves crashing against the rocks. I don't remember the exact route after that. On two occasions I thought he had given me the slip, but somehow I always managed to find him again. He was so intent upon his path that I doubt he ever looked back, but I still took pains to minimize his chances of seeing me. Eventually I almost literally crashed into his bicycle, which he had parked under a tree, and I had a very bad few moment when I realized I had no idea where he had gone from there.

The roar of the surf was quite close and I moved toward it, almost ending my life my stepping out into empty space over a gaping wilderness of broken rock. I stood there gasping, staring down at what could quite easily have been my death, and I saw something move along the cliff face.

It took a few minutes to find the path, which was concealed by a small maze of brush, but once past that, the descent was surprisingly easy. I almost tripped over a fallen tree limb, and broke off a cudgel sized piece to tuck through my belt. It was a poor weapon, but the best I could fashion on short notice. Approximately three quarters of the way down, the rock wall folded forward in a jagged lip, behind which lay the artfully concealed mouth of a sea cave. I wished that I had had the forethought to bring a torch, but it was too late for useless regrets.

I made my way inside more by touch than sight. Once or twice I thought I heard a distant voice, but the crashing waves shuddered through the earth and overwhelmed my ears. I stumbled more than once, skinned a knee and both elbows, bumped my head against an overhanging rock. It was surprisingly dry inside, but the darkness was oppressing, and despite my resolve, I began to consider turning back before I got hopelessly lost.

Then there was an abrupt turn in the passageway and in the distance I saw a faint glow of artificial light. It was the flickering of a lantern, and it guided me over the next few score steps. I approached cautiously and peered around the edge of an upright wall of stone. Perched up on a rock shelf was a small cage of metal bars, inside of which a human form lay huddled in one corner.

There was no sign of Lembic, but I heard another fragment of human speech, unmistakable this time. It was a woman's voice, and I thought it might be Shirley. Moving with great caution, I crouched and advanced to another hiding spot several steps closer, hoping to have a better view of the interior of what appeared to be a good sized cavern. It did provide a wider view, but there was nothing to be seen except rocks and hints of further passageways, and I could no longer even see the cage I had spotted from the entranceway.

I slipped the cudgel out my belt and held it ready, drawing little confidence from its presence, and stepped out into the open. There was no cry of alarm, even after I advanced another few steps and climbed up a smooth slope of stone. From here I could see the cage again, although its occupant was concealed behind a spur of rock. I also saw another human form, this one standing with its arms upraised against an interior wall. It was Rachel, and her wrists were chained to pins set into the stone.

Her head was down and she remained motionless and at first I thought her dead. I glanced around cautiously, but saw no sign of Lembic, so I sprinted across the intervening space and crouched at her feet. "Rachel," I whispered. "It's Edward. Are you all right? Can you hear me?"

She didn't move at all for the first few seconds, and then her head came up very slowly. "Edward? Is that you? Are you a part of this then?"

"No, of course not." I stood up and peered at her chains. There wasn't much light here, but they looked quite new and quite strong. "I'll get you out of here somehow."

"The key," she said softly. "It's over there. On the rock. He left it there."

I turned and looked about and almost immediately saw it sparkling in the flickering light. "Hold on."

The shackles were new and freshly oiled and the lock turned easily. Rachel half fell forward into my arms and I felt her hands around my waist and wondered if I would have to carry her from the caves. But more importantly, where was Shirley? I was about to ask that very question when a voice disturbed me.

"You fool!" It was Lembic. I turned to see him emerging from a deeper passageway. "You mustn't let her loose! She's not safe yet!"

I pushed Rachel away and turned to face him, raising the cudgel over my shoulder. "Stay away from us, Lembic. The game is up. Tell me where Miss Appleton is or so help me, I shall bash your head in."

That was a threat I was never to carry out. Something hit me on the side of the head that very moment, and I fell heavily, slid down across a crumbling ledge, and took a blow in the ribs that drove all thoughts from my mind except for the incredible need to draw a fresh breath. Even when I overcame that brief paralysis, I could only lie there, enthralled by the wonderful pleasure of having a working set of lungs. I felt that I might be content to lie there forever, in fact.

But something caught me by the right ankle and dragged me back the way I had come, then twisted my leg so that I flipped over onto my back. Rachel stood over me, and even in the poor light of the cavern, I could see the transformation that had come over her and I realized my rescue had been much too late. It was recognizably her face, but distorted in an absolutely feral manner. The eyes positively glowed and her brows had thickened. The ears protruded from the side of her head like those of an animal, and her mouth was partly open, revealing teeth like none I had ever seen before, neither human nor animal, but something else.

"Rachel?" The sound of my voice seemed to trigger something and she leaned down suddenly, her jaws widening, and my arms came up defensively. I felt her knees on my thighs and she seemed disproportionately heavy for a brief second, and then she was gone so quickly that I blinked in disbelief. An incredibly loud hissing echoed through the cavern and there was the sound of a struggle.

My lethargy was suddenly gone and I leaped to my feet in time to see the end. Rachel was locked in battle with a much larger figure, too large to be Lembic. Her hands clawed at the man's face as he pressed his arm to her chest and forced her back against the cavern wall. Then, shockingly, it was over. His free hand moved to her throat and there was an odd popping sound as Rachel's head was literally torn from her body.

My stomach was still unsettled from the previous day's excesses, and now I lost today's contents as well. I found myself sitting on the cold stone with my arms around my knees, and a heavy hand resting on my shoulder. I looked up into the face of the man whom I knew as Josef Straban, my benefactor.

"She was one of them, wasn't she? Rachel, I mean."

He nodded. "Only recently turned. Your friend is at rest now."

I gathered my wits and rose to my feet. "Lembic must still be around here somewhere."

Straban shook his head. "She killed him before she attacked you, but he will not rise. I might have saved him had I arrived sooner, but the ocean air diluted your scent and I was thrown off the trail."

Then I remembered Shirley. "Miss Appleton. Is she all right?" I wasn't sure that I wanted to know the answer to my question.

Straban handed me the set of keys I had used to free Rachel. "She is unconscious but appears unhurt. She is not like this one." He glanced at Rachel's mutilated body. "It would probably be best if she were taken from this place before she sees something which would haunt her dreams."

"Yes, of course."

Shirley was bruised and dehydrated and remained disoriented even after I carried her from the cage and used some tepid water to bathe her face. She could not stand without assistance, so I wrapped an arm around her waist and started to lead her away. Straban had not moved since he had first spoken to me. "Aren't you coming with us?"

"No. There is one more for whom I must wait. I shall see you later at the hotel."

I took another step, then stopped again. "There is one thing I must know." He made no objection, so I rushed on. "Dracula's journals refer to a faithful servant who was rewarded with the gift of eternal life. The man's name was Josef. That was you, wasn't it?"

For a few seconds, I thought he would not answer, but he did, and not as I had expected. "No, I am not that man, though I use his name. Josef Straban was killed by Jonathan Harker and Quincey Morris in the Borgo Pass. At my request, he sacrificed himself in my place while I traveled another route. We were very similar in build and appearance, and apparently my old nemesis never saw him clearly before the final dissolution." He sighed, but his voice was suddenly stronger and contained a hint of pride. "I am Vlad Tepes, Count Dracula."

Needless to say, I was stunned. I will never know how long I might have stood there if Shirley had not suddenly stirred at my side. "Someone is coming," she whispered urgently.

Dracula crossed the distance separating us almost as if by magic and pushed us back into the shadows. "Stay out of sight. It is the one I seek. Tonight the long journey finally ends."

We retreated behind a small protruding rock and crouched low. I felt Shirley's hand in mine and we clasped out fingers together. Dracula vanished effortlessly. The only sound was the muted rumbling of the ocean and an occasional dripping from somewhere deeper in the earth. Each second stretched endlessly and I felt that I would scream if only to break the tension, and then a man stepped into view, the man whom I was almost expecting.

Quentin Moore.

Even before I saw his face, I recognized the smooth animal grace with which he moved. He bent over something I could not see, and later learned was Lembic's eviscerated body, and then found Rachel's crumpled form. There was no hint of concern in his voice or manner when he turned and called out to us.

"Palmer? It is you, isn't it? I can smell your presence. You are a surprisingly resourceful man. I am quite impressed. Come out and let us talk. You know what I am, and now that I have a better understanding of your talents, perhaps we can find some common ground. I can offer you immortality, you know. And power. Secret power, admittedly, but satisfying for all that."

I didn't answer, and Dracula remained concealed.

"Why so reluctant, Palmer? Is it the girl? If you want her, you shall have her. For centuries, if that pleases you. We can reach an accommodation. Let us meet like gentleman and work out the differences between us."

He sounded earnest, but I knew in my soul that if I placed myself in this man's power, I would be destroyed utterly. Instinctively I hated him and everything he stood for, and had I been alone, I might have damned all and stood up to challenge him. Undoubtedly he would have killed me easily.

Instead it was Dracula who stepped out into the lamplight. "Good evening. It has been a long time since last we met, Quincey Morris."

And Quentin Moore hissed and retreated a step.

The ensuing battle was no doubt as epic as the struggles of Ajax and Achilles before the walls of Troy, but I can tell you little of it. The two figures closed on one another and seemed to merge into a single shape, and almost immediately one of them knocked over the lantern and the entire cavern was thrown into abrupt darkness. Shirley and I crouched for what seemed eternities but was probably only a few minutes, while the two men – if that is the right term - fought in almost complete silence only a few arms lengths away. Not another word passed between them, but we could hear the impact of their bodies against the walls of the cave and an occasional bestial growling that made my skin crawl. Then there was a sudden, more complete silence. Even the ocean seemed to have muted itself and my heartbeat drummed in my ears as Shirley pressed close against me, trembling.

And then a hand touched my shoulder.

"Come. I will show you the way from here. It is done."

And Vlad Tepes, Count Dracula, led us from that cavern of horror and we emerged into a nightscape in which the wind was gathering its energy in anticipation of an oncoming storm.

"You can find your own way back. I must dispose of what remains inside."

I wanted to leave, but I also wanted an explanation. "I don't understand this. If you have known what was hidden here all along, why bring me into it?"

He shook his massive head. "I had not known, and had I investigated personally, I might have been recognized, or in some fashion warned Morris that he was sought."

"So you used me."

"Regrettably, yes. But only to bring an end to this. He was the last one left except for me. And now it is time for our kind to disappear from this world."

"The last? But what about Mina. Or Florence?"

He stirred impatiently, but then sighed. "You have a right to know, I suppose. Return to your hotel and take care of the young lady. I will call upon you once more, and I shall bring your answers with me."

"Why can't you come with us and tell us now." I think at this point I had moved beyond fear. The fact that I was shouting with anger at a man, no, a creature of such power must have terrified me somewhere inside, but having witnessed three violent deaths in a matter of minutes, I was not acting entirely rationally.

"Because first I must deal with the bodies, Mr. Palmer." His voice deepened with irritation. "Unless you would prefer to explain these matters to the police yourself?"

Some of Shirley's strength returned once we were outside in the night air, sufficiently that we commandeered Lembic's bicycle and rode together back to the hotel, although with frequent pauses while she regained her breath. I offered to escort her to her room, but she insisted on waiting with me until our benefactor appeared. She said she wanted to hear what he had to say but I think the truth was that she feared being alone. I ordered a variety of food and drink through room service and once she had eaten enough to restore her somewhat, I cautiously asked if she wanted to talk about what had happened and after a brief pause, she nodded.

"Not that I can tell you much. It was Lucy who had the brilliant idea." Her voice caught. "Poor Lucy. At least it was quick for her." I waited patiently while she stared into the distance for a moment. "She suggested that we make inquiries with a local solicitor and the innkeeper provided a name. Unfortunately, he dismissed us summarily, but his secretary offered to help."

"Miss Dobbit," I said quietly.

She blinked and nodded. "That was her name, yes. You know of her?"

"We are acquainted." I didn't elaborate, and she resumed her narrative.

"Miss Dobbit said she knew someone who might be able to be useful. She described a roadside picnic area and suggested that we meet a friend of hers there at dusk that evening. Rachel was somewhat apprehensive, but Lucy was adamant and so we found ourselves sitting alongside the road as the sun fell.

"We were about to abandon our mission when a dark figure emerged from the trees. Lucy lowered her window but we kept the doors locked. He identified himself as a Mr. Moore and indicated that he had some information which he thought might be useful to us. We had all agreed that we would remain in the motorcar throughout the interview, but Lucy inexplicably opened the door and stepped outside, and almost upon the instant, she and Moore had disappeared.

"Naturally Rachel and I followed, calling her name and feeling quite apprehensive. Then I found her, stumbled over her actually, and even in the darkness I could tell that she was dead." Shirley's voice broke for a second, but she regained her self control almost immediately.

"I heard Rachel cry out a moment later and realized that I could no longer see her. I grew disoriented and perhaps a bit hysterical, and I ran through the brush aimlessly for some time. Then I was struck on the back of the head, I think, and when next I opened my eyes, I was in that cage in the cavern, and Rachel lay beside me. She was. . . quite dead and an awful little man was," she hesitated, bit her lip and looked away, "he was amusing himself with her body." It was undoubtedly Lembic she had seen; I felt no sympathy for the man and wished only that I had been able to kill him myself.

She was silent for a long time after that and I thought she would say no more. But finally she roused herself. "Hours must have passed, perhaps an entire day. Then the same man brought food and water and dragged Rachel's body from the cell. When I saw that he was chaining her to the wall, I thought him mad, but before he had finished, she began to stir." Her voice crackled with tension now. "I think if he had waited another few moments, she would have killed him, and probably me as well. As it happened, it was only with great difficulty that he managed to finish attaching the chains. Her face was horrible, Edward. It was still Rachel, of course, but a Rachel transformed into a creature of pure evil, hating and hungry and entirely bestial."

"A vampire. She became a vampire."

"Yes, I suppose so. I fainted then, I believe, and have only flashes of memory after that until I opened my eyes and saw you hovering over me. What is going on, Edward? I must know."

So I provided her with a very brief version of what I knew of the history of Dracula and his long time foe. She listened patiently, without interrupting, although at times she appeared stunned. When I finished, a figure stepped out of the shadows at the far end of the room.

It was Dracula, and I have no idea how he entered my rooms unobserved nor how long he had watched us.

"I have done what needed to be done. All that remains is for you to play out the remainder of your small parts."

"What are you talking about?" I was still defiant, but my earlier bravado had slipped away. This creature could have killed us both without warning, could still do so with impunity.

"I suggest, Miss Appleton, that you stay as close to the truth as possible. It might be best if you insist that you eluded your attacker at the roadside, but fell in the darkness and struck your head, rendering yourself unconscious until this evening, when Mr. Palmer discovered you and escorted you to safety."

"But what of the others?" I detected not the slightest trace of fear in Shirley's voice and was irrationally proud of her.

"Your friend's body has been restored to its proper condition. It will appear that she was abducted and murdered by Mr. Lembic. I have taken the liberty of ringing up Inspector Gladdings, identifying myself as Mr. Quentin Moore, and entertaining them with an interesting and not entirely untrue story. I told them that a chance conversation led me to believe that my employee was involved in the recent disappearance of two young women and that a search of a certain section of the seacoast might profit them. I promised to meet them there. Alas, they will arrive too late, and find that Mr. Lembic and Mr. Moore fought on a treacherous ledge and fell onto the rocks, where the sea battered their bodies almost beyond recognition."

"Miss Dobbit may have to answer some awkward questions," I ventured.

"She will have to deal with them as best she may. Surely you feel no sympathy for a woman who agreed to lure the young ladies to their deaths?"

"No, but I rather liked Mrs. Dobbit, her mother. I would hate to see her turned out of her house."

"Mrs. Dobbit's allowance will continue so long as she lives. There is no one left to countermand it."

"Then Florence Stoker, that is, Enheduanna, is dead as well."

He answered by removing a small journal from his pocket and tossing it onto the bedclothes. "All the answers I have for you are contained there. Do with it as you wish. It is time for me to go."

"Go where?" I asked impulsively.

"To my homeland. I have read the documents which you obtained from Mrs. Dobbit and have satisfied myself that she has left no others of her kind behind. Noel may be technically a thrall but he remains mortal. I am the last now, Mr. Palmer, and it is time for my kind to pass from this Earth. I wish to end where I started, in the land of my ancestors."

He moved toward the door then and I rose, perhaps to intercept him. I am not sure exactly what I planned. But he was gone so swiftly that it was as though he had never been there, and when I stepped out into the corridor, there was no sign of him or anyone else.

So here is the last volume of this adventure, James. Some of the pages are water stained but all of the text remains legible.

The Journal of Vlad Tepes

April 10, 1912

It is unusually bright and sunny in Cherbourg today, so I have taken shelter inside a small tavern near the wharf. I have a considerable wait before the ship arrives, so I have decided to set pen to paper once more, although I have not kept a journal for many years now. I have run from defeat in the past, but this time there will be no choice. One of us must perish. Our confrontation will be on the high seas, and there will be no possible retreat for either of us.

I will not dwell on my past failures. Suffice it to say that once Enheduanna and her allies believed me dead, I was able to slink back to my holdings and lick my wounds; the humiliation of my defeat has taught me a bitter lesson. Mine is a proud family, however, and I was overcome by a great melancholy from which I recovered only very slowly. When I finally bestirred myself to seek intelligence of my enemy, I discovered that Mina Murray was no more, presumed dead along with her husband and most of those others who assisted her against me. I bore them no ill will but could not find it in my heart to mourn them, and I never for a single moment believed that she was gone.

During the next few years, I expended considerable effort to locate her. Lord Godalming's dragoman was in my pay, as well as two of the guards at Seward's asylum, but none of these were able to tell me anything useful. Van Helsing had disappeared as completely as had the Harkers. Other agents forwarded to me endless news accounts of mutilated bodies and missing persons, but I could detect no pattern of attack, nothing to indicate a more than human hand in these crimes. I cast my net wider on the assumption that she had left England, and for several months charted the path of several suspicious events in Germany, but the trail vanished with the arrest of a cunning madman.

Two years passed before the first hopeful sign. In 1888, news of the murders in Whitechapel reached even to the remote parts of Transylvania. I returned to London for the first time since my ignominious defeat, and was nearly attacked by a vigilante group one night as I searched for evidence linking them to her, or more likely to one of her get. By chance I was able to examine the fourth victim briefly before the alarm was raised. The evidence was inconclusive, and the method of attack was certainly not her style, but I still believed there was a connection and concentrated my search in the London area. Then the murders stopped and I was stripped of even that tenuous clue.

I made the arduous Atlantic crossing in 1894 aboard a freighter carrying breeding stock for an American rancher and spent three years searching for her or Morris in the New World. I might have remained there longer except that I chanced to see my name mentioned in the newspapers. Someone named Bram Stoker had written a book titled *Dracula*, and from the brief description, I knew instantly that this was no coincidence. I returned to England a few months later – the shorter sailing times are a godsend - and at last discovered her new identity, but I dared not approach unprepared. I could not risk forfeiting victory again.

For more than ten years I gathered information. I was circumspect. I altered my appearance and assumed more conventional dress. Even then I watched her directly only through the eyes of others, and I replaced my agents frequently to prevent her from sensing my presence through them.

In all honesty, I must admit that I waited longer than was necessary. I became fascinated with her latest effort. Her creation of Florence Stoker was unlike anything she had attempted in the past. She played the dutiful wife and mother – Noel was obviously not her natural child - superbly and varied her hunting ground so widely that I might never have suspected her true identity if she had not betrayed herself by causing her husband to "write" the account of our adventures. Although many of those around her must have been more or less her creatures, I was unwilling to use the glamour to look into their minds and discover the truth. Hers is a much more powerful talent, and she would surely have detected my touch had I done so, although I have learned to mask my taint during these past few years. Even those with fey powers no longer sense my presence unless there is physical contact.

And so the time passed and I did nothing, might have let her slip away if it had not been for a chance encounter just a few weeks ago. I was prowling the streets restlessly when I heard a child crying softly from within a darkened alley. I investigated and found a young girl crouched over the body of a dead prostitute. She was pulling at the dead woman's clothing and alternately sobbing and demanding. "Get up, Ma, get up!"

I startled the child but caught hold of her with the glamour, soothing her as best I could, superimposing the image of a kindly face I snatched from her memory over my own rough features. "What happened girl? Tell me!"

"The bad lady hurt my ma," she told me tearfully. And a quick examination of the dead woman confirmed what I already suspected. I left the youngster in the care of a startled but malleable police constable. This encounter reminded me that even though she had taken on a more human appearance than was her custom, she was still driven by the hunger and not content to confine her attention to what livestock was within reach. My inaction was at least indirectly responsible for the child's bereavement. I could wait no longer.

It was not a simple matter to obtain an invitation into their home in Belgravia. I watched the servants come and go for weeks until one day the housekeeper returned from the market with her arms overflowing. I offered her my assistance and applied a touch of the glamour. She invited me in for tea, which I consumed quickly. I was afraid to tarry too long lest my scent betray my visit. That very night I stealthily entered the house again. I had thought to strike quickly and silently and, to my horror, I almost slaughtered an innocent, for the woman lying in Florence Stoker's bed was a stranger to me, and a living mortal. I almost fled in confusion, but fortunately delayed long enough to touch the imposter's mind. That set me on my present course.

I will board the *Titanic* today when it stops briefly in port. My name is to be Youssef Nasur and I will be traveling in steerage. When we dock in New York, either she or I will be no more.

April 11, 1912

Happenstance almost disrupted my plans today. We docked briefly in Queenstown and I unwisely came up on deck for a few minutes. One of the cabin attendants was walking along the passageway while looking back over her shoulder at a young lady who stood at the rail. I was not quick enough to prevent her from running into me, and there was an almost exquisite moment of contact. She was fey.

Her face contorted in an expression of shock and terror and she fled from me, raced down the gangplank, and disappeared ashore. I cannot guess how much of my nature she gleaned from that brief contact, but it was certainly enough to endanger my mission. So I played sentry for the rest of the morning and early afternoon, waiting for her to return to the ship. I would not kill the woman even now, but I had no compunction about frightening her again if necessary so that she would quit the vessel. It was far too important that my opponent not escape into the New World.

Fortunately, she had not returned by the time we cast off in the early afternoon.

I found my quarry during the early evening. She is traveling under the name Martha Hiltunen, and in second class, much to my surprise. I would have thought her grown so accustomed to luxury that she would refuse to relinquish it even now, but perhaps I am being unfair. Or perhaps it is simply that she would not fit in with the first class passengers, most of whom seem to know one another. Indeed, within their portion of the ship, it appears the entire voyage will be one unending party.

The ship is indeed impressive, even to one with eyes as old and well traveled as mine. Its makers unwisely challenge the gods when they call it unsinkable, but if ever there was a vessel to which that term applied, this might well be the one. Its appointments, at least in the first class section, are luxurious, and even the steerage area is moderately comfortable. I share a compartment with several young Finnish immigrants who eye my cloak and turban with suspicion but not hostility. They are unaware that I speak their tongue so there has been no conversation between us.

I feigned sleep for most of the day and only went up to the deck at dusk. Third class passengers are confined to a small portion of the ship near the stern, but once darkness falls, I have little difficulty slipping away. With care I can spy upon the other passengers, although portions of the ship are so well lighted that I could not enter without great risk of betraying my presence.

There are almost nine hundred crew members aboard, so it was not difficult to find a uniform which fit me, and in that guise I mingled freely in the second class areas, although I was still barred from first class. The passengers in that section made a point of knowing, and rewarding, those of the crew they see regularly. I overhead one gentleman tell another that he had taken passage aboard the *Titanic* only because he thought Captain Smith the most able seaman he had ever met. My unfamiliar face would almost certain bring questions I could not answer.

I was standing in an alcove when I noticed a very young male child wandering apparently unattended near the starboard railing. The lad swarmed up the rail with surprising agility and leaned forward to stare down at the rushing waters. His position was precarious as there was a considerable swell and he cried out when a particularly violent gust of wind cost him his balance. I had taken only two steps forward when a slender figure rushed from the adjacent passageway and snatched him back. A second figure, a young woman, emerged a second later, gathered the child into her arms, and scolded and consoled him in regular alternation.

A crewman came up with a lantern in response to the commotion, and in its light I saw the face of the child's savior. It was she whom I sought!

I followed surreptitiously and heard her introduce herself as Martha Hiltunen, but then the press of people that had allowed me to move closer ebbed away and they were out on the open deck where I could not approach without risking discovery. Taking advantage of a darkened recess, I pretended to smoke a cigarette and watched them. She seemed to be getting on famously with the child, and I wondered if she had already marked him as her next victim. I would have to visit the livestock in the hold before we reached New York, but the voyage was short enough that it should not be necessary for her to feed en route, particularly if she had been sensible enough to satisfy her physical needs before leaving port. But perhaps she still hunted for the pure pleasure of it. My surveillance of her recent activities suggested otherwise, but my agents could easily have been fooled. They had not warned me of her flight to the New World until the very last moment, or of the imposture she had arranged to conceal her departure. How much more might they have failed to notice?

With some difficulty, I shadowed her throughout the evening. She returned to her stateroom shortly before midnight, and in all that time she was never alone. Just before entering, she paused and looked around warily, forcing me to retreat before her sharp eyes discovered me. I realized then that this was going to be more difficult than I had anticipated. An ocean voyage had seemed ideal. We would be isolated, with relatively few people about, and the ocean would swallow forever whatever evidence of our battle remained. It seemed so simple. In reality, the *Titanic* is an enclosed city in itself, and even worse, a city locked in a perpetual holiday. Portions of the crew are always awake and active and even the passengers seem determined to be in constant motion.

I considered the possibility of breaking into her stateroom, but it was not likely that I could do so and deal with her before creating enough of a disturbance to draw the attention of others. Indeed, I was still not certain that I could overcome her under even the best of conditions. The specter of failure continues to haunt my thoughts.

April 13, 1912

I fear this pursuit must continue beyond the voyage. It required a surprising amount of effort to find the elusive Miss Hiltunen this evening. She has found favor with one of the first class passengers – a married man traveling without his wife – and dined in fine style. Although I was able to spy on her briefly, there was too much light and traffic for a prolonged stay, and I was forced to retreat toward the stern when a drunkenly amorous couple seeking privacy stumbled into my hiding place.

I watched for her to return, but abandoned my post when dawn approached. It is unlikely that she would claim a victim, particularly a man of considerable stature, under these circumstances, but I suspect she allowed him to escort her back to his stateroom. A touch of the glamour would leave him with pleasant but false memories, and possibly even an irritating love bite which he would likely consider a badge of honor. It is unusual but not unheard of for her to spare her victims.

A few more days should not matter to me, but I worry that she will somehow escape when we dock in New York. My travels in that country have demonstrated how easy it would be for one of our kind to disappear there, and countless lives could be lost before I located her again. The Martha Hiltunen identity will no doubt give way to a new one quickly. She is too wary to leave a trail that obvious.

April 14, 1912

As I write these words, I am uncertain whether they will ever be read. It is only a matter of time until my refuge is gone and the cold North Atlantic waters close in. They cannot hurt me, of course, for I have no true warmth for them to steal, but the leather covers of this journal can only protect the pages for a limited amount of time.

Let me try to set down the events that have happened today, events so momentous and tragic that even I have difficulty remaining calm while I recall them. I did not leave my compartment at all during the daylight hours. Although it was cloudy and would have done me no great harm, the sunlight nevertheless bleeds away some of my strength, and I was resolved to remain ready at all times to consummate my campaign against my old enemy.

When I emerged just after the sun had dropped to the horizon, the crowds were much more attenuated than previously. The temperature had dropped dramatically and was hovering just above the freezing point, forcing most of the passengers to shelter indoors. That was no hardship in first or even second class, of course, and the steerage passengers were so crowded that they provided much of their own heat.

There were no lights in the cabin allotted to Martha Hiltunen, nor had I expected there to be. Although I knew she was as inured to the cold as I, it seemed more likely that she was inside, mingling with the crowd. I reclaimed my crewman's uniform from where I had concealed it and, disguised as well as I could manage, I made my way through the interior of the ship. My movements were quick and purposeful, and everyone assumed I had legitimate business where I ventured, although I was careful to avoid approaching any of the officers.

It was just after eleven when I finally found her sitting with a half dozen other women in one of the second class lounges. She glanced in my direction as I entered and I hastily turned and exited without changing expression. I doubted that she had had a clear look at me, and she had never seen me clean shaven, so I believed myself undiscovered. An officer named Lightoller was coming toward me and I passed him with a nod, but I sensed that he had stopped and glanced at my retreating back curiously, so I left the area directly rather than risk discovery of my impersonation.

I hastened toward the stern of the ship where the starboard well deck, which served as an inadequate recreation area for the third class passengers, had been deserted most of the evening. The temperature had continued to fall, and even those who habitually remained up and about at this time of night had retreated to the warmth belowdecks. I had come here to think, but I never had the opportunity.

She was waiting there for me. Apparently her senses were more acute than I had realized.

"Good evening, Vlad." Her voice was level but I sensed excitement. "Somehow I knew you still walked in this world. My mind insisted that I had seen you die, but my heart knew otherwise. Are you still resolved to destroy me then? I cannot believe this meeting is coincidental."

"We cannot go on as we have, my lady. There must be an ending."

"And you have abrogated to yourself the right to make this decision for me as well as yourself?"

"You have shown scant concern for all the lives you have ended across the centuries. Why should I feel qualms about taking yours? You and I and perhaps Quincey Morris are the last of our kind, and we are past our time."

She laughed. "Then you know about him."

"There were reports of attacks in the area where he was buried. It was not difficult to determine the truth."

"Oh, Vlad, you were ever so pompous when I first met you, and that is one quality that remains unchanged. Twice before we have crossed our metaphorical swords. What makes you think the outcome this time will be any different?"

"Perhaps because this time you are no longer as anxious to go on as you once were."

Her face changed suddenly, startled, even apprehensive, and I thought I had touched an even deeper nerve than expected, but a split second later I realized I was not the cause of her reaction. The deck shuddered under my feet and a high pitched tearing sound disturbed the night. I staggered but did not fall, and turned in time to see an enormous white shadow emerge from the darkness and pass by, showering chunks of ice and snow onto the deck in such copious amounts that I was forced to retreat amidships. It was a gigantic iceberg and we had clearly struck it a glancing blow.

I looked around for Enheduanna, but she was gone.

There was a good deal of scurrying about, mostly passengers disturbed at their rest. Several crewmembers were in evidence as well, and at least one officer. I avoided them all as best I could and moved away from the stern, but it was almost midnight by the time I found her again, standing by herself staring off into the darkness. Despite the chill air, the number of passengers on deck had steadily increased. I could hear music drifting back from the first class lounge and a constant murmur of voices. The only sign of panic I observed was when an oil stained crewman rushed up to an officer and shouted "we need more stokers". She heard him as well, and jumped at the sound of the name under which she had hidden for so long.

I descended toward her by means of an enclosed stairway, but she had vanished again when I reached the bottom. Frustrated, I started toward her cabin, but had to make way when several crewmembers pounded along the corridor toward me in considerable haste. By the time I reached my goal, it was difficult to proceed because the stewards were turning out the passengers and sending them up onto the deck. I retreated and saw that they were starting to uncover the boats. Most of the passengers seemed either amused or annoyed, and I shared their opinion that Captain Smith was being over cautious until I noticed an almost imperceptible tilt to the deck.

Confusion grew more prevalent with every passing minute. Some of the passengers and many of the crew appeared apprehensive, but most of the former acted put upon and some openly balked at the increasingly acerbic orders from the stewards. I did notice that emergency or not, the three passenger classes remained separate. I was not dressed as a crewman this evening, and one of the stewards berated me when I decided to seek my quarry belowdecks, insisting that everyone should remain above in case it became necessary to leave the ship "for purely precautionary reasons". After assuring him that I was merely going to roust my traveling companion from his bed, he grudgingly turned away.

The sky was suddenly illuminated by the explosion of a rocket, and I think that more than anything else convinced me that the situation was more serious than it appeared. But my own mission transcended the moment. The increasingly chaotic conditions aboard might work to my advantage. I was determined to find my old enemy now, in the bowels of this foundering ship, and ensure that she at least should never set foot in one of the boats.

But how to find her? Her cabin was empty, the door closed but not secured. Someone was trapped in the adjacent room by a jammed lock, and I paused long enough to use a fire axe to break it down and set him free. A steward ran up at that moment, berated me for damaging the ship, and insisted that I would be presented with a bill when we arrived in New York.

Having assured myself that she was not to be found in the second class staterooms, I joined the now thinning flow of passengers headed upward. Another rocket burst as I reached the deck, and I noticed that at least one of the ship's officers was now armed. They were separating the men from the women, which was going to make my task even more difficult, but there was still enough milling about that I was able to slip away. I passed a group of musicians who were making their way toward the forward boat deck near the grand staircase, and ascended to the next deck. The tilt forward was more pronounced now and I saw that at least one of the lifeboats had been lowered.

I made my way systematically from one boat station to the next, descending to the main deck when necessary, searching for my nemesis. As long as I made no attempt to enter one of the lifeboats, no one seemed interested in my movements. It was possible by now that she had already left the *Titanic*, and if so, my chance was probably gone. When I reached Boat #8, an elderly woman in a black dress rushed past me, lost her footing, and fell over the rail. Purely by instinct I reached out, caught her by the ankle, and pulled her to safety. She stood up and ran off without a word of thanks.

A few moments later I reached the vicinity of the boat deck. The band had reassembled and were playing another inappropriately cheery ragtime tune. Enheduanna stood just beyond them, motionless, a little apart from everyone else. As I started toward her, her head rose. She must have seen me because she faded back into the darkness.

But this time she was unable to evade me for long. I watched the door to the gymnasium close and followed, and the crowd parted before me as though sensing the seriousness of my purpose. Once inside, I saw her immediately, standing on the far side of the room, leaning forward over a wicker chair. We were alone except for the rows of mechanical horses and stationary bicycles.

"It seems that nature intends to do your work for you, Vlad."

"Perhaps. Certainly we are most unnatural creatures." I let the door close behind me as yet another rocket burst in the distance. "It must end here. I cannot allow you to leave this ship."

She laughed. "Do you really think you could stop me? Have your powers grown so much in these last few years that you can accomplish what has always before been beyond your reach?"

"We are not the same. Our strengths and our weaknesses vary, and the outcome is uncertain. But yes, I believe that I will succeed, and then I will make an end of Morris and myself as well."

She made an exasperated sound. "Why? Why would you abandon endless life?"

I felt a surge of anger and welcomed it and the strength it brought. "It is not endless life, Enheduanna. We hover somewhere between life and death and partake truly of neither. The only thing that is endless is the torment."

"Untrue. We can taste the best of both. I enjoy everything that life has to offer. The sunlight no longer bothers me, I have seen my own face, raised a child, even earned the love of a mortal man without recourse to the glamour. I have been a good wife and mother, an asset to society, and a good companion to my acquaintances."

"And by night you hunt down and kill those whom by day you call friends!"

"Not true!" Her own anger stirred and she stepped out from behind the chair, her fingers curling into fists, her features rippling as her true face fought to express itself. "I kill only so that I may live. I hunt those who endanger me, or take my prey from the useless dregs of the mortal world."

"And who judges them useless? You? What gives you that right?" I moved a step forward as well, and I felt her gathering the power of the glamour. The very air crackled with energy.

"Power makes right, Vlad. You told me that once yourself, when you were still mortal. And if I remember correctly, you had already taken more lives in your mortal form than I harvest in a millennium. Who are you to name my sins or call me to task for them?"

I nodded. "My soul is as fouled as your own. I never claimed otherwise. The world will be a better place when both of us are removed from it."

"Your heart has softened as much as your head, Vlad. Look at them!" She gestured through the windows toward the milling crowd pressing about the lifeboat. "They are cattle! Their lives are so brief that I am at best a petty thief when I steal some few years. And sometimes I reward the best of them, as I once did you."

"This is no reward you have given me. It is a curse that afflicts both of us, and from which we shall only be freed by a true death."

"Someday, perhaps, but not today, Vlad, and not by your hand." And then she was upon me. She struck first with the glamour, and her power was much greater than mine, but not enough to breech my defenses, as she must have known. It aided her cause in that it was a distraction and an irritation, and while I mustered myself to drive her out of my head, she assailed my body. I had seen her true face before, although I have never seen my own, and if any passenger had happened to glance into the gymnasium during the next few moments, they might have believed the devil himself was aboard the *Titanic*.

I was thrown from my feet and slammed into one of the mechanical horses. Her rage was terrible to see and she reduced my cloak to ribbons as she sought to claw my flesh. I responded in the same fashion, and we rolled back and forth across the linoleum floor, which was soon streaked with our tainted blood. My left ear was a bloody ruin and a deep gouge ran from my right shoulder down across my ribs. Eventually my greater physical strength worked to my advantage, and I shattered her forearm when she unwisely lunged toward my throat. It would knit within a few hours, of course, but in that instant she reeled back, clearly disconcerted, and rushed from the gymnasium before I could interfere.

I saw her vanish down a staircase and set out in pursuit. Three sharp reports echoed above the shouting crowd – pistol fire, I guessed. The most recent rocket had almost extinguished itself, and none followed. Fortunately, most if not all of the ship's lights continued to glow. Unfortunately, by its light I realized that in addition to the forward tilt, we were beginning to list.

I pursued Enheduanna to the lower decks, moving forward into first class territory. She ran with preternatural quickness, always a few steps ahead of me. A steward stepped out between us at one point, but his eyes were wide with fear and I think he saw nothing but his own death. Another man, a passenger, was lying in a corridor, bleeding profusely from the head. I might have stopped, but I could not take the chance that she might escape me.

Just beyond, the floor was awash, and the water level was visibly rising.

I caught up to her in the first class foyer, beneath the main ballroom. Or more correctly, that is where she turned to face me. The water was already up to our waists, but through some strange geometry of the ship, it was pouring down onto us from above as well as rushing in from below. There was debris all around us, floating, falling from above, and occasionally flying through the air as the encroaching water breeched another barrier.

She had to shout to be heard above the din. "If we perish here, Vlad, at least it will be a magnificent ending. I have seen wonderful and terrible things in my time."

"You ARE a wonderful and terrible thing, Enheduanna, and I say again your time has passed."

I meant to rush her then, but fate intervened once more. Some impediment to the water gave way at that instant and a great dark wave poured into the chamber. I was swept from my feet and slammed against the far wall, slid along it some way until I found an irregular surface to which I could cling while the surge passed. Then the water became relatively calm and I was able to turn. The flood was already chest high and rising quickly. I allowed myself to float and realized that the ceiling was now effectively a wall. The angle of the deck was impossible unless the stern had been lifted completely out of the water.

I turned toward Enheduanna and saw her holding herself steady by gripping a portion of what had once been a magnificent chandelier. She was staring at something floating in the water just beside her. It was a child. The current pushed the limp form in my direction and as it floated past, obviously dead, I recognized it as the young boy she had pulled back from the rail two days previously. The mass of water around us acted as insulation, and it was now quiet enough to speak almost normally.

"Perhaps you are right, Vlad. The death of strangers never touched me in the past, but of late, the passing of those I have known has become a great burden. Bram truly loves Florence in his way; did I tell you that? I never used the glamour to shape his affection. So does Noel, although I may have tainted the purity of his feelings by promising him eternal life and by shaping his mind while he was an infant. And I have had friends, true friends. Ellen Terry, for one, and William Gilbert and Oscar Wilde and even Philippa Balcombe."

"They were never your friends, Enheduanna," I said. "They were Florence Stoker's friends. Our kind cannot know true friendship. That is part of the curse."

She was silent for several seconds, and the water continued to rise. "I have lived through countless centuries, Vlad. It has been a very long journey."

"It is long past time to stop then. Time to rest."

"I will not take my own life, you know. You will have to seize it from me, and I will resist until you overpower me."

"I understand." I relinquished my own hold and prepared to push off through the water toward her, but at that instant the air was filled with a torturous screaming that seemed a physical being. The entire ship shuddered and then the wall, or rather the ceiling, in front of me disintegrated and a great dark shape blotted out the stars and I realized that the forward funnel had broken loose and crashed into the deck, shattering everything in its path. The chamber collapsed in around us and the water rose above my head and an oppressive silence fell.

Since it was unnecessary for me to breathe, I was not discomforted by the lack of air. At first I thought I had been trapped by the wreckage, but I found an escape route around a piece of twisted debris. Incredibly many of the lights were still functioning beyond that point, and I swam awkwardly forward, searching for Enheduanna.

I found her almost by chance.

She called herself immortal and in one sense she truly was. But nothing lasts forever, and even our kind perishes eventually. Her body was caught between a portion of the funnel and the reinforced decking. Her eyes remained open, but there was no light in them, and I could see enough of the terrible damage done to her body that I felt certain she could not repair herself. I had anticipated this moment for more than a century, shaped myself to its achievement, but I had always expected that it would be my hand that dealt the final blow, rather than blind fate.

I felt cheated. I also felt regret. Her passing removed a great shadow from the world, but I felt no joy.

The lights went out a moment later. Shaking off my reverie, I turned toward the stern of the ship, planning to climb up above water level. But there was no time. I felt a great rushing all about me and realized that the *Titanic* was experiencing its final spasm.

I am not certain how much time passed before I extricated myself from the wreckage and floated upward a seemingly interminable distance until I reached the surface. Perhaps as much as an hour. I emerged to find myself surrounded by the frozen corpses of scores of men, women, and even children. There were faint shouts and I could see lights in the distance, but none turned in my direction. I dared not swim to one of the boats when it was so obvious that all those exposed to the water had died. And truthfully, I was overcome by melancholy. I did not regret Enheduanna's passing, but I regretted its necessity.

There were a number of small icebergs nearby and I swam to one of them. I did not relish the prospect of spending a day floating in the sunlight and knew I could find enough shadow there to shelter me even if it meant carving a tunnel into the ice. Shortly after dawn I remembered the journal in my pocket and unzipped its case, which had proven to be nearly water tight. I have now brought this account up to date.

My future is uncertain. I tried to alter my form and become a great fish so that I could swim back to England but that power is denied to me unless I am on solid land. The Titanic is gone now, fallen into a maelstrom, and I can no longer see or hear anything of the lifeboats. I float off toward my destiny like Dr. Frankenstein's monstrous creation, and perhaps to no happier an end. If I survive, I must still track down her last surviving creation, Quincey Morris. If not, then humankind will have to find its own solution. At the moment, I am indifferent.

July 10, 1920

I had not expected to add anything to the preceding account, but I imagine the good Mr. Palmer would be very unhappy with me if I failed to explain my rescue. On the night following the calamitous end of the *Titanic*, I saw lights approaching through the mist. I secured this journal as best I could within my clothing and swam out to meet it. It was a Russian tramp freighter named *Burma* and its lookouts were more worried about ice than in finding survivors or bodies. I had no difficulty climbing aboard and concealed myself in the cargo hold. On the second day following, we reached port in New York and I slipped ashore.

My return to England was uneventful, and most of what followed has been recorded elsewhere. The ring and passwords I secured from a woman who watched over one of Enheduanna's document caches in France. I had been there when my mistress had struck a deal with the woman's several times removed grandmother. My agents had brought me news of Morris' return to England, although they had lost track of him following his arrival, and I feared that he had followed our dark mistress to the New World. I chose Mr. Palmer after investigating his character and learning that he was reputed to be honest, intelligent, and tenacious, and he has demonstrated those qualities to me.

I have left him in charge of our story to do with as he sees fit. Personally, I believe it would be best if he burned the documents and went on with his life. Humankind has a hard enough road to travel without the knowledge that there were once beings among them who considered them nothing but clever prey. Disbelief is likely in any case, and Palmer might ruin his life by insisting otherwise. Perhaps, as with *Dracula*, it might be presented as fiction.

I am fated to be remembered as a sinister figure of utter evil, as Enheduanna intended. Ironically, I take comfort from this, because in whatever form it may take, I SHALL be remembered. Her anonymity is secure forever.

EPILOGUE

Letter from Edward Palmer to James Chatsworth, dated January 14, 1937

Dear James,

Just a quick note to let you know that we succeeded in our quest. Shirley and I arrived in Knightsbridge a week ago now, and found lodgings not far from where Mrs. Stoker resides. We sent a note expressing our admiration for her husband's work and our desire to pay our respects, but a servant replied that Mrs. Stoker is too ill to receive visitors.

Fortunately, your friend Charles was able to help us, indirectly at least. He introduced us to a young student of art history named Vincent Price whom we convinced to intercede on our behalf. Price has won the lady's favor and within the week he arranged for us to call upon Mrs. Stoker.

"She is a delightful lady. Advised me to seek a career on the stage of all things. But you must not stay long. She tires easily and her mind is not as strong as it once was."

We were ushered into a darkened sitting room by a servant who plainly disapproved of our presence. Our hostess was dressed formally, welcomed us politely, and poured tea with a shaking hand. Shirley held up our end of the conversation, as I was quite frankly a bit overwhelmed. When we spoke of *Dracula*, she became quite animated, insisting that people were plotting to steal the monies rightfully due her by making moving pictures based on the story.

Shirley changed the subject and she calmed somewhat, although she remained mildly agitated. Then she began to visibly tire and I took a chance. "You and my mother once had a mutual acquaintance."

"Oh, and who might that have been, young man?" She had settled back into her chair and her voice was ever so slightly slurred.

"Mary Whitlow. My mother knew her only slightly."

Her body stiffened almost imperceptibly and her eyes fastened upon me so intently it was almost a physical sensation. "I have not heard that name in a long time."

"She disappeared, I understand. No one ever found out where she went. I don't suppose you might know?"

There was a long silence in which her eyes loosened their grip on me and almost seemed to turn in upon themselves. I thought she would never answer and made as if to rise and leave, but Shirley touched my arm and I waited. Eventually her lips moved, but her voice was so soft I had to lean forward to hear the words. And her voice was thinner and her diction altered.

"Yes, Mary's gone. But she's loyal, she is. She's waiting patiently for her reward what's been promised to her." And then she was silent again.

Shirley and I left without disturbing her.

And so it ends, James. Assuming he was as good as his word, Dracula has also gone to his final rest. I suppose that he was right, that creatures such as he and Enheduanna have no place in our world. We do such terrible things to each other by ourselves that mere monsters of the night such as they seem pale threats in the great scheme of things. But even the fiercest of nightmares can stimulate us at times, inspire us to fight the darkness. I cannot help but think that with their passing we lose much of the dark inspiration that allows us to seize upon our fears, give them form, and face them forthrightly. Perhaps I have allowed my obsession with this story to cloud my judgment, but I think the world is a less interesting place in their absence.

I remain your steadfast friend,

Edward Palmer.

www.ingramcontent.com/pod-product-compliance
Lightning Source LLC
Chambersburg PA
CBHW072109170626
46813CB00004B/1490